# THROUGH

# THESE EYES

D1519835

## TOM BRADFORD   MICHAEL RISLEY

*This book is dedicated to the men and women behind the badge who lay their lives on the line to protect and serve.*

*The authors would like to acknowledge the tireless efforts of Jennie Risley. Undaunted, she took thousands of longhand chicken scratch pages and transformed it to the book you see today. We thank you.*

# 1

Pink transmission fluid poured from underneath the dark blue Chevrolet Monte Carlo and trickled down the asphalt street. The high-speed impact with a concrete light pole had left the car's front end a twisted mass of metal and chrome. Steam from the engine, mixed with dust from the street, rose up into the night air and swirled around the top of the street light.

With its lights flashing and siren screaming, a sheriff's department Crown Victoria rolled to a squealing stop ten yards shy of the disabled Monte Carlo. Before Baxter could get the sheriff's car in park, the driver's door of the low rider opened and an overweight Mexican teenager bolted into the upper middle class neighborhood seeking refuge. He wouldn't get far. Every car out on patrol had joined in the chase and in minutes, the entire neighborhood would be saturated with cops.

Baxter got out of the sheriff's car with service weapon drawn, ready to fire, and focused on the murky silhouette still in the front passenger's seat of the Monte Carlo.

"Don't move! Let me see your hands, let me see your hands!"

After Baxter shouted the command, there was silence and a misty rain started to fall. Defying Baxter's orders, a set of feet wearing white Nike high-topped basketball shoes kicked open the door. Baxter's right index finger quivered on the trigger of the 9mm Glock, watching as the passenger leaped out of the Monte Carlo. The headlights of the sheriff's car along with the street light gave Baxter a good look at the person escaping into the night. Light reflected off the metal object in the teenager's hand.

*Okay, that's him; he matches the description put out by dispatch. Hispanic male juvenile, five feet nine inches tall, one hundred fifty pounds, dark blue denim pants, white Los Angeles Dodgers uniform jersey, armed with a silver handgun...*

Baxter took a deep breath, exhaled, and squeezed off two rounds. Both shots missed their mark; leaving the smell of gunpowder fused with burnt rubber from the wrecked Monte Carlo to drift in the air. The suspect had a thirty-yard advantage and Baxter started to sprint after him. They ran through the backyards of Southern California "cookie cutter" homes; two stories with tan stucco exteriors and dark brown tile roofs. At 10:30 in the evening most of the back patios and backyards were unlit.

Baxter was in good shape, but the fleeing kid was better. A quarter of a mile into the chase, Baxter's lungs felt like they were going to explode. Baxter lost sight of the suspect when the kid darted into an unlit backyard and then disappeared into the abutting dense shrubs and bushes.

Out of breath, heart racing, and adrenaline pumping, Baxter stopped to focus on the surrounding backyards. Something was moving and making a squishing sound on the wet grass. Between the moonless night and the misty rain, it was difficult to see anything. Forty feet away, in a backyard to the left, there was more movement. *There he is!*

"Sheriff's department! Put your hands up! Sheriff's department! Put your hands up!"

Reacting to Baxter's yelling, the kid clad in the Dodgers jersey made an abrupt turn towards Baxter. When the boy turned, Baxter saw silver in his right hand. Baxter fired one round into his chest. The force of the bullet jerked the boy's body into the air. He fell backwards onto the wet grass.

"Don't move; let me see your hands!" Baxter shouted. The body remained motionless.

Baxter, with short measured steps, and the Glock still aimed at the boy, entered the backyard and walked towards the fallen figure. From ten feet away Baxter could see a red stain on the boy's white jersey. Standing over the body, Baxter saw syrupy blood flowing from the chest wound. The boy's left hand was tucked underneath his left leg. His right hand was plainly visible, holding nothing.

*Where's the gun?*

The sheriff's department helicopter appeared overhead. Flying at two hundred feet above the ground, it began making a series of tight left-handed circles over the backyard. Each circle took four seconds to complete. From inside the cockpit the observer deputy controlled the craft's searchlight, brightly illuminating the shooting scene below and keeping the searchlight trained on the body of the shot boy. As the helicopter circled, the body would be bathed in bright light for two seconds, followed by a strobe light effect of darkness for two seconds.

Five feet from the boy's right hand, Baxter saw something silver lying in the wet grass. A sickening feeling formed in the pit of Baxter's stomach.

*It's not a gun...it's a cell phone.*

When the helicopter's searchlight shined directly on the body, Baxter could see the boy fighting for each precious breath of life. Blood was starting to ooze from the corner of his mouth. When the body was cloaked in passing darkness, Baxter could hear the boy's guttural gasping, along with the sound of blood gurgling from the sucking chest wound.

It startled and confused Baxter when a whimpering dog came up to the body. The white and tan Jack Russell Terrier nudged its nose against the face of the shot boy.

*Shit, something's not right here.*

Becoming more nauseous by the second, Baxter feared the worst. A transmission came in on Baxter's walkie-talkie, confirming those fears.

"Highland units, be advised, the armed robbery suspect from the Circle K is now in custody and the weapon recovered. The Hispanic male juvenile is wearing a white Dodger's jersey and blue denim pants."

*God help me, I've shot the wrong person and he's about the same age as Nate.*

Her hands trembled as she put the Glock back in its holster. Deputy Michelle Baxter fell to her knees and started to gag.

A pair of uniformed sheriff's deputies entered the backyard and ran over to the fallen boy. He now had no pulse and was not breathing. Where the "G" on the jersey should be, they saw the chest wound. In timed intervals, they pumped up and down on his torso.

Baxter wiped the vomit from her face with the sleeve of her uniform. Her mind went numb and her body felt paralyzed as she watched the two deputies try to bring the boy back to life.

*Save him, please save him. Don't let him die.*

Wrestling with the gusting winds coming down off the foothills, the sheriff's department helicopter continued to circle overhead. The whine of its engine and the *whop, whop, whop* of its rotor blade cut through the surreal scene unfolding on the ground below. The boy's cell phone started to ring.

# 2

"Carmen, where are you?"

"Vince and I are at the country club, his Christmas party. The music is loud in here. Let me go outside so I can hear you better, Laura."

Carmen Costa had a glass of red wine in one hand and her cell phone in the other. She walked outside and stood under the covered entrance. The chilly December wind passing over her bare shoulders made her shiver. On the other end of the call was her next-door neighbor and good friend, Laura Grogan. "Okay, Laura, that's better, but I hear a lot of sirens in the background. What's going on?"

"Emergency vehicles, Carmen, they're everywhere."

"Why? Where are they at?"

"They're in your driveway and on the street in front of your house."

"What?"

"I think something's happened to Mario."

"What do you mean; you think something has happened to Mario?" Carmen said. Her hands started to shake and she held the glass away from her body trying to keep the splashing wine off her new dress.

"I'm upstairs, in my bedroom. I'm looking out the window into your backyard. Mario's on the ground; a bunch of paramedics are circled around him. I think he's been shot."

"No, that can't be. Are you sure it's Mario?" Carmen asked, trying to convince herself that Laura was mistaken.

"It's Mario," she answered, fighting back the tears in a failed attempt to remain calm for her friend.

"Stay on the phone. Vincent and I will be there in twenty minutes."

Carmen let go of the glass of wine and covered her mouth with her left hand. Shards of glass went flying; the crimson liquid splattered her highheels and ankles.

Unsteady on her feet, and leaning against the wall for support, she went back inside and saw her husband, Vincent, talking to his partner in the accounting firm. Vincent Costa watched his wife come into the dining room and from the anguished look on her face, knew that something was wrong. He excused himself and hurried towards her; she collapsed into his arms, crying.

"Laura's on the phone," Carmen said between sobs. "She says Mario is in the backyard. Paramedics are working on him; she thinks he's been shot."

Gritting his teeth in a losing effort to maintain his composure, Vincent clutched his wife's hand, leading her out of the dining room, through the lobby, and out into the parking lot. He opened the passenger door of their silver Lexus coupe and helped his weeping wife into her seat. He started the car and peeled out on the rain slickened asphalt.

"Is Laura still on the line?"

"She should be."

"Put her on speaker phone."

Carmen positioned the phone on the wood paneled console between the gray leather seats.

"Laura, this is Vince, are you still there?"

"Yes," she answered, above the noise of the sirens and sheriff's helicopter.

"What in the hell is going on at our house?"

"It's Mario, I think he's been shot by a cop."

"By a cop? Laura, that doesn't make any sense. Start at the beginning—tell me everything you know."

"I was upstairs in the bedroom, reading. I heard what sounded like a gunshot coming from the walking trails that run behind our backyards. I jumped out of bed and looked out the window. I saw a sheriff's deputy walking over to someone in your backyard."

"How do you know it was a sheriff's deputy?" Vincent asked.

"Well, it wasn't a regular person. They had on a uniform. It was olive colored. The police wear black uniforms and I know that the sheriffs wear olive uniforms."

"Why do you think it's Mario?"

"It's Mario—I just know it is. Does Mario ever wear a white Los Angeles Dodgers jersey?"

Vincent looked over at his wife; her eyes were wide with terror. He sighed in resignation and answered, "Yes."

Laura Grogan gave Vincent and Carmen several moments to absorb the impact of what she had just told them. She took a deep breath and then went on with her account. "A police helicopter started circling over your house. Two more deputies ran into your backyard. They both went over to Mario. I think that maybe they were giving him CPR. Then the paramedics arrived and now I can see them working on Mario. Oh my god!"

"What?" Vincent asked, now consumed with horror over his neighbor's sudden outburst.

"No, no, no," Laura said, her voice trailing off into a whisper.

"Laura, what the hell is going on?"

"The paramedics, they're packing up their stuff, they're leaving. Mario is just lying out there in your backyard, all by himself."

Vincent Costa made a fist with his right hand and began pounding the dashboard of the car.

"Vince, tell me he's not dead. Please, tell me my baby's not dead," Carmen pleaded with her husband.

Vincent stopped beating on the dashboard and reached across the console to comfort his wife. He had no answer for her.

Five minutes from their home, the only sound breaking the silence in the Lexus was the *swish-swoosh-swish-swoosh* of the windshield wipers. They soon came to the street that went into their subdivision, but it was blocked by a marked San Bernardino County Sheriff's Department vehicle. Its light bar flickered red and blue. Vincent slowly drove up to the sheriff's car. He could see his house thirty yards away. In front of his house, he counted four-marked sheriff's cars, two ambulances, and one fire engine. They all had their emergency lights flashing. The red, yellow, blue, and white lights eerily reflected off the wet asphalt.

Carmen let out an ear-piercing shriek and started to open her door. Vincent stopped her. A muscular African American deputy, in sheriff's department rain gear, got out of the car and went to Vincent's door. Costa lowered the window and rainwater dripped in.

The deputy leaned into the open window, glanced over at a sobbing Carmen, and said, "I'm sorry, sir, I can't let you go any farther."

Vincent gave his name and said, "We're going to our house."

"Which house is yours, sir?"

"It's the one with the damned yellow tape all around it," Costa answered. His voice was thick with sarcasm and contempt. "Now please let me through. My wife and I need to get to our son."

"I'm sorry, sir, I'm afraid I can't do that."

"Yes you fucking can, deputy. Something has happened to our son. You are going to let my wife and I get to our house."

"Sir, I appreciate the frustration you and your wife are feeling, but I can't let you proceed any farther."

"Look, deputy, you're really starting to piss me off. I don't think you understood correctly. My wife and I are going up to our house to see about our son. You do whatever you have to do. Arrest me, I don't give a shit."

"Sir, I really don't want to arrest you, but you're not leaving me much of a choice. I think it would be best if you just gave me a moment to contact my watch commander."

"I think that's a fine idea, deputy, why don't you go do that."

Vincent watched the deputy walk back to his vehicle and Carmen stared at her house. She said nothing and tears rolled down her cheeks. Moments later, another marked sheriff's vehicle made the short drive from the Costa residence to the roadblock. A uniformed female got out of the car and walked up to the driver's door of the Lexus.

"Mr. Costa, Mrs. Costa, my name is Sergeant Susan Kemp. I'm the watch commander for the Highland Station."

"Sergeant, please, my wife and I just want to get to our house so we can see about our son, Mario."

"Mr. Costa, I'm afraid that's not going to happen. I'd like to take both of you down to sheriff's headquarters so that we can talk."

"No, we're not leaving. Whatever you have to say to my wife and I, tell us right now, right here."

"Okay," Kemp said. She paused, trying to find the words on how to break the devastating news. "There has been an incident at your house involving your son."

"An incident? One of your goons shoots our son and you have the fucking nerve to call it an incident?"

"Mr. Costa, why do you believe that your son has been shot by a sheriff's deputy?"

Costa took the cell phone from the center console and held it up, just inches from the face of Sgt. Kemp. "Our next door neighbor, Laura Grogan, heard a gunshot, and looked out her bedroom window. She saw a deputy with his gun pointed, she saw our son Mario on the ground in our backyard. She called us on the cell phone. We've been talking to her this whole time. We know paramedics were in the backyard working on Mario. The last thing she told us was that the paramedics had packed up and left. Anything else you'd like to know, sergeant?"

Kemp struggled to put on her best poker face, stunned at the revelation of the next-door neighbor who had witnessed everything.

"Mr. Costa, Mrs. Costa, your son has been shot and he did not make it."

# 3

Sergeant John Tate turned down the thermostat, shut off the lights, and walked upstairs. At the top of the stairwell, the wood flooring creaked underneath the weight of his feet as he walked into the three bedrooms, checking on his five sleeping girls. Going into the master bedroom he passed by his wife, Kathy, who was reading in bed and went into the bathroom to brush his teeth. While gargling with Listerine, his sheriff's department cell phone started ringing.

"Tate," he said, walking back downstairs to the kitchen.

"John, this is Susan Kemp over at the Highland Station."

"Hey, Sue, what's going on?"

"Is it snowing up there?" Kemp asked.

Tate pushed aside the curtains and looked out the kitchen window. "Yeah, still snowing a little bit. It's been coming down most of the evening. What's it like down the hill?"

"Light rain, probably in the mid-fifties," Kemp said. "I've got to tell you, John, I've lived in Southern California all my life and I never get over this weather. Rain down here, snow up there in Big Bear. What's your elevation? Eight thousand feet?"

"Closer to nine thousand feet where I'm at. So what's up Sue? I know you didn't call me at eleven o'clock in the evening to talk about the weather."

"You and your team still first up?" Kemp asked.

"Yes."

"We've got our hands full down here with an officer involved shooting."

Tate's leather homicide investigation notebook sat on the counter, next to the cookie jar. Years of use had worn smooth the customized beveling, but the scent of cowhide was as strong as when his wife gave it to him after he was promoted to detective. He picked it up, took a pen out of an empty coffee can, and sat down at the kitchen table.

"What's the deputy's name?" Tate asked.

"Michelle Baxter."

"Michelle Baxter, I don't think I know her," Tate said, bouncing his pen up and down on the notebook. "Wait a minute, isn't she the wife of Jordan Baxter? The guy that used to work for us then went to law school at night and became a prosecutor?"

"That's her," Kemp said, letting out a sigh. "You know the rest of that story?"

"Wasn't he killed in Afghanistan about six months ago?"

"Yes."

"Does this one look like a good shoot?" Tate asked.

"I don't know, John.  Excuse the language, but it's a real cluster fuck."

"Why?"

"She shot an innocent sixteen year old Hispanic kid who was just out in his own backyard."

"Did the kid make it?"

"No."

"What's his name?" Tate asked, writing in his notebook.

"Mario Costa."

Tate rubbed the bridge of his nose and said, "Yeah, Sue, I'd say that does have all the makings of a Class A cluster fuck.  What do we know so far?"

"About twenty two hundred hours dispatch got the call; an armed robbery at the Circle K, Baseline and Victoria.  Suspect is a Hispanic male, approximately seventeen years old, five feet nine inches, one hundred fifty pounds, wearing dark denim pants, and a white Los Angeles Dodgers jersey. Suspect is armed with a silver handgun, last seen leaving south on Victoria in a dark blue Monte Carlo low rider."

"Damn, Sue, they ought to change the name of that Circle K to *Stop and Rob*. How many times has it been knocked over?"

"Hey, an all night convenience store in the shitty part of town, John. Michelle is about to come off her shift. She gets the call and is in the area. She proceeds over to, as you would say, the *Stop and Rob*. She spots a dark blue Monte Carlo traveling east on Greenspot. She lights him up and the chase is on. The pursuit heads east towards the nicer subdivisions—they're hauling ass. The Monte Carlo makes a violent turn and front ends a concrete light pole. The driver immediately ditches on foot, off into the night. Michelle attempts to detain the passenger. He boogies on foot through the residential neighborhood. Michelle gives chase. This kid matches the description from dispatch: Hispanic male, seventeen years old, about five feet nine inches, one hundred fifty pounds, blue denim pants, white Los Angeles Dodgers jersey. The kid's got a silver handgun."

"So where does this Mario Costa kid fit in the picture?" Tate asked, flipping through the pages of his notebook.

"This is where things get real sketchy. We haven't talked to Michelle, she requested her union lawyer. What we do know is that Mario Costa was in the area, his own backyard. Mario is Hispanic, sixteen years old, five feet nine inches, about one hundred fifty pounds. He was wearing a white Los Angeles Dodgers jersey."

"How do we know that he's not the kid who knocked over the *Stop and Rob* and he was running for the safety of his crib?"

"Couple of reasons, John. First, Mario didn't have a gun. He had a cell phone. Second, another one of my guys apprehended the other kid wearing a Los Angeles Dodgers jersey. That kid had a gun. The store clerk made a positive ID."

"She shot the wrong kid?" Tate asked in disbelief.

"Yup."

After a minute of silence he said, "Sue, we do indeed have a cluster fuck on our hands. How is Michelle doing?"

"She's way beyond being a mess. Crying, keeps talking about how the Costa kid was no older than her son Nate."

"What about the kid's parents?" Tate asked, pouring a cup of cold coffee from the pot and sticking it in the microwave. "Were they home when all this went down?"

"No," Kemp answered. "They were at a Christmas party in San Bernardino."

"Have they been notified?"

"Oh yeah— they've been notified. Right now they probably know more than I do."

"You're losing me there on that one, Sue. I don't understand," Tate said. He winced as the first sip of hot, stale coffee burned his tongue.

"The parents' names are Vincent and Carmen Costa. They were getting a blow by blow narrative in real time."

"How the fuck does that happen?" Tate asked. The second sip of coffee went down better than the first.

"Their next door neighbor, a gal named Laura Grogan. She was in an upstairs bedroom and heard a gunshot. She looks out a window, into the Costa's backyard, and sees a deputy with a service weapon drawn. She sees Mario lying on the grass in the backyard. She correctly assumes that the deputy shot Mario. Grogan immediately calls Carmen Costa at the Christmas party."

"Shit."

"Shit, pretty much sums it up, John."

"Now let me guess," Tate said. "The Costas immediately leave the party and head for home. They don't get anywhere near their house because you've set up a crime scene perimeter. What is now a bad situation takes an even uglier turn for the worst."

"You nailed it," Kemp answered. "Vincent Costa gets into it with one of my guys who won't let him enter the crime scene. Under the circumstances I really don't blame Costa for being pissed."

"What kind of contact have you had with the parents?" Tate asked.

"At the perimeter things were escalating between Costa and my guy. I made contact and told them why they couldn't go to their house. I wanted to get them down to headquarters. They refused, so I told them their son had been shot and did not survive."

"Is that all you told them?"

"Yes."

"Good, I'll talk to them later on tonight. Where are they right now?"

"I was finally able to convince them to go down to headquarters," Kemp said. "After I broke the news, Mrs. Costa cried herself to the point of physical exhaustion. Mr. Costa goes back and forth between denial and anger. He's got a lot of questions and he's demanding answers."

"Oh, I bet. If I were in his shoes, I would too. I'll talk with him. Where are you at now, Sue?"

"I'm at the Costa residence, sitting on the scene until I can turn it over to you. You have an estimate on your arrival here?"

Tate looked up at the clock on the kitchen wall, "It's twenty three thirty hours now. I should be there by zero one hundred."

"Sounds good, John. Anything you want me to do?"

"No, Sue, just keep the scene secure," Tate answered, walking back upstairs into his bedroom. "Besides your people, who's on scene now?"

"Crime scene tech has been here about ten minutes and the deputy coroner just arrived."

"How about the media?" Tate asked.

"Not yet."

"Won't be long, they'll be on this like stink on shit," Tate said, ending the call with Kemp.

Kathy Tate glanced up from her book and asked her husband, "Bad?"

"It doesn't get any worse," he answered, going into the walk-in closet to pick out a shirt, suit, and tie. "One of our people shot and killed a sixteen year old kid, mistaken identity, the wrong kid."

"I'll tell the girls in the morning that you got called out and we have to wait on putting up the Christmas tree," she said, watching her husband dress.

"Don't wait on me, who knows how long I'll be on this one." He gave his wife a kiss on the cheek while he straightened out his tie and shirt collar.

Tate walked out of the master bedroom and into the other bedrooms. His little angels were sound asleep, comforters pulled up to their necks. Tate gently kissed five sleeping foreheads and went back downstairs into the kitchen.

John Tate had been with the San Bernardino County Sheriff's Department for twenty-five years, the last seven heading up a homicide investigation team. Half of Tate's twenty-five years as a cop had been spent investigating murders. In addition to investigating homicides, Tate and his three detectives investigated his department's officer-involved shootings.

Tate sat down at the kitchen table, took out his cell phone, and started making the calls and assignments. His first call was to Lieutenant Mike Lenihan, "Hey boss, did I wake you?"

"Nah," Lenihan answered, "just watching Sports Center."

"We've got an officer involved shooting in Highland," Tate said. "Gonna be a big mess, I gotta get on the road. I'll keep you advised."

He went to the hallway closet and grabbed his wool overcoat. His mind became consumed with thoughts of what Michelle Baxter, Carmen Costa, and Vincent Costa must be going through at this very moment. He left his house and stepped into the lightly falling snow. His shoe prints left a trail in the fine white powder from his front porch to his unmarked sheriffs' unit. Tate opened the door, started the car, and turned the heater on to full blast. It was going to be a long night.

# 4

Tate drove past half a dozen television news vans as he approached the perimeter of the crime scene. The uniformed deputy that had denied access to Vincent and Carmen Costa waived him through. He pulled into the driveway of the Costa residence and reached over to the passenger's seat for his wool overcoat. Getting out of his car, he immediately felt the great variation in temperatures between his home in the snow-laden San Bernardino Mountains and that of the City of Highland, located at the base of the mountain range. He threw his overcoat back into the passenger's seat and shut the car door. The force of the door closing caused lingering snow on the car's roof and trunk to fall onto the concrete driveway.

While opening the front door to the house he wiped his shoes back and forth over the welcome mat, trying his best not to track in mud. He entered the tiled foyer of the large two- story home. The smell of pine was strong. Walking into the living room, he saw the freshly cut Christmas tree with stacks of wrapped presents lying beneath it. He took a moment and admired the tree's decorations. Prominent on the tree were two ornaments, each bearing the photograph of a young boy. They looked like brothers.

"Did you have any problems getting down the hill?" a voice from behind Tate asked.

Tate turned around, "Oh, hey, Sue—not too much of a problem. A little slipping and sliding; black ice was the biggest problem."

"Were you chained up?" she asked.

"Nah, I don't believe in snow chains, just slows me down."

"You know you're crazy, John."

"Yeah, so I've been told."

Sergeant Susan Kemp walked into the kitchen and from a marble counter top picked up her investigation notebook, steel mag-light flashlight, and travel mug of coffee. "All right, John, I'm out of here. It's all yours."

"Thanks, Sue. Do you know anything more since you briefed me on the phone?"

"No, nothing of significance."

"Michelle Baxter is still at the Highland station?" Tate asked.

"Yes."

"And the Costa's are at headquarters?"

"Yes."

Kemp walked out the front door and Tate went into the kitchen. On a dinette set he saw an opened pizza box, two slices of pepperoni pizza remained. On the wood floor, just off to the side of the dinette, he spotted a blue dog bed. Inside the bed, there was a white and tan Jack Russell Terrier. He was shaking and curled into a ball with his nose tucked under a small-embroidered pillow.

"Hey, buddy," Tate said, reaching down to pet the scared dog. "Too bad you can't talk. You could probably tell me what the hell happened here tonight."

Tate heard familiar voices coming from the backyard, through the patio slider, and into the house. He stood up and caught sight of his detective, Scott Kane, with crime scene technician, Randy Bell. Kane was writing in his leather notebook and Bell was adjusting his .35 mm SLR camera.

Tate walked over to Kane, looked down at him and asked, "Scooter, have you and Photo Boy done a preliminary walk through of the scene?"

"Yes, Sarge," Kane said, looking up at his boss.

Tate was on the tall side at six feet three inches. He also had a nickname for most of the people he worked with. When John Tate gave someone a nickname, it was a sign of acceptance. If you worked with or for John Tate, and you had no nickname—that's when you should be worried.

"Have you thrown down any placards yet?" Tate asked.

"No, sir," Kane answered.

"Okay, Scooter, what is this crime scene telling us?"

"First off, it's pretty obvious. Our deceased, Mario Costa, is home alone with the dog. Looks like the kid ordered up a pepperoni pie for dinner."

"No shit, Scooter, and we sent you to detective school to make that brilliant deduction?" Tate said to Kane, giving the detective a little good-natured ribbing. In the business of investigating homicides, day in and day out, a sense of humor went a long way in taking the stressful edge off the gruesome duty.

Kane passed through a sliding glass door leading out to the concrete patio area and backyard. Tate and Bell followed.

"The glass slider was two thirds of the way open," Kane said. "With temperatures in the mid-fifties and a drizzly rain falling, whatever the kid was doing outside, he didn't plan on being out that long."

Standing on the concrete patio, Tate focused on the Costa's quarter acre grass backyard, the neighbor's yards, and the walking trails that abutted the properties. "Damn, it's darker than hell back there," Tate said.

"Very," Kane agreed. "There's a set of light switches on the inside wall next to the sliding glass door. One switch turns on the exterior patio lights. The other switch turns on a spot light type of fixture that shines into the backyard. Both lights were off."

"Well, like we said, it appeared that the kid wasn't going to be outside that long," Tate said.

"Exactly, Sarge."

Tate walked out into the Costa's backyard. Paper and plastic medical debris left by the paramedics littered the yard. In the rear left quadrant of the backyard, he set his eyes on the figure lying in the grass. Tate made his way to Mario Costa, Kane and Bell followed right behind him. The rain had stopped, but the freshly mowed grass was still wet. Tate breathed in and smelled the grass clippings that were beginning to cling to his shoes and pants legs.

Standing over Mario Costa's body, Tate shook his head from side to side and rubbed his right hand around his temples and forehead. Mario was wearing Levi's blue jeans. The front and back of the pants were soiled from the body purging itself upon death. Mario's once white jersey was now a deep crimson color. The blue Dodger's script had turned a sickly shade of purple. Mario's open hazel eyes held the death stare. A small amount of blood had trickled and dried up on the corner of his mouth.

"Want us to start putting placards down?" Kane asked, breaking the silence.

"Yes," Tate managed to say with his jaw clenched.

Crime scene technician Randy Bell reached into his duffel bag and pulled out a bright yellow plastic placard. The placard bore the number "1". Bell bent down and placed the placard six inches from Mario Costa's jet-black hair. He then slowly walked around the body, taking pictures with his camera, from multiple angles and positions.

The three then paced the five feet from Mario's body to the cell phone. Droplets of sticky blood hugged the blades of nearby grass. From his duffel bag, Bell took out a placard bearing the number "2". He placed the placard next to the cell phone and took photographs.

Scott Kane picked up the cell phone. It had a silver metal finish and measured five inches by three inches—the kind that folded out with a small keyboard. "Nice phone," Kane said as he inspected it.

"A phone's a phone."

"No, Sarge, this one's nice, top of the line. It's got all the latest bells and whistles."

"When did the kid use the phone last?" Tate asked.

Kane scrolled through the call history log of the phone. "There's an outgoing call at ten seventeen and an incoming call at ten thirty three."

Tate opened up his leather notebook and held it in his left hand. Holding a flashlight in his right hand, he shined it onto the pages. "From my telephone briefing with Sue Kemp it looks like the kid made that out going call just minutes before he was shot. That incoming call— Baxter had already shot him. Scooter, you say it's the same number?"

"Yes, sir."

"Read it out loud to me."

Kane read out the number from Mario's cell phone as Tate handed the flashlight to Bell, so that he could jot down the number in his notebook. "Okay, Photo Boy, go ahead and bag it."

Randy Bell gave the flashlight back to Tate and took a brown paper bag from his duffle bag. With a magic marker, Bell wrote identifying information on the bag. He took the cell phone from Kane and placed it inside the bag; sealing it with clear sheriff's department evidence tape and marking it with the date and his initials.

"Baxter fired one round?" Tate asked.

"Yes," Kane answered.

"Have you located the casing?"

"Yes, Sarge."

"Let's go take a look."

With Kane leading the way, they walked forty feet from the Costa backyard to a dirt-walking trail. Waving his flashlight back and forth, Kane pointed to the small brass shell casing glistening in the light.

Bell placed yellow placard number "3" next to the shell casing. He photographed the casing and placed it in a brown paper bag, then marked, and sealed it.

From the spot where Michelle Baxter had fired the fatal shot, Tate stared into the Costa backyard at the body of Mario Costa. He said in a low voice, "What a mess. She didn't have that good a look."

After collecting the shell casing, Kane and Bell went back to Mario's body and began the process of taking the exact measurements of the crime scene. They measured the dimensions of the backyard. They determined the distance of Mario's body from the back sliding door, from the spot where the shell casing was recovered, and from the neighboring bedroom window, where Laura Grogan had witnessed the shooting. With these calculations, Detective Scott Kane would prepare a crime scene diagram— a piece of evidence in any subsequent criminal or civil trial.

Tate went back inside the house and sat down on a black leather couch in the living room. He glimpsed over at the Jack Russell Terrier still lying in its doggie bed. Tate called out and the dog obediently trotted over to him. He then spent a few moments stroking the dog's coat. The dog rested up against his legs as he reached into his suit jacket for his cell phone. Flipping through the pages of his notebook, Tate found the number that Scott Kane had read off from Mario's cell phone. He punched the number into his cell phone.

"Sir, my name is Sergeant John Tate with the San Bernardino County Sheriff's department. I know its two o'clock in the morning, but who am I talking to?"

A groggy, sleep-filled voice answered, "My name is Jack Reed. What's the problem Sergeant? Please tell me everything is okay with Mario Costa."

"How do you know Mario Costa?" Tate asked.

"He and my son Archie are good friends. They go to school together."

"Why would you think something is wrong with Mario Costa?"

"He never called my son back. We've been worrying about him all night."

"Tell me about it," Tate said, writing in his notebook.

"What happened to Mario?"

"Please, Mr. Reed, just tell me what you know."

"My son and Mario are gamers. You know, playing video games on the TV or online with their computers. At ten o'clock this evening, they were supposed to go on line to play one of their virtual reality games. About that time, Mario called our house, the number you just dialed."

"Did your son talk with Mario?"

"No, Archie didn't get to the phone in time and it kicked over to voice mail."

"Did Mario leave a message?"

"Yes."

"What'd he say?"

"He just wanted Archie to know that before he could log onto the game he had to take his dog, Payaso, outside to go do his business. He asked

Archie to call him back on his cell phone. He said he'd have it outside with him."

"Did your son try to call him back?"

"Yes."

"When?"

"Oh, I don't know, pretty quickly after Mario left his message here for my son. I'd say within minutes."

"Did Archie speak with Mario?"

"No, Mario didn't answer his phone and never called back. That's why we've been worrying about him all night. Sergeant, is Mario okay?"

"No, Mr. Reed, he's not."

"Are his parents with him?"

Tate thought about his response and then answered, "Yes."

"Can you tell me more? What do I tell my son?"

"Mr. Reed, please understand that it wouldn't be appropriate for me to give you a whole lot of details right now. I know you'll hear about it on TV tomorrow. There's been a shooting; Mario was killed in that shooting."

"Oh my God," Reed said, after seconds, but what seemed like minutes of silence.

"Yeah, keep them in your prayers," Tate said concluding the call.

Before leaving the Costa residence, he spent a few more moments petting the dog and looking intently at the Christmas tree. "Merry Christmas ole' boy," he said to the dog as he looked at the Christmas ornament imprinted with the photograph of a young Mario Costa.

# 5

At four o'clock in the morning, the drone of a janitor's floor buffing machine echoed through the still hallway of the sheriff's headquarters building. Inside a conference room, Vincent and Carmen Costa waited. Vincent stood at a window, lifelessly staring into the night. He took off his suit coat, then his necktie, and draped them over a chair. Carmen, her eyes puffy and red, sat in a chair at the conference room table. She dabbed at her eyes with a Kleenex and added it to the pile of used facial tissues sitting on the table, next to a Styrofoam cup of cold coffee.

"How are we going to tell Joseph?" Carmen asked her husband.

"I don't know, I don't know," he answered, without a trace of emotion.

Joseph Costa, at age twenty, was their other son; a junior at Cal State Fullerton and the star pitcher for the school's baseball team.

Sheriff's Chaplain Robert Parks knocked on the door of the conference room and walked in.

"Is there anything else I can get you folks?" he asked.

"No, I don't think so," Vincent answered.

"I just spoke with Sergeant John Tate; he is pulling into the parking lot."

"Chaplain?"

"Yes, Mrs. Costa."

"Would you please stay here with us?"

Parks went over to the table and picked up the tissues along with the cold cup of coffee. He threw them in a wastebasket, walked back to the conference table, and sat down in a chair next to Carmen Costa.

"There's no way this can be happening. My baby can't be dead," Carmen said to the Chaplain, the tears once again filling her eyes.

Parks struggled to find a response and could only reach over and touch her on the shoulder with empathy.

"This just doesn't make any sense," Vincent said in disbelief. "There's got to be some kind of mistake. It can't be Mario. Why would a cop shoot Mario in our own backyard?"

As Costa finished his sentence, the door to the conference room opened and Sgt. John Tate walked into the room.

Vincent Costa turned from the window, looked at him, and with an edge in his voice, asked, "Are you Sergeant Tate?"

"Yes, sir."

Costa took a seat next to his wife and Chaplain Parks. Tate sat at the head of the table, opened up his leather notebook, and took out a pair of business cards. "I'm very sorry about your son, Mario," Tate said, to start the conversation.

Carmen Costa looked straight at Tate, desperation coursed through her veins, "Please, Sergeant Tate, please tell us Mario is alive, please tell us he's okay."

"I can't, Mrs. Costa. Your son, Mario, was shot this evening and he died from those wounds."

Denial shifted to grief as she screamed, "No, no, no!" and buried her head into the shoulders of her husband. They held each other close and sobbed for ten minutes.

Vincent Costa then wiped his nose with a tissue and cleared his throat, "Sergeant Tate, was our son killed by a cop?"

"Yes sir, Mario was shot by a deputy with our department."

"How can that be?" Costa said, shaking his head. "Mario has never been in trouble with the law."

"It had nothing to do with your son being in trouble with the law."

"Then why did they have to shoot him, Sergeant Tate?"

"There was an armed robbery of a convenience store on the other side of town; this lead to a vehicle pursuit between our department and the robbers. They wrecked their get-away car in the subdivision next to yours. Our deputy then engaged in a foot pursuit with the armed robber."

"Sergeant Tate, you're not suggesting that Mario was involved in the robbery are you?"

"No, Mr. Costa, Mario had no involvement in the robbery."

"Then why did your people have to shoot him?"

"The foot pursuit went through your neighborhood. The suspect our deputy was pursuing had on a white Los Angeles Dodger's jersey. Your son was in your backyard—he also was wearing a white Los Angeles Dodger's jersey."

Vincent glared at Tate. It took a couple of minutes for the impact to set in, "The deputy confused my son for the armed robber?"

"We haven't talked to the deputy yet. But, I would have to say that the deputy certainly thought your son was the armed robber."

"Don't play word games with me, Tate. The bottom line is your people shot and killed the wrong person, my son."

"Yes sir, that is correct."

"Vince, I'm confused. Is he saying that just because Mario was wearing a Dodgers jersey, he's dead?"

"I think that's exactly what he's saying," he answered his wife. His eyes were hot and his voice firm.

"Do you know why my son was in the backyard?" Carmen asked.

"Yes, ma'am, he was taking your dog out."

Vincent Costa shifted his glare from Tate to the map of San Bernardino County, which was hanging on the wall of the conference room. Tears welled in his eyes. Carmen Costa again buried her head in her husband's chest, muffling the sounds of her sobbing. The only other noise in the room was the soft buzz of the overhead fluorescent lighting. Chaplain Parks got up from the table and searched for another box of facial tissues.

Tate left the table and walked over to the window, giving the Costa's room to grieve.  He peered out the window and witnessed the morning sun just starting to peek above the mountains to the east.  He sighed and thought to himself—*this job really sucks sometimes.*

"Sergeant Tate?"

"Yes, Mr. Costa."

"What's his name?"

"Whose name, sir?"

"The man who murdered my son, what's his name?"

"I'm sorry, Mr. Costa; I can't give you that information."

Vincent gently moved his wife's head from his chest.  He got up from the table and walked over to Tate.  Costa stood face to face with Tate, separated by no more than an arm's length distance.  "I'm his father; you have to tell me the name of the monster who murdered my son."

"I can't do that, Mr. Costa."

"Why?" he asked.  The conversation had now escalated into a full-blown confrontation.

"The Peace Officer Bill of Rights prohibits me from releasing that information at this stage of the investigation."

"He has rights?'

"Yes, sir, the deputy has rights."

"Where were my son's rights when he was gunned down in his own backyard?"

"I can appreciate your feelings, Mr. Costa."

"I can't have his name, that's bullshit, Tate!"

"No sir, that's the law."

Carmen Costa got up from the table, went to her husband, and grabbed his hand, "Vincent, please, all this yelling and arguing isn't going to bring Mario back."

"What's going to happen to this deputy?" Vincent asked Tate.

"Your son's death is a homicide, like any homicide, there will be a criminal investigation and I am in charge of the investigation for the sheriff's department."

"Tate, the man murdered my son— he should be in jail right now."

"Mr. Costa, all we know right now is that one of our deputies shot your son. That's why there's an investigation. When the criminal investigation is completed, the sheriff's department will submit the reports to the District Attorney. They will decide what should legally happen to the deputy who shot your son."

"So the District Attorney will then file murder charges?"

"Mr. Costa, it's way too early to make those determinations. When the DA gets our investigation, they will have decisions to make. First, they will determine whether the deputy was justified in using deadly force. If the deputy had legal justification for the use of deadly force, no criminal charges will be filed. If the deputy had no justification, then the DA will decide if there is enough evidence to file criminal charges; manslaughter or murder."

"C'mon, Tate, how can the murder of my son be justified?" Vincent said, letting the words hang in the air.

"Mr. Costa, no two people should have to go through what you and your wife are going through. However, I'm not going to argue with you. I'm just trying to answer your questions the best I can."

"Yes, Sergeant Tate, we understand that," Carmen Costa said. "Where is Mario now? Can we at least say good-bye to him?"

"An autopsy will be done on your son Monday afternoon. When that is completed the coroner's office will release his body."

"No," Carmen said stiffly. "You can't do that to my baby. I won't let you do an autopsy on him."

"I'm sorry, ma'am, we have to, it's part of the criminal investigation and it's required by law under these circumstances."

Carmen Costa's red face, from crying, turned pale. She rushed out of the conference room, down the hallway, and into the restroom. She went into a stall, leaned over the commode, and started throwing up.

# 6

Michelle Baxter sat alone in the watch commander's office at the Highland Station. There were no windows in the room, so she couldn't see the steady stream of sheriff's department vehicles going in and out of the parking lot. However, the quiet of the room did allow her to hear the flurry of activity just outside the door. She recognized the voices of her sergeant, lieutenant, and captain. The tone of their dialogue reeked of stress and intensity.

Physically and emotionally worn out, she took a long drink of water from her thermos and closed her eyes. She just wanted to go home and hug her seventeen-year-old son, Nate. Dark bags encircled her eyes and when she opened them, she glanced down at her watch. She decided to give him a call, even though he was probably still in bed.

"Nate, did I wake you up?"

"Well, yeah, it's like six o'clock in the morning," the drowsy voice answered.

"I hope you didn't stay up too late waiting for me."

"Just 'til around midnight. Between you and dad, I've pretty much got the cop routine figured out. If you're not home when your shift is over, and you don't call, it probably means you're working like some kind of major crash or crime scene and you can't get to a phone.  You know, you get home when you get home.  Where are you now?"

"I'm still at the station."

"When will you be home?"

"I don't know."

"Mom, you don't sound too good, is everything alright."

"No, Nate, everything's not alright.  I shot someone last night."

"Are you crying, mom?"

"He was just a kid, probably your age."

"Is he going to make it?"

"He died, Nate."

"Are you okay?"

"I'm tired, I'm scared, and I miss you."

"When will they let you come home?"

"I have no idea.  I don't think they're even close to being finished with me.  My union lawyer should be here any minute now.  Then I've got to talk to the detectives and I'm pretty sure department policy says I have to talk to the department shrink."

"Shrink?"

"Psychologist."

"Oh—why do you need a lawyer?  Are you in trouble?"

"I don't know, son, I really don't know.  I'm scared."

"Is there anything I can do?" Nate asked his mother.

"Yes, give your mom a great big hug when she walks through the door."

"I love you, mom."

"I love you too, Nate.  Like you say, I'll be home, when I'll be home."

She didn't know what she would do without her son.  He had the same first name as his father, Jordan.  To avoid confusion, they had called him Nate, his middle name.  Since Jordan's death, six months ago, they had become even closer as a mother and son.  In the days, weeks, and months ahead she would need her son more than ever.

The door to the office opened and a disheveled looking middle-aged man with an awful comb-over entered.  In one hand his pudgy fingers held a king sized container of coffee. In the other, a dog-eared yellow legal pad. He set them both down on the desk and held out his right hand.

"Morning— I'm your lawyer, Maury Stein."

"Michelle Baxter," she answered, reaching over and shaking hands with her lawyer.

"You don't look like a Baxter."

"Excuse me?"

"Your skin color, you don't look like a Baxter."

"You know what, pal, I've just met you and I really don't think I care much for you. Yeah, your right, I don't look like a Baxter. That's probably because I'm Hispanic and my maiden name is Paz. My husband was a gringo; any other racist questions?"

Unfazed by Baxter's biting response, Stein asked, "How long have they had you in this room?"

"I don't know, probably five hours now."

"Are you tired?"

"Very."

"Do you just want to go home?"

"Yes."

* * *

Tate pulled into the drive through lane of King Taco, a mom and pop Mexican fast food joint located across the street from the sheriff's headquarters. King Taco usually did a booming business with the cops and other county workers, but at 7:00 a.m. on a Sunday morning, he drove straight up to the window and placed his order.

Tate handed the young Hispanic woman working the window a ten-dollar bill. She returned the favor by giving him a paper bag containing two overstuffed chorizo and egg burritos. He maneuvered his unmarked sheriff's car into a nearby parking stall and took out one of the burritos. Tate's stomach growled in anticipation of the much-needed nourishment; he'd been working all night and had not eaten in twelve hours. Laboring through the night was part of the job description for a homicide investigator. In Tate's line of work, nine out of ten times, all the bad stuff happened at night. He unwrapped one of the burritos and the smell of spicy Mexican sausage permeated the car as he ate the burrito with a minimum number of bites.

After wiping the remnants of the burrito from his face, he laid his head back against the headrest, and closed his burning eyes. Sleep was a rare commodity for the homicide investigator working a fresh case. His tired mind wandered and he thought about where the night had taken him and where the day ahead would lead him. There was nothing pleasant about working a homicide investigation, especially when the shooter was a deputy. Tate didn't like investigating his own people. It came with the job, but it still sucked.

He took a five-minute catnap, then started the car, and made the four mile drive to the sheriff's Highland Station. On a typical Sunday morning the station's parking lot would be empty—but not this Sunday morning. Tate drove into the parking lot and had a hard time finding a spot; he counted all the unmarked department vehicles. *Damn, there's enough brass here to sink a battleship*, he thought to himself.

After coming across a parking spot, he grabbed his suit jacket, leather notebook, and the bag containing the King Taco burrito. He went inside the station and walked past a conference room. Without being noticed, he stopped and peeked inside. Sheriff's department officials, all way above Tate's pay grade, were thrashing out the troubles that the Costa shooting would bring to the department.

Tate rapped on the door to the watch commander's office, "C'mon in," said a male voice with a thick New York accent.

Tate walked in and saw Maury Stein sitting at a chair behind the desk with Michelle Baxter sitting at a chair in front of the desk. He introduced himself and took a seat next to Baxter.

"Sergeant, it's been a long night for my client. She's tired and just been through a very emotional incident. I don't think we're going to get anything productive done this morning."

Tate, knowing the department's protocol on officer-involved shootings, asked Baxter, "How long has Sergeant Kemp had you on ice, here in this room?"

"Since midnight," Baxter answered.

"Hungry?"

"Yeah."

Tate handed her the bag with the King Taco chorizo and egg burrito, "I brought you a little breakfast."

"Appreciate it, Sarge," Baxter said to Tate as she took the foil off the burrito and began eating.

After a few bites, she looked up. Tate could see tears starting to well in her eyes.

"What was his name?" she asked Tate.

"Mario Costa."

"Have you spoken to his parents yet?"

Tate detected a slight Hispanic accent in her soft voice, "Yes, I just left them over at headquarters."

"Ugly?"

"Very," Tate answered Baxter.

Baxter pushed away the half-eaten burrito. Her breathing became hurried and short, the way someone does when trying not to cry.

Tate offered her a tissue and said, "Michelle, me and my team are working the criminal investigation. When we're done, it's going to get sent over to the District Attorney's office for them to review. They will decide what, if any, criminal charges will be filed against you."

"Sergeant Tate," Stein said, interrupting. "These are all legal issues that I need to discuss with my client before we proceed any further. Because she's beyond the point of exhaustion, that conversation is not going to happen today."

"I understand that counselor, but I've got a job to do here too. So why don't you just let me finish saying what I need to say to Deputy Baxter?"

Stein looked at Baxter and said to his client, "Can you go on for a little while longer?"

Baxter blew her nose into the tissue and nodded her head up and down in the affirmative.

"Michelle, I want to explain to you what we're doing here. As I said, my team is only focusing on the criminal aspect of the shooting. I'm not doing the Internal Affairs investigation. Someone else from the department will do that.

"I don't care about things like, when was the last time you qualified at the range? What kind of ammo did you have in your gun? Or, how much sleep did you get the night before the shooting? IA cares about that stuff, not me.

"What I need from you is a detailed explanation of why you made the decision to shoot the kid. I need to see this shooting through your eyes.

"Now, it is up to you to decide whether you want to talk to me and my detectives. We only take voluntary statements. I'm not going to force you to talk, like IA does.

"But I can tell you, without us knowing why you shot the kid; the DA will not legally justify the shooting."

"My client may decide that she doesn't want to give a statement," Stein said as he stopped writing on the tattered yellow legal pad.

"I understand that, counselor," Tate said, his patience with Maury Stein wearing thin. "Michelle, before you arrive at that decision, make sure your mouthpiece over there explains to you the consequences of not giving us a statement."

Michelle Baxter wearily watched the exchange between the two men. She ran her hands through her short black hair. Her light olive colored uniform shirt bore several small dried stains of Mario Costa's blood. Her dark green uniform pants bore the bits and pieces of her own dried bile.

Tate took a pair of business cards out of his leather notebook and handed one each to Baxter and Stein. He made his way towards the door and said, "Give me a call when you want to talk."

As Tate was leaving the office, Michelle Baxter spoke for the first time in fifteen minutes, "Sarge."

"Yes, Michelle."

"Thanks for the breakfast."

Maury Stein left soon after Tate. He instructed his client to come to his office on Tuesday, so they could discuss all the legal issues Baxter would be facing from the shooting.

Baxter then left the watch commander's office, went to the restroom and splashed cold water on her face. Wiping her face dry with a paper towel, she fixed her eyes on the mirror. She looked terrible. Just twenty-four hours earlier, she had taken pride in her youthful complexion and facial features. She always thought she looked younger than her forty-two years. Not today, not right now. *You look like shit* she said to the mirror.

With a couple of moistened paper towels, Baxter tried to scrub away the blood and bile stains on her uniform. The stains wouldn't come out and she started to feel nauseous again as she tossed the paper towels into the trash. Doing her best to avoid the department brass, she went back into the office to wait on the department's psychologist.

Five minutes later a woman about the same age as Baxter walked into the office and introduced herself as Dr. Rebecca Morgan.

"How are you doing, Michelle?"

"I'm okay."

"No you're not."

"Look, Doc, I just shot and killed an innocent person, a sixteen year old kid. What in the hell am I supposed to say?"

"You're not supposed to say anything, Michelle, there's no script here you have to go by."

"I have a son almost the same age."

"What's his name, Michelle?"

"Nate."

"Have you talked with Nate today?

"Yes, by phone, a couple of hours ago."

"How about your husband?" Morgan asked, glimpsing at the wedding band on Baxter's finger.

"I lost him six months ago," Baxter answered as she wiped her eyes with the back of her uniform shirt sleeve. "He was killed by a car bomb in Afghanistan."

"I'm so sorry, Michelle."

"I am too."

"Michelle, I've been doing this a long time. You will be going through a lot of emotional stuff because of the shooting. I can promise you that.

That's why I'm here for you. It's important for you to talk through these issues."

"I appreciate it, Doc, but I am okay. I really don't need you or anybody else."

"Michelle, don't suppress or deny your feelings. That's not a healthy road to go down."

"Look, Doc, you've done your job. Just go back and tell the brass that I am going to be fine. I'm out of here."

# 7

"What time was Joseph leaving for LAX?" Carmen Costa asked her husband as they travelled on the 91 freeway from San Bernardino to their son's apartment in Fullerton. Her voice was low and showed no signs of emotion. They were the first words she had spoken since leaving the sheriff's department headquarters.

"My mom's flight from Seattle gets in at noon. He'd probably leave around ten."

Carmen looked at her watch, "By the time we get to his apartment it's going to be nine o'clock. How are we going to handle this?"

Vincent stared straight out the windshield, keeping the Lexus at a steady eighty miles per hour in the fast lane. They were one of the handful of cars on the freeway; Sunday morning was one of the few times it was not bumper-to-bumper all the way into Los Angeles.

"We'll tell him, you stay with him. I'll drive into LAX to pick up my mom."

Mary Costa, Vincent's mother, was flying in that morning for the holidays. Because they had expected a late night at the Chamber of Commerce Christmas party, Joseph volunteered to pick up his grandmother at the airport and drive her to the family home in Highland.

Vincent exited the freeway and maneuvered into the parking lot of an AM-PM convenience store. He went inside and returned with two sixteen ounce Styrofoam cups of coffee. Carmen held the steaming cups while they drove across the street into the parking lot of Joseph's apartment complex. They sat in silence for several minutes, holding hands. Just before he opened the car door, Vincent gave a supportive squeeze to his wife's hand.

Most of the complex's residents were students attending nearby Cal State Fullerton. Joseph shared the apartment with two other members of the school's baseball team and both of his roommates had gone home for the Christmas and New Year's break.

Vincent knocked on the door. After a couple of moments, Vincent started to knock a second time when his son came to the door. In his calloused hands, Joseph held a bowl of Captain Crunch cereal. He took the spoon out of his mouth and a little bit of milk dribbled down his chin and onto the dimple that melted the hearts of college girls.

"Mom, dad, what are you guys doing here?" Joseph said, surprised to see his parents standing outside the door. "I told you I was going to pick up grandma at the airport."

"We've got some bad news," Vincent said, biting his lower lip.

"What's wrong?" Joseph asked, leading his parents into the apartment.

Carmen walked into the small kitchen area, pushed aside an empty Burger King bag, and sat down at the dinette table. Vincent went to the living room, picked up the TV remote control and turned down the volume on the NFL pre-game show.

Vincent looked his son in the eyes. "Joseph, your brother died last night."

"What?"

"Mario's gone."

"No, no way," Joseph said, turning to look at his mother.

Unable to speak, she nodded her head up and down.

Joseph picked up a worn out baseball that was lying in the corner of the room and gripped it with all his might. His well-built, six foot four body wilted as he tried to take in the news. He fought back the tears, he hadn't cried since he was ten years old. "What happened?"

"A sheriff's deputy shot and killed him," Vincent said.

"A sheriff's deputy? That's crazy, pop."

"Well, that was our first reaction."

"Mario's a good kid, he's got good friends. They don't run around doing stupid stuff."

"It wasn't anything he or his friends did," Vincent answered.

"So what happened? It's not like the police just go around shooting people for no reason."

"I don't know, Joseph, maybe they do."

"Huh?"

"The best we can tell, last night a convenience store over in the bad part of town was robbed. There was a car chase, then a foot chase. A deputy was chasing the robber through the backyards of our neighborhood. Mario was out in the backyard, letting Payaso do his business. The deputy saw Mario, mistook him for the robber, and shot him."

"That's bullshit, pop, how could the cops just shoot the wrong person?"

"The robber was Hispanic, about Mario's age and build. The kid had on a Dodgers jersey. Mario had on his Dodgers' jersey."

"The one I just gave him for his birthday?"

"Yes."

Joseph stared at the muted television picture. A tear rolled down each of his cheeks. After three minutes he said, "Why did I have to give him that damn jersey?"

Carmen got up from the dinette, walked into the living room, and sat down on the couch next to her son. She held him close and said, "Stop thinking like that, Joseph. It's not your fault."

Joseph gave in to the tears. His mother held him, and in a barely audible voice, he said, "Mario didn't even like the Dodgers or baseball. I should have never gotten him that jersey."

Carmen ran her fingers through her son's wavy black hair, "He loved that jersey, not because he liked the Dodgers or baseball. I couldn't get it off him long enough to run it through the wash. He loved it because you gave it to him and you were his hero."

Joseph wiped his nose with the back of his hand. His mother gave him a tissue. "Why are you both lying to me? He can't be dead." Vincent sat down on the couch next to his wife and son. They all embraced and sobbed, sharing their grief and heartache.

Joseph's tears soon turned to anger, "What are they going to do to the deputy who killed Mario?"

"We don't know," Vincent answered.

"Something has to happen, he murdered my little brother."

"All we know is that they are doing an investigation," Vincent said.

"He's gotta pay for killing Mario."

"Please, Joseph, it's too soon to be worrying about that. Let's just get from one hour to the next." Vincent gave them each a kiss and reached into his pocket for the car keys. "I've got to go pickup Grandma."

Vincent left the apartment and shielded his eyes from the bright morning sunlight. He took a deep breath and opened the car door. *Please God, help me keep it together.*

* * *

Nate Baxter drained the pasta into a colander in the sink and jumped backwards, trying to avoid the splash of steam and hot water. He gave the pasta a couple of good shakes and went over to the stove to stir the pot of simmering red sauce. The garage door opened and he heard his mother's car drive in.

"Nate?"

"I'm in the kitchen, mom."

Michelle Baxter walked into the kitchen, sniffed at the robust aroma of garlic, and saw her son peeling a cucumber. "What are you doing?" she asked.

"Cooking."

She looked at her son and faked a smile, "Put that peeler down and come give your mother a hug."

"Are you okay, mom."

"Yeah, I'm fine," she said, holding her son close and clutching him tightly. "Do I have time for a shower?"

"Fifteen minutes, I've still got to finish the salad."

"Thank you for fixing dinner, Nate."

"I kinda thought you would be tired when you got home." When he stared into his mother's eyes, he recognized that stressed and frazzled look—he often looked like that in the morning after pulling an all-nighter, studying for an exam.

From the kitchen's pantry, Michelle got a black plastic trash bag and made her way up the stairs. The second floor of the big house was quiet, too quiet. Nate's bedroom and bathroom was downstairs. She and Jordan had the second floor all to themselves. A large master bedroom, his office, and her craft room. She walked by his office and peered in; it was just as he'd left it.

In the bathroom, she turned on the shower and started to undress. She balled up her uniform shirt and pants, putting them in the black trash bag. Bile from her stomach worked its way through her esophagus and throat as she sealed up the bag with a twist tie.

She washed her body once, twice, then a third time. The soap could wash away the remnants of her vomit and the boy's blood, but no amount of scouring could cleanse her mind. She put the bar of soap back in the holder, leaned both of her hands up against the tile, and started crying. The hot water splashed off her hair, rinsing away the soap and tears.

Toweling off, she stared at the steamed over mirror and didn't know the face that looked back at her. In the six months since Jordan's death, she had aged so much. The emotional healing process after his death had been hell, and now this. Sifting through clothes in her dresser drawers, she put on an Ole Miss sweatshirt, a pair of sweatpants, and went back downstairs.

Nate had the pasta, salad, and bread on the table waiting for his mother. Before she sat down, Michelle went to the wine rack and grabbed a bottle of red wine. With the bottle of wine in one hand, a wine glass and corkscrew in the other, she sat down at the table with Nate.

"This is good, Nate," she said, twirling the stringy pasta on her fork and taking a bite. "When did you learn to cook?"

"I've been watching grub TV."

"Grub TV?"

"Yeah, you know, The Food Network."

"That's pretty desperate, Nate, no baseball games on TV, so you have to resort to watching the Food Network."

"Tell me about it."

Michelle took a long sip of wine and gazed at a painting on the wall, "He was so young, that could have been you, Nate."

"Mom, you did what you thought you had to do."

"It was all just so horrible. The car chase, the foot pursuit; I was so scared that I'd never see you again."

Talking about the facts of the shooting made him uncomfortable, so he changed the subject. "When do you have to go back? Are they giving you some time off?"

"Oh yeah—they're giving me some time off. I don't know when I'm going back—if ever. I'm on administrative leave."

"What does that mean?"

"Well, if I was a crook, I suppose you could call it house arrest."

"You can't leave the house?"

"I can leave the house; I just need to carry my cell phone in case they want to know where I'm at."

"For how long?"

"I don't know. It could be a good long while. I'll find all that stuff out on Tuesday when I talk to my lawyer."

"Are they paying you?" Nate asked, as he took the dinner plates from the dining room into the kitchen.

"Yes," she answered. "Nate, let me take care of cleaning up."

"No way, mom— this is my deal from start to finish."

Michelle got up from the table and kissed her son on the forehead, "Good night, I'm going upstairs, I'm exhausted."

"Good night, mom. I love you."

"I love you, Nate," Michelle said, willing herself up the stairs with the wine glass and a second bottle of wine.

Not much of a drinker, the bottle of wine she downed at dinner was her first full bottle of wine since they celebrated their anniversary last year. Never before had she started on a second bottle of wine.

In the office, she sat in his chair. She breathed in the comforting smell of leather and the faint scent of his Brooks Brothers cologne. Holding the wine glass in the palms of her hands, she looked at the framed photographs on the wall. Jordan in his Ole Miss Football uniform, his sheriff's department uniform, and getting sworn in as a Deputy District Attorney. On the desk sat his favorite family photograph. Taken when Nate was ten, they were having a snowball fight in Lake Arrowhead. Next to the framed photograph rested one of Nate's trophies from when he played Little League baseball.

Halfway into the second bottle of wine, she knew she was drunk. She had hoped that the alcohol would take the pain away, but it provided no relief—the images from the boy's backyard were still in her mind. A little unsteady on her feet, she went into the master bedroom and got ready for bed.

She had been up for thirty-six hours and fell into a deep sleep the moment her head touched the pillow. The sleep did not last long. She woke up in a cold sweat. She kept seeing the boy; helplessly watching him fight for each tortured last breath of life. It played in her mind, over and over and over again. It would not stop. The *whop-whop-whop* of the sheriff's helicopter circling over the boy—she could hear it. The helicopter's searchlight shining down on the body, alternating between light and dark—she could see it. She reached over to the nightstand for the bottle of wine.

# 8

On Monday morning, the protesters and the media were camped out at the entrance to the sheriff's headquarters building. Since the night of the shooting, all the Southern California media outlets had made the death of Mario Costa its lead story. Parked alongside the street in front of the building were the remote reporting vans of KNBC, KABC, KCBS, and KTLA. Each van's satellite transmitter reached into the air. From a distance, they looked like a herd of giraffes.

Fifty members of Stop Police Abuse (SPA) kept up an angry vigil outside the entrance. SPA was a local Hispanic activist group whose platform centered around what they believed to be the sheriff's department's excessive use of force on members of the Hispanic community. About a dozen of the enraged protesters waved signs that read: *Stop the Abuse, No More Police Murders, Leave Us Alone,* and *Bad Shoot-Bad Cop.*

Inside the building, from his second floor office, Sheriff Larry Covington and his second in command, Assistant Sheriff Frank Peters, glared down at the commotion outside.

"I see our friends are back," Covington said.

"Yeah, they're more jacked up than usual. We had to confirm early on that we shot the wrong person—an innocent kid."

"Fuck 'em," Covington said, leaving the window and making his way to his desk. "Those wing nuts would still be out there even if we had shot the actual robbery suspect."

"Probably," Peters answered his boss.

"What are they demanding from us now?" Covington asked, not looking up from the stack of documents he was signing.

"They want the name of the deputy. They also want you to explain why a white deputy had to shoot and kill an innocent Hispanic kid. They're just stirring the pot, playing the race card."

"You know, Frank, I'd like to go out there and bust their bubble. Those assholes outside automatically assume that when a deputy shoots a Hispanic, the shooting deputy has to be a white guy. But we can't do that, can we?"

"No, boss, the Peace Officer's Bill of Rights is crystal clear on that issue. Until the DA makes a decision, we can't release any information on the deputy; not the name, not the gender, and not the race."

"What's the background on Michelle Baxter?" Covington asked. "I don't know much about her. The last time I saw her was at her husband's funeral."

Peters opened the personnel file in his hand and briefed his boss. "She's forty-two and has one son. From what I understand, the kid is one hell of a baseball player. She's a local girl. Her maiden name is Paz. She never really knew her parents, was raised by a maternal grandmother. She grew up in the Hispanic Mt. Vernon neighborhood—that's a pretty rough area."

"What do you think our friends outside would make of that?" Covington said with a hint of contempt in his voice.

"That's probably not what they want to hear. In any event, Baxter has an AA degree in criminal justice from Valley Junior College. She then joined the department, seventeen years with us, a solid record as a patrol deputy. I don't see that she's ever put in for detective or tested for sergeant. She's just a good career patrol deputy."

"Been involved in any other shootings?" Covington asked.

"None."

"Any prior citizen complaints?"

"No, sir, nothing that amounted to anything. Just the standard pissed off person who didn't think they deserved a ticket."

"Looks like she's had a very vanilla career."

"Yes, sir, up until Saturday night."

Covington's secretary came into the office and announced, "Sergeant Tate's here."

"Bring him in," Covington said.

Late Sunday night, Tate had taken his first break from the investigation. He drove to his home in Big Bear, grabbed a few hours of sleep, showered, put on a fresh suit, and then went back down to headquarters. Tate entered the office, shook hands with his superiors, and sat down in a chair next to Peters.

Covington leaned back in his leather chair, clasped his hands together behind his head and asked Tate, "How's it looking?"

"It's a mess, sir."

"Before we start, let me get the DA on the phone. He needs to be a part of this." Covington put his desk phone on speaker mode and dialed the direct private line for Anthony Garcia, the elected District Attorney of San Bernardino County.

"Morning, Tony."

"How are you guys holding up over there?" Garcia asked. "I drove by your shop coming in this morning and saw our friends from SPA."

"It's a real shit- fest, Tony."

"I only know what I've read in the paper and seen on TV. Who's the deputy?" Garcia asked.

"Michelle Baxter."

"Oh, no, don't tell me that, Larry," Garcia said, letting out his breath with a tone of disappointment.

"You know her?" Covington asked.

"Of course I do, her husband, Jordan, was one of my prosecutors. Last year his reserve unit was called to active duty in Afghanistan. About six months ago, he was killed by a car bomb. Remember, Larry, I was sitting right next to you at his funeral."

"Yeah, he was a good cop for us, before he went to work for you," Covington said. "Tony, I've got you on speakerphone and I'm here with Peters and Sergeant John Tate. I think you need to be in the loop on this thing, since it's going to be coming your way when we're done with the investigation. Tate and his team are working the criminal side and I've asked him to bring us up to speed. Why don't you go ahead, John?"

Tate flipped through his notes, organized his thoughts, and began the briefing. "To start at ground zero, we interviewed the clerk from the Circle K at Baseline and Victoria, in the City of Highland. Saturday night at approximately twenty two hundred hours the clerk says a navy blue Monte Carlo pulls into the parking lot right in front of the entrance. Your typical low rider gangsta car with all the windows heavily tinted.

"A Hispanic male, approximately seventeen years old, gets out of the front passenger seat and walks into the store. The clerk describes him as being five feet nine inches tall, weighs about one hundred and fifty pounds. He's wearing a white Los Angeles Dodgers uniform jersey and blue denim pants.

"The Hispanic juvenile goes to the beer cooler and grabs a twelve pack of Bud Light. He goes up to the counter and the clerk asks to see his ID. The suspect then pulled a silver handgun from the waistband of his pants and demanded cash. The clerk empties the money drawer and gives the cash to the suspect. With the cash and the beer, the suspect splits out of the store and jumps into the front passenger's seat of the Monte Carlo. The car hauls ass out of the parking lot and speeds off into the night."

"How much?" Covington asked Tate.

"Excuse me, Sheriff; I'm afraid I don't understand your question."

"How much money did the suspect get away with?"

"Let me see," Tate said, going through his notes. "Seventy-four dollars."

"Seventy- four fucking dollars," Covington said, shaking his head. "Why is life so damn cheap?"

"These are crazy times," Garcia said on the other end of the telephone line.

"The clerk immediately dials nine-one-one," Tate continued with the briefing. "Dispatch broadcasts the call; Baxter is in the area and starts to roll that way.

"Baxter sees the navy blue Monte Carlo travelling eastbound on Greenspot. She lights up the Monte Carlo and the chase is on. Baxter radios in that she sees a hand come out of the front passenger window. She hears the pop, pop, pop and sees the muzzle flash. They're taking shots at her.

"The chase goes through residential neighborhoods. The Monte Carlo takes a sharp turn too quickly, over corrects, and slams head on into a concrete light pole.

"We haven't interviewed Baxter yet, so now I can only tell you what I heard when I listened to her belt recorder."

"Have you tried to interview her?" Peters asked.

"We tried, but she still needs to think it over with her mouthpiece."

"Do you suppose she'll talk?" Garcia asked.

"I don't know," Tate answered.

"Larry," Garcia said. "There's no way I can justify this shooting without her complete statement."

"I know, Tony. Let's hope she gives us an interview. Sorry we interrupted you, John, go ahead."

"In listening to her belt recorder I can hear her get out of her unit. She right away orders someone to halt. This is followed by the sound of two rounds being fired from her service weapon.

"For the next two minutes you can hear the sound of her running, her breathing becomes more labored. She stops, and thirty seven seconds later, you hear her once again order someone to halt. This is almost immediately followed by the sound of one round being fired.

"After she fires the shot, her breathing is very quick and heavy. You can hear her walking through grass. You can then hear her throwing up."

"John," Garcia asked. "What's the name of the kid she shot?"

"Mario Costa, sir."

"The media is reporting that the only thing in the kid's hands was a cell phone."

"That is correct, Mr. Garcia."

"Did we apprehend the actual suspect who robbed the Circle K?" Garcia asked.

"Yes, sir," Tate answered. "Another deputy with the Highland Station, who was involved in the chase, took into custody a male juvenile Hispanic. The kid had a handgun on him. Yesterday we did a live line-up with the Circle K clerk. He positively ID'd the suspect as the robber. We've also got in custody the kid who was driving the Monte Carlo."

"Do we know why Costa was in the area?" Garcia asked.

"Yes, sir, he was in his backyard taking his dog outside to piss."

"This is a fucking mess."

"I agree, Mr. Garcia," Tate said. "This is a fucking mess."

"She shot the wrong kid," Covington said, closing his eyes and rubbing them with his thumb and index fingers.

"Larry, we've got to have Baxter's statement."

"I know, Tony."

"When will the reports be coming my way?" Garcia asked.

Covington looked at Tate and answered, "The minute Tate finishes the criminal investigation."

"I can hardly wait," Garcia answered with sarcasm.

"I bet," Covington said as he ended the call with the DA.

Covington got up from his desk and went into the adjoining private bathroom. He looked into the mirror and straightened the knot in his tie. He walked back into his office, put on his suit jacket, and said to Peters and Tate, "Alright gentlemen, let's get this over with."

On the outside foyer of the building, Covington stood at a podium bearing the shield of the San Bernardino County Sheriff's Department. Assistant Sheriff Frank Peters stood to the right of Covington. Sgt. John Tate flanked Covington to the left. Covington looked out into the crowd of reporters and angry protesters and began his prepared statement.

"Saturday night, at approximately ten p.m., an armed robbery occurred at the Circle K convenience store located at the intersection of Victoria and Baseline, in the City of Highland. In an effort to apprehend the suspects, members of my department engaged in a vehicle and then foot pursuit of the suspects. At this time, the two suspects responsible for that robbery are in custody at Juvenile Hall.

"During the foot pursuit, one of my deputies shot a sixteen-year old male juvenile. As has been reported, the shot was fatal. The deceased victim was not involved in the armed robbery. Regrettably, we shot the wrong person."

The fifty SPA protesters began shouting out, "Murderers!"

Covington let the fuming crowd vent for several moments. The television cameras captured every detail for the noon newscast. When the outcry subsided, Covington continued with his statement.

"My heartfelt sympathy and those of every member of this department goes out to the grieving parents and family members of the young victim. Standing to my left is Sergeant John Tate who is assigned to our Homicide Division. Since the shooting, Sergeant Tate and his team have been conducting a criminal investigation on this homicide. When completed, that investigation will be submitted to the District Attorney's office. The DA will determine whether or not the shooting was justified."

"Justified my ass," an angry SPA groupie interrupted and shouted.

"What can you tell us about the deputy who killed the boy?" a reporter asked.

"Nothing," Peters answered. "Every sworn peace officer has protections under the Peace Officer Bill of Rights and until the District Attorney reaches a decision, any information on that deputy is confidential and privileged."

"That's a bunch of bullshit," a SPA follower holding a protest sign said. "What's to stop that deputy from going out tonight on patrol and shooting someone else?"

"The deputy has been placed on administrative leave and will remain off duty until the District Attorney's office makes a decision on the criminal investigation and our department concludes its Internal Affairs Investigation," Peters said.

Martin Bustamonte, the president of the local SPA chapter and spokesperson for the organization stepped out from the crowd and angrily pointed his finger at the three standing by the podium.

"Sheriff Covington, isn't this just another example of racial profiling by your white deputies?"

"That's not an accurate statement, Mr. Bustamonte," Covington answered.

"Sure it is, Sheriff. Word on the street is that both the robbery suspect and the kid you shot are similar in height and build. They both were also wearing Dodgers jerseys. So, just slap a Dodgers jersey on us and we all look alike?"

*You ignorant son of a bitch*, Covington thought to himself.

# 9

"Hey, you were just on the noon news," Coroner's Clerk Donna French said to John Tate as he walked into the coroner's office.

"What a pain in the ass that was," Tate said and signed in on the coroner's logbook.

"How come they didn't let you talk?" she asked.

"It was fine by me; I didn't even want to be standing out there. There was way too much brass for my liking."

"You here for the post on the kid that got shot?"

"Yes," Tate answered.

"That whole thing sounds fucked up."

"You've been getting quite the potty mouth lately, young lady. But yeah, it's all fucked up. Is Photo Boy here yet?"

"Yup," French answered. "Bell is suiting up."

Tate walked from the reception area towards the secured door and French buzzed the door open. In the hallway, leading to the dressing room, the subtle smell of human decomposition wafted in the air. Tate always thought it smelled like walking by a dumpster and getting just a faint hint of the stench and rot inside.

"Hey, Photo Boy," Tate said to Forensic Tech Randy Bell.

"What's up, Sarge?" Bell answered, already dressed in his protective gear.

Tate sat down on a wood bench next to a row of lockers and put on a surgeon's gown over his dress shirt. He then positioned a paper hat over his hair and paper booties over his shoes.

The protective clothing served two purposes. It prevented cross contamination, insuring that those present at the autopsy didn't contaminate the body being autopsied. The protective clothing also acted as a shield against the spewing body fluids of the deceased.

Tate and Bell pulled the paper masks down over their faces, left the dressing room, and made their way towards the autopsy area. The disgusting odor of decomposition was no longer subtle, it was overpowering.

"Damn, must have been a bad weekend," Bell said. "This is about the busiest I've seen it."

"It's always like this, the week before Christmas," Tate answered. "Between murders and suicides, a lot of folks just can't seem to get into the holiday mood. Or if they do, they sure express it in a different way."

The hallway leading to the autopsy room was lined with six rolling stainless steel cutting tables. On a typical day there might be only two or three. A yellow body bag sat on each table. Inside each bag somebody's mother, son, or brother, waiting its turn to be sliced and diced by the Forensic Pathologist.

Walking into the autopsy room, they heard the piercing whine of the Forensic Pathologist's best friend. It reminded Tate of the sound of the high-speed router in his wood workshop—only this was the sound of the bone-cutting saw. The stench of bone being cut smelled like scorched hair.

The autopsy room could accommodate four autopsies at the same time. Three were currently in progress. Tate and Bell went to the fourth cutting table where Mario Costa's body sat inside the yellow, still zipped, body bag.

From a cutting table eight feet away, a nauseating and revolting odor swept over the entire autopsy room.

"Oh, shit," Bell said, wincing. "They just cut into a floater."

"Nothing worse than a floater," Tate answered. His eyes burned and he tried hard not to gag. "Water and decomp don't mix well."

Forensic Pathologist and Medical Examiner, Samantha Dunn, walked up to the cutting table, grinned at the two, and said, "You boys ready to start?"

"Holy crap, Doc, you should have warned us about the floater."

"You're tougher than that, John. It's just stink."

"Yeah, Doc, it's stink that stays in your hair for days," Tate said.

Dunn unzipped the yellow body bag and casually asked, "Is this the kid your department shot?"

"Yes," Tate answered and for the next ten minutes gave the doctor a briefing on the particulars of the shooting.

While Tate briefed Dunn, Bell took photographs of the clothed body. The clothes were removed, marked as evidence, and Bell then took photographs of the unclothed pasty looking body.

Dunn picked up a scalpel and made the "Y" cut—stretching from both nipples to the sternum and then to the bellybutton. She peeled back the skin, exposing meat and ribs.

"How are the girls doing?" Dunn asked Tate.

"They're doing fine, Doc."

"Are they looking forward to Christmas?"

"Definitely, and I'm looking forward to spending some time with them. They were decorating the tree this morning. As I'm walking out the door they made sure to remind how nice it would have been to have daddy's help."

"That's got to tear at your heart, John."

"It does, Doc."

With a pair of ordinary garden pruning shears, Dunn cracked the ribs, revealing the heart, lungs, and liver. The chest cavity was full of blood.

"Blood clot—hematoma," Dunn said. "The bullet came in from front to back, hit the right lung, and then the heart. There it is, right there, imbedded in the spine."

Dunn removed the disfigured lead bullet and handed it to Bell for evidence.

"Cause—single gunshot wound to the chest. Death—within minutes," the doctor said into her tape recorder.

Dunn gathered up the cut rib bones, along with the internal organs, and arranged them in a clear plastic bag. She then positioned the plastic bag in the body's exposed chest cavity. She concluded the autopsy by closing up the chest cavity and stitching back together the skin from the "Y" cut. From start to finish, thirty minutes.

"Y'all have a good Christmas," Dunn said to Tate and Bell as she made her way to the next table and the next autopsy.

Tate and Bell returned to the locker room to throw away their paper protective gear, now spattered with blood and other bodily fluids. Sitting on a bench, hunched over, and hanging his head down, they walked past Chief Medical Examiner Ken Felts.

"Morgue Dog, what is up brother man?" Tate said, slapping Felts on the back.

Felts slowly raised his head, looked at Tate, and answered, "Hey John, hey Photo Boy, how are you guys doing?"

Outside of work, Tate and Felts were close friends. On days off, and if Tate's girls were in school, they liked to get their minds right by fishing and hunting in the San Bernardino Mountains.

"We just got done with the post on the kid shot by the department. Nothing remarkable evidence wise, just a run of the mill post," Tate answered his friend.

Felts continued to stare blankly at the row of metal lockers.

"Hey, are you okay, man?" Tate asked.

"Just a bad day, John."

"You do a post on a baby or something?" Tate asked.

"Two. First, a nine-month-old girl—she and her mother were hit by a drunk driver. Poor little thing was burned beyond recognition. Followed that up with a post on a two year old—a shaken baby case. The boyfriend was watching TV and got pissed off at the kid's crying."

"It's a fucked up world, Ken," Tate said.

"Ain't that right, brother," he answered.

"Wanna go fishing after the holidays?" Tate asked.

"Sure, John, just give me a call."

While driving from the coroner's office back to sheriff's headquarters, Tate made a cell phone call to Vincent and Carmen Costa. He told them that Mario's body would be released to the mortuary that afternoon.

When the call was ended, he said to himself, *Yup, it's a fucked up world.*

\* \* \*

"Thank you for allowing me to come over at this most difficult time," Martin Bustamonte said, sitting in the Costa's living room. "Our organization extends its deepest condolences."

"My family and I appreciate your kind words," Vincent Costa replied.

Vincent, Carmen, and Joseph sat on a couch. A wing-backed chair was positioned on each side of the couch. Bustamonte sat in one chair; Vincent's seventy-one year old mother, Mary, sat in the other.

"Have you decided when the services will be held?" Bustamonte asked.

"We just got notification today from the sheriff's department that Mario's body is being transported to the mortuary," Vincent said. "We know it will be Christmas Eve, but we plan on having a public memorial for Mario on Thursday afternoon and then a private burial service."

"Is your family aware of our organization, Stop Police Abuse?" Bustamonte asked. He was overweight with slicked back hair and talked with a thick accent, even though he was a third generation Mexican-American and had only been south of the border a handful of times.

"In all honesty, we've never heard of your group," Vincent answered, with no hint of an accent.

"We are an activist group committed to fighting police abuse against members of the Hispanic community. We have chapters in Los Angeles, San Diego, Riverside, and of course here in San Bernardino."

"I wasn't aware there was a problem," Vincent said, beginning to question his decision to allow this guy in the door.

"Surely, you must be joking, Mr. Costa."

"No, I'm not, Mr. Bustamonte."

"The police are targeting our brothers and sisters in the Hispanic community," Bustamonte continued. "They profile us in making traffic stops, they use excessive force when they arrest us, and while we're unjustly jailed, they beat us."

Vincent shifted uncomfortably on the couch and exchanged glances with his wife before turning again towards Bustamonte, "Well, Mr. Bustamonte, perhaps our Hispanic brothers and sisters should stop committing crimes and the problem goes away."

"With all due respect, Mr. Costa, it's the police who are committing the crimes. Mario's murder is the latest and most egregious example of their excessive use of deadly force," the activist said as he made eye contact with each member of the Costa family. Nobody spoke for several moments; Mary started sniffling and held a tissue to her eyes. Joseph got up off the couch and went over to console his grandmother.

Vincent glared at the now unwelcome visitor and said, "Mr. Bustamonte, I'm not comfortable with where this conversation seems to be going."

"Pop, he's right, they murdered Mario!"

Their son's sudden outburst of emotion surprised Vincent and Carmen. They knew Joseph harbored a great amount of guilt over giving his brother the Dodgers jersey. Since the shooting, Joseph had kept that guilt bottled up inside, refusing to discuss anything related to the facts of his brother's death.

"Alright, Mr. Bustamonte, what do you want from us?" Vincent asked in a calm but rigid voice.

"We want to take an active role in your fight for justice over Mario's murder."

"No you don't," Vincent said, interrupting Bustamonte. "You and your group just see an opportunity to use our son's death as a way to further your cause. Quite frankly, a cause I'm not so sure I agree with."

"Pop—let him finish."

"Joseph," Carmen said, giving her son a mother's disapproving look. "Don't you talk to your father in that tone of voice."

"They murdered my brother and now someone has to pay."

The tension and anger in the room was too much for Vincent's mother. Mary Costa got up from her chair and went upstairs to the guest bedroom.

"What kind of role does your organization want to take?" Vincent asked.

"Well, first off, we'd like to have a respectful presence at Mario's memorial on Thursday."

"A respectful presence? What does that mean?" Vincent asked.

"About two hundred of our members from all the Southern California chapters plan on attending. No signs, pickets, or anything like that. They will be wearing black armbands in Mario's honor. With all the anticipated media coverage we think it would paint a compelling picture."

"No, absolutely not," Vincent said.

"Pop—you can't do that, it's open to the public."

"Joseph, you stay out of this," Vincent said, shooting a piercing glare his son's way. "No, Mr. Bustamonte, you and your group are not going to turn our son's memorial into a three ring circus."

Bustamonte looked defiantly at Vincent, "I don't know if I can stop them."

"You'd better."

Carmen knew she had to steer the contentious exchange in a different direction. "Are there other things your group can do?" she asked.

"Yes," Bustamonte answered, "We can put pressure on both the Sheriff and the District Attorney."

"And what would that accomplish?" Vincent asked, now calmed down a bit.

"Hopefully, from the Sheriff, find out who this monster is and assurances that he's been fired from his job. From the District Attorney, we want the filing of criminal charges against this monster; until we get that, we'll be on their steps every day."

"Mr. Bustamonte, I can't stop your group from pressuring the Sheriff and DA. I just know that I don't want to have anything more to do with you or your group."

"Mr. Costa, why do you seem to have such a problem with SPA?"

"You and your group are a bunch of ignorant racists. Just because my family and I have the same color skin, and similar sounding last names, you automatically assume that we have issues with white people."

"That's not true," Bustamonte said.

"It is and you know it," Vincent answered. "I inherently believe that law and order is good. I inherently believe that the police are good. I'm tired of seeing all the little gang banger Hispanics with tattoos and pants hanging down around their asses. They are the people you defend— I want no part of it. It's one of those punks that started this whole thing when they robbed the liquor store."

"But what about the police shooting your son?" Bustamonte asked.

"That's my fight, my families fight, not yours. My wife and I won't sleep until there is justice for our son's killer. We don't need or want your help—it'd be best if you left now."

Bustamonte got up from the wingback chair, shook hands with Joseph, and walked to the front door. Before leaving, he looked back at Vincent and said, "You're right about one thing—you can't stop us."

# 10

"Michelle, are you listening to a word I'm saying?" Maury Stein let go of the pen in his right hand and asked his client. "I'm trying to explain to you my strategy for keeping your ass out of hot water."

"Yeah, I'm listening, Maury," Michelle lied to her attorney.

Her temples throbbed and her eyes burned. Feeling dehydrated, she took another long sip from her bottle of water. It was the rum's revenge from the night before.

Nate had talked her into watching Monday Night Football, the Chargers versus the Raiders. Whenever the Chargers were on television, Nate and his father had always watched the game together. Jordan had been a tight end at Ole Miss, all SEC Conference in his senior year. Coming out of college the San Diego Chargers drafted him in the fourth round. He was a lock to make the Charger's roster until a severe shoulder injury, during the last week of training camp, ended his dream of playing in the NFL. With his degree in criminal justice, Jordan went to work as a deputy with the San Bernardino County Sheriff's Department.

While watching the game with Nate she made four trips from the family room to the kitchen, and the rum. The bottle of rum had been tucked away in the back corner of the pantry for the better part of two years; she had forgotten that it was even there. When she first noticed the bottle, earlier in the day, she remembered Jordan had bought it for a family gathering. She felt confident that Nate had not caught on. Mixed in her red plastic Ole Miss tumbler, the rum and diet cola looked innocent enough.

"Are you drunk?" Stein asked her.

"You know, you can be pretty offensive sometimes," she answered.

"Well, what do you want me to say? Your breath smells like a fucking distillery."

"I'm okay, I was watching the game last night with my kid and I had a few drinks. I'll remember next time to get your permission."

"Look, I just need your full attention here. We're going to be talking about a lot of stuff that will have a huge impact on your life."

"I understand, Maury; you've got my full attention."

"Alright, any time a cop shoots someone in the line of duty; three independent roads have to be travelled. I like to label them civil, administrative, and criminal. Are you with me so far?"

"Yes," she said, shaking her head up and down in the affirmative and taking another long drink off the water bottle.

"Let's go down the civil road first. I think from your perspective that will be the least of your worries."

"Okay," she said finishing off the bottle. "Can I have more water?"

Stein got up from his chair, walked to a small refrigerator in the corner of his office, and took out a bottle of water. He handed it to her with an irritated look on his face and continued with his explanation.

"The kid's family is going to be filing a civil lawsuit in federal court, you can count on that. You'll be a named defendant, along with the sheriff's department. Bottom line is that the department is going to be writing out a check that has a shit load of zeros on it."

"I don't have that kind of money," Baxter said, rolling the water bottle back and forth between the palms of her hands.

"You won't have to pay a dime. You killed the kid in the course and scope of your employment as a sworn peace officer. The taxpayer's are going to pick up the tab."

"I guess that's somewhat of a relief," she said. "Will I have to sit there at the trial?"

"If it went to trial," Stein answered, his pudgy fingers brushed dough-nut crumbs off his tie. "This shooting is ugly, one of the worst I've ever seen. Ain't no way your department lets a jury near it."

"Damn, Maury, you make it sound like I'm some sort of demon. You don't think I feel like shit for killing him?"

"Hey, I'm not here to hold your hand and make you feel good. That's why the department gives you a shrink."

"You're a son of a bitch."

"Probably the nicest thing I'll be called all day," he said, paying no attention to his client's icy scowl. "Now, let's talk about the administrative road; how things will pan out between you and the department. Is this your first shooting?"

"Yes."

"Do you have any prior incidents of non-lethal force? You know, tas-ers, stuff like that?" Stein asked, as he turned over a page in the dog-eared yellow legal pad.

"Nah, not really, just had one incident when I was working the jail right after I got out of the academy."

"What happened?"

"An inmate pinched my ass; I beat the shit out of him."

"That doesn't count."

"You think they're gonna fire me?" she asked.

"I doubt it," Stein answered. "Oddly enough, it's possible to kill the wrong person and still be within department policies. If they should find that you did violate policy, with your clean record, maybe thirty days with no pay."

"I'm a mess, Maury," Baxter said, staring at the lawyer's framed diplo-mas and awards on the wall because she didn't want him to see her start tearing up. "His face haunts me at night, I don't sleep."

"Michelle, like I said, save that talk for your shrink. Let's focus on the eight hundred pound gorilla in the room—the criminal investigation."

"You really are a fucking asshole."

"My wife says she loves me. Has Tate tried to contact you since we saw him last?"

"No."

"Good, I think it's in your best interest to not talk to him."

"Why, the truth's the truth? I've got nothing to hide about what happened Saturday night."

"Michelle, you killed someone, you are the suspect in a homicide investigation."

"Yeah, Maury, I understand that."

"Number one rule in the world of criminal defense— never let you client talk to the police. Nothing but bad can come out of it."

"But it's not like I started my shift that night with the intent to kill anyone," Baxter said as she crossed her right leg over her blue jeans and started picking at the soles of her running shoes. "I was defending myself."

"Yes, you were," Stein said. "But it takes us into a very gray area under the eyes of the law."

"Okay, I know that the criminal investigation will be given to the DA and he will decide what to do," Baxter said, struggling to form cogent thoughts in her brain. The consequences of her little bender with rum made it difficult. "The department gives us training on this kind of stuff and they told us that usually the DA will justify our use of deadly force. They'll give us a clean bill of health, a stamp of approval. But, they made it very clear to us that the DA has to have our statement to justify the shooting. The DA has to know what was going through our mind when we decided to shoot."

"Yes, Michelle, that's usually how one of these plays out: Deputy shoots someone and tells the DA they had to do it in self-defense. DA agrees and justifies the shooting. Game over, book closed, everybody goes home happy. But this one's different, Michelle."

"Why? I shot because my life was in danger."

"Well," Stein said, "most officer involved shootings are a little cleaner."

"Are you saying mine was a bad shoot?" she asked, feeling her heart thumping rapidly.

Stein stopped writing on the legal pad, put down his pen, and looked his client in the eyes, "I'm not an expert in police training and tactics. I don't know if this is a good shoot or a bad shoot. It sure looks a little stinky to me. But, who the hell cares what I think? What I'm worried about is whether the DA and twelve jurors think this is a bad shoot. We can't take that chance."

"Alright," she asked, "What are the possible scenarios if I do give a statement?"

"You explain in detail, every reason, and every thought process that was going through your mind as to why you believed you needed to shoot. The DA agrees and the shooting is justified. That's your homerun."

She polished off the second bottle of water, tossed it into a trashcan next to Stein's desk, and asked, "What's the downside?"

"The DA doesn't agree with your way of thinking. He concludes that the reasonable person, the reasonable deputy, under those exact circumstances would not have shot and killed the kid."

"And?" she asked.

Stein answered, a little too loudly, "And, the DA files criminal charges against you."

"What kind of charges?"

"Most likely, Voluntary Manslaughter."

"If convicted, would I go to prison?"

"Yes."

"How long?"

"Eleven years."

"I can't do eleven years in prison," Baxter said after thinking it through for several minutes. "What if I don't give a statement?"

"My bet is the DA would not file criminal charges."

"Why?" she asked.

"Without your statement they wouldn't have enough evidence to convince a jury that you are guilty. They have the burden of proof; they have to show the jury what you were thinking. The only way they get that is if you give a statement. In addition, there is always the wild card of you testifying at trial in your defense. They have no idea what your story would be—an unknown, and prosecutors hate unknowns."

She got the picture of her predicament and thought out loud, "So, everything revolves around my statement. It can be incredibly good for me, with the DA justifying the shooting. Or, it can be incredibly bad for me, maybe the DA doesn't like what I have to say and he files criminal charges against me."

"Bodda-bing-bodda-boom," Stein said. "You win the prize."

She mulled it over for a moment, got up out of her chair, and walked over to the small refrigerator. She grabbed a bottle of water and while twisting off the plastic cap asked, "But if I don't give a statement, there is absolutely no possibility of the DA justifying the shooting. Won't people always be questioning my actions?"

"Yeah," Stein said. "I suppose a big black cloud would always be hanging over your head. But it sure beats the possibility of doing time in prison."

"I don't know, Maury, I'm the one who has to go to the market or the gas station. People will be thinking *there goes the cop who shot the wrong kid, and she won't even tell us why she did it*. I mean, I've already killed him, which I've got to carry with me for the rest of my life. To throw that extra baggage on me, I don't know if I could live like that."

"Think about your son, Michelle. You could also be the one who spends a lot of time in state prison. That's no way to live either."

"I guess I've got a decision to make," she said.

"Yes, you do," Stein answered. "My job is to mitigate your risk. I know it's not the perfect situation for you, but I do think it's in your best interest. No statement—fuck 'em."

Baxter got up and started to leave the office, "I'll sleep on it and I'll give you a call when I've reached a decision."

"If you decide to talk, I need to be there," Stein said. "That's not up for negotiation."

"Why do you need to be there?"

"Well, for starters, I am your lawyer."

"Besides that."

"I can run interference, keep Tate honest."

"Why do you need to keep Sergeant Tate honest? All I have to do is tell the truth."

"You ever hear that old saying—'Sometimes the truth hurts'," Stein said as he stood up from his desk and led his client out of the office.

Baxter got into her Toyota Camry and drove out of the lawyer's parking lot. *Two hours with that bag of shit is way too long*—she thought to herself. She scanned both sides of the road for a fast food joint. It was lunchtime and her alcohol-saturated system pleaded for food. She saw a Burger King, pulled into the parking lot, and went inside. A fitness fanatic who ran at least six miles a day, she closely watched her diet, always eating healthy. However, not today—right now her body begged for grease to soak up the alcohol. In her hung over state, the Whopper and onion rings were a religious experience.

There were a couple of liquor stores close to her home. Before leaving for her lawyer's office, while Nate was still in bed, she threw the empty rum bottle away—wrapping yesterday's newspaper around it and putting it in a plastic supermarket bag.

When she pulled into the liquor store she froze with terror at the car driving into the parking stall to her right— a dark blue Chevrolet Monte Carlo with tinted windows. Overcome with panic, she put the car in reverse and sped out of the parking lot. Peeking in her rear view mirror at the Monte Carlo, she saw an elderly African-American female with gray hair getting out of the driver's side and walk into the liquor store.

Baxter steered into the parking lot of a liquor store just up the street and slammed on the brakes. Her hands had a death grip on the steering wheel. She sat there for several minutes before she was composed enough to go inside for her liquid coping mechanism.

# 11

"Are we gonna take dad's SUV?" Nate asked his mother.

"You mean your SUV," she answered.

"Yeah, I guess, but I'll always think of it as dad's."

"Don't forget your parka, it's going to be cold up there," Michelle said.

"Do you wanna drive?" Nate asked.

"No, you can drive, it's your car."

"You trust me on the mountain roads? There might be some ice and snow."

"Of course I trust you." Her answer was a half-truth. She had another hangover and she didn't trust herself.

They threw their winter gear into the back of the Ford Expedition and with Nate driving they were soon on the 210 Freeway headed west from their house in Rancho Cucamonga for Lake Arrowhead. It was Wednesday, the day before Christmas Eve. For as long as Nate could remember, they always went up to Lake Arrowhead on this day.

Perched five thousand feet high in the San Bernardino Mountains, Lake Arrowhead was a small mountain community with the feel and flavor of a European alpine village. Going up to Lake Arrowhead had always been a Christmas tradition for their family. They took pleasure from the snow, the smell of fresh pines, the village's Christmas decorations, last minute shopping, and snowball fights.

They had driven in silence for ten minutes when Michelle said to her son, "You're awful quiet over there."

"Just concentrating on my driving."

"Something bothering you?" she asked.

"I don't know—it's just that dad's always been with us."

"I know how you feel."

"Would he still want us to go up there?"

"He would insist on it," she said.

"Are you going to let me throw snowballs at you?" Nate asked with a hint of mischievousness in his voice.

"When does ball practice start?" she asked, dodging the question.

"Right after New Year's."

"Have you heard anything from Cal State Fullerton?"

"The admissions office or the athletic department?"

"The athletic department—with your grades and SAT score, getting in has to be a no brainer."

"Coach Rogers got a call from their baseball people the other day. They want some more video tape on me."

"You think they're going to make you an offer?"

"Hard to say, I think there's a good chance. Last year's starting third baseman graduated and went pro. Coach said me and some other kid out of Bishop Amat are their top third base prospects."

"Any thoughts on going pro?"

"Some."

"How's that looking?" she asked.

"Coach Rogers says he's been getting some serious calls from the Atlanta Braves."

"Does he have any idea what round they might take you?"

"Probably between the tenth and fifteenth rounds."

"I don't think your signing bonus will be enough for you to buy me a new house and let me retire," she said with a grin.

"Definitely not," he answered.

"What did your father think?"

"Dad said there was good and bad about both. He said if I went pro, I'd have a shot at the majors. But, I'd probably spend five years in the minor leagues, making nothing, living on a bus, and eating off the dollar menu. He said if I went the college route I'd go to the pros as a much more complete and developed player. Plus, I'd get a free education. Downside is if I get injured in college—game over, no pros."

They drove in silence for five minutes. Michelle chewed on a fingernail and then wiped the corners of her eyes.

"Nate, I'm so sorry. I'm never going to be able to take the place of your father."

"What do you mean, mom?"

"When it came to baseball and you, he was everything. He taught you how to play; he went to all your games, you guys talked about your future. I can't fill that void, but I'm going to try my best."

"I know you will, mom. We just have to stick together and get through all this stuff."

"Nate, you're a good kid."

"I am, aren't I?" he said, smiling at his mother. "Is this where I get off the freeway?"

"Yes."

After thirty minutes on the 210 Freeway, Nate steered the Expedition onto Highway 18 and started the steep climb up the mountain. The narrow two-lane road, lined with an array of boulders and pine trees, twisted and turned along the edge of the mountainside. For good reason, it also went by the name of Rim of the World Highway. Driving up the mountain, motorists could peer down thousands of feet into the San Bernardino Valley and see for miles all around. It was indeed like driving along the rim of the world.

The fickle winter mountain weather cooperated that day for Michelle and Nate; sunny and crisp with good visibility. When the mountain weather did turn for the worse, driving conditions could become downright nasty. Snow, fog, and ice with zero visibility. The only way to navigate the roadway would be to open the car door, look down, and follow the fluorescent yellow median strip.

They started seeing snow on the ground at the four thousand foot level; clean and white, it majestically draped the branches of the pine trees. The cinder-lined roadway was clear and free of black ice.

"We picked a good day to come up," Nate said.

"Yes, it's beautiful up here," his mother answered.

After thirty minutes on the mountain road, they arrived at the Lake Arrowhead Village. The mountain community was a popular Southern California tourist destination, especially during the holiday season, and the parking lot was full. Nate circled twice around the lot looking for a spot.

"There's one," Michelle pointed out.

Nate squeezed the big SUV into the small parking stall; the tire's made a crunching sound driving over the snow. Being careful not to bang their doors against the neighboring cars, they got out and put on their Gore-Tex parkas and leather gloves.

"It's cold," Nate said, watching the steam flow out of his nose and mouth.

"Invigorating," she answered. The frigid temperature felt good to Michelle and helped to snap her brain out of its alcohol induced fog.

A concrete sidewalk snaked along the rocky shoreline of the crystal blue waters. They strolled in silence for fifteen minutes, each absorbed in their own thoughts, and admiring the beauty of the expansive lake and its panoramic shoreline. Large two and three story chalet style homes sat on the prime lakefront acreage. Many affluent Southern Californians owned weekend mountain retreats in Lake Arrowhead.

"This is so peaceful," Michelle said, breathing in a heavy dose of the crisp mountain air that left a slight burning sensation deep in her lungs.

Behind his mother's back, Nate reached down and grabbed a handful of snow. He made a snowball and playfully tossed it at his mother. It hit her on the back of her parka and broke up into pieces.

"You rat."

"Why are you acting surprised? You knew it was coming."

For Michelle, acting surprised was part of the yearly, let's hit mom with a snowball routine.

"Let's check out the shops," she said to her son.

They walked from the shoreline to the shops. Charles Dickens Era Victorian Christmas decorations adorned the shopping area. The long line to see Santa Claus meandered outside the shops. Little boys and girls all bundled up bravely fought off the cold; anxiously waiting to place their orders with the big guy.

They stopped to look in the windows of the upscale clothing boutiques and art galleries. Christmas music softly played from the well-hidden speakers. An inviting aroma soon seized their attention.

"Wow, something smells good," Nate said, walking towards the shop where the smell was coming from.

"Warm butter and chocolate," Michelle said, sniffing the air.

They peeked into the window. Inside, a middle-aged woman wearing an apron and hair net labored over a gray marble slab. In each hand, she held a spatula. Nate and Michelle watched as she worked the thickening brown glob, back and forth, with the spatulas.

"Mmm, fresh homemade fudge," Nate said. "I gotta have me some of that."

"We're going to eat lunch in just a few minutes."

"I don't care."

"Do you know how many miles I'll have to run just to work off one bite of that stuff?"

"Repeat, mom, I don't care," Nate said. He opened the door and the smell of fresh warm fudge rushed out. "I'll be right back."

Nate came out of the candy shop a few minutes later with a content smile on his face and a hunk of the sweet luscious goodness on a sheet of wax paper. He broke off a piece and plopped it in his mouth. Michelle put up only a token of resistance when her son broke off a piece and put it in her mouth.

Nate finished the fudge as they walked to the crowded Mexican restaurant.

"Your dad was right," she said while they waited for a table. "You're a walking, talking eating machine."

Nate gave his mother a shrug of his shoulders and wiped a stray bit of fudge from the corner of his mouth.

Once seated, the server came over and set down a bowl of tortilla chips and salsa.

"Can I get you something to drink?" the server asked.

"Coke," Nate answered, just before he put a chip loaded with salsa into his mouth.

"And for you, ma'am?" the server asked, looking at Michelle.

Michelle debated the question in her mind. She knew what she wanted—a rum and diet. She felt confident that Nate hadn't caught on to her drinking—why risk it.

"Iced tea," she answered.

Waiting for their food to arrive, Nate polished off the chips and salsa. He looked at his mother and said, "Earth to mom."

"Just thinking," she said.

"About what?" he asked.

"Whether or not I should talk."

"You lost me, mom."

"Okay," she said, thinking about how to explain to Nate, in laymen's terms, her legal dilemma. "Technically, the boy's death is a homicide. That makes me the suspect in a criminal homicide investigation."

"But you were just doing your job."

"Yes, I was, but it's not that black and white."

"Does your lawyer think you should talk?"

"No, he thinks I should stay quiet. It's his opinion that there could be a real downside to me giving a statement."

"Are you going to take his advice?"

"I don't know—I think he's a douche bag."

The server interrupted their conversation, giving Michelle a taco salad, and Nate a chile relleno with rice and beans.

"So what are you going to do?" Nate asked, while pouring a liberal amount of hot sauce on his food.

"I think I'm going to give them a statement."

"Why?"

Michelle picked at her salad with a fork. "It's horrible that I shot and killed him—I relive it in my sleep every night. But, I don't think I did anything wrong. I've got nothing to hide."

"Exactly," Nate said. "You did what you thought you needed to do. You believed your life was in danger. I don't understand the downside to telling the truth."

"My lawyer says the downside is if the District Attorney thinks I shouldn't have shot him and that I didn't have legal justification."

"What would happen then?" Nate asked.

"They could file criminal charges against me."

"Like what?"

"Most likely, Voluntary Manslaughter."

"Would they send you to prison?"

"They could."

"How long?"

"Up to eleven years."

Nate pushed his empty plate away and looked out the window, staring at the people walking by. "Okay—I see the problem. How does not giving a statement solve that problem?"

"My lawyer is confident that without my statement the DA will not file criminal charges. He says they won't have enough evidence and wouldn't take the risk of finding out my story for the first time while I'm testifying."

"I don't know, mom, I'm not a lawyer or anything, but it sounds like you giving a statement has a lot of risk."

"It does, Nate."

"So why would you do it?"

"Because I'm afraid if I don't, I won't be able to live with myself."

"I don't understand," Nate said.

"I can't go the rest of my life being scorned. *Oh, there goes that lady cop who shot and killed the wrong kid. She didn't co-operate in the investigation. She doesn't even have the decency to tell us why she did it.*"

"Yeah, but you eliminate any chance of going to prison."

"Nate, I can't live like that. I didn't do anything wrong. I was just doing my job."

Michelle picked the check up off the table and slid her body out from the booth.

"C'mon, let's go back to the candy shop and get a piece of fudge to take home."

"No argument from me on that one," Nate smiled.

After another walk by the lake, they left Lake Arrowhead in the mid afternoon. To leave any later would risk black ice forming on the mountain roads. They made it down the mountain without incident and Nate pulled onto the 210 freeway, heading west for their home in Rancho Cucamonga. Rush hour traffic was heavy and the normal thirty-minute drive would take them one hour.

"Mom?"

"Yes, Nate."

"The selfish side of me says you shouldn't give a statement. I don't want you to do anything that might lead to something bad happening to you."

"I understand, Nate. I think that's a normal human reaction."

"But," he said, changing lanes to let a speeding car pass, "You have to do what you believe is right."

"Even if it could lead to a bad result for us?" she asked, looking at her son.

"Well, yeah, that's pretty much what you and dad have been teaching me for seventeen years. If you believe giving a statement and telling your story is the right thing—then that's what you have to do. Go for it."

"Let me think about it some more," she said. "Your support means everything to me. Thank you."

After dinner, she cleaned the kitchen and took Tate's business card out of a drawer. She held the card in her hand, contemplating her decision. She reached for her cell phone and punched in his number.

"Sergeant Tate?"

"Yes."

"This is Michelle Baxter."

"What can I do for you, Michelle?"

"I want to talk to you."

"Okay, when?"

"As soon as possible—I know tomorrow's Christmas Eve, but can we do it tomorrow?"

"Sure, not a problem," Tate said. "I'm working tomorrow. What time?"

"Is nine o'clock at headquarters okay?"

"Perfect. Michelle?"

"Yes, sir"

"Will your lawyer be there?" Tate asked.

"No," she answered.

"Does your lawyer know you've decided to give a statement?"

"No."

"You sure you want to do this alone?"

"Yes, Sarge, this is my call."

"Okay, Michelle, see you in the morning."

She put the phone down and walked over to a cabinet—the rum cabinet. She took hold of the half-empty bottle. She reconsidered, stopped, and slid the bottle back; making sure it was concealed behind the cans of soup. *Sorry, my friend, not tonight— I need to be clear-headed in the morning. I can do without you for one night. I hope.*

# 12

Detective Scott Kane lifted the pink little girls' bicycle and passed it up to his boss. Standing in the bed of Kane's pickup truck, John Tate took the bicycle from Kane and looked for a place to load it.

"Are we going to have room for everything, Sarge?" Kane asked.

"Not a problem, Scooter," Tate said, re-arranging the boy's bike, Christmas tree, and a box of ornaments to make room for the second bike.

"What else do we have left?" Tate asked, jumping from the bed of the pickup truck and onto the asphalt of the sheriff's headquarters secured parking area.

"Just the food," Kane answered. "Bell's inside boxing it all up."

"Does Mrs. Jackson know that you and Photo Boy are coming over?"

"Yeah, she got pretty emotional when I told her what we were doing. She says without us there wouldn't be a Christmas for Mikey and Ashley."

Ellie Jackson was the maternal grandmother to Mikey and Ashley Turner. Mikey was eight years old and his sister was six. Sam Turner, the children's father, was an alcoholic and methamphetamine addict. Rhonda Turner, the children's mother, was also addicted to methamphetamine and sold her body to support their meth habits.

On Thanksgiving night, Sam and Rhonda were "tweaking" in their dirty little two-bedroom apartment. Rhonda told Sam that he needed to get a job because she wasn't going to turn tricks anymore. This pissed off Sam and they started arguing. Mikey and Ashley, who were used to their parents fighting, watched TV in the bedroom they shared.

In a meth-induced frenzy, Sam went to the kitchen and grabbed a dull steak knife. He walked back into the living room and stabbed Rhonda nine times in the chest and abdomen. For good measure, he slashed her throat.

Mikey turned up the volume on the TV to drown out the sounds of their mother screaming and pleading for her life. When the screams stopped, Mikey and Ashley came out of the room. Their father had fled the apartment, leaving behind the bloodied lifeless body of their mother. Mikey called 911.

Tate and his homicide team had worked the case. An anonymous phone call came into the sheriff's department; tipping them off that Turner was hiding out in the small desert town of Baker. Turner didn't go quietly when they found him hiding underneath the bed in a sleazy hotel room. Tate and his boys won the fight. Healing from a broken arm and two fractured ribs, Sam Turner was spending Christmas in jail, facing capital murder charges.

"You sure you don't want to go with us, Sarge?" Kane asked as he secured the loaded pick-up bed with bungee cords.

"I'd like to, but I can't," Tate said. "Michelle Baxter should be here any time now for her interview."

Randy Bell walked out of the building, carrying a cardboard box.

"What do we got in the box, Photo Boy?" Tate asked.

"Turkey, ham, canned stuff, and lots of candy," Bell answered.

"Outstanding," Tate said. "I really need to thank everyone for giving those kids a good Christmas."

"Michelle Baxter's here, I took her into the conference room," Bell said.

"Okay, thanks, Photo Boy. Y'all tell Mrs. Jackson to let us know if there's anything else we can do for Mikey and Ashley."

Tate went back into the building and stopped by his office before going to the conference room and Michelle Baxter. He took a micro-cassette recorder out of a desk drawer and his National Rifle Association coffee mug from the credenza. Tate rarely, if ever, washed the mug and the inside always had a dried coating of coffee.

The coffee pots were just outside the door to the conference room. Tate poured himself a cup and yelled into the open door of the conference room, "Baxter, need any coffee?"

"No, sir, I'm good," she answered.

Tate walked into the conference room and shut the door behind him. Michelle Baxter was sitting in a chair, dressed in blue jeans, running shoes, and an Ole Miss sweatshirt.

"Did you go to the University of Mississippi?" Tate asked.

"No, sir, my husband did."

"How did he end up way out here?"

"Jordan played tight end at Ole Miss. The Chargers drafted him in the fourth round. He injured his shoulder during his first training camp, so long NFL. Luckily, he had his degree in Criminal Justice and the department was hiring."

"I'll be darned, I didn't know that about Jordan," Tate said.

"He was my Field Training Officer. That's how we first met." She rubbed her fingers over the white gold wedding band and looked away from Tate.

"Hey, Michelle, I was real sorry to hear about Jordan's death. I was a couple of years ahead of him at the academy, so I never really got to know him or work with him. I hear he was a great cop and a good Deputy DA."

"Thanks for the kind words, Sarge. It's been a tough year."

"You sure you want to do this without your lawyer?" Tate asked.

"Yeah, I'm sure. I didn't do anything wrong, so why do I need a lawyer? Besides, the guy is such an asshole."

"No comment," he said, smiling at Baxter's candid and accurate statement about Maury Stein.

Tate placed the micro-cassette recorder on the table and took a fresh tape out of his shirt pocket. He slid it into the machine and pressed the start button. Tate began the interview by stating the date and time. He then advised Michele Baxter of her *Miranda* rights. While he did this, she folded her hands across her chest and stared up at the ceiling tiles.

"You okay, Michelle?"

"I don't know. I've given the *Miranda* advisals to hundreds of dirt bags. Just kind of makes me feel like a suspect."

"Technically, you are a suspect, Michelle."

"I was just doing my job out there."

"With those rights in mind, do you still want to talk to me?"

"Yes."

"Alright, Michelle, let's talk about the shooting. I want to know what you were seeing, what you were hearing, and how that impacted your decision to shoot. I want to see this thing through your eyes. Make me feel what you were feeling."

"I got the call from dispatch, at twenty two hundred hours, right before shift change."

"Up to that point how had your shift been?" Tate asked.

"It was actually a pretty quiet night. I would say the highlight of the shift was getting hit on by a couple of homeless dudes down by the park."

"Where were you when you received the call?"

"I was in my unit, travelling on Victoria, about two miles south of the Circle K. I told dispatch to show me enroute, did a u-turn, and headed north on Victoria for the crime scene."

"I've listened to the dispatch tape," Tate said. "What were you thinking when the call came in?"

"My first thought was this always happens at the end of a shift. My second thought was this is going to be a little more than two bums hitting on me."

"Why did you think that?"

"Well, for starters, the location of the Circle K. When the sun goes down the gang-bangers own that neighborhood. Then, the description of the car—typical gangster ride. I also knew we had at least two suspects, the kid who went into the store, and the wheelman. I knew the punk who robbed the store had a gun. Yeah, this had all the makings for some serious shit."

"What happened next?"

"At Victoria and Greenspot I see a dark blue Monte Carlo going east on Greenspot. I turn left onto Greenspot, activate my lights and siren, and get up behind the Monte Carlo."

"Did the vehicle pull over?"

"No, he steps on the gas and tries to lose me. We're now doing between seventy and eighty. That's when things really got hairy."

"Can you explain that?"

"I see a hand come out the front passenger window. I then see three muzzle flashes and I hear the pop- pop- pop. I'm thinking to myself—*these crazy motherfucker's are shooting at me.*"

"Where did this happen?" Tate asked.

"Still on Greenspot, but now we're approaching some residential areas. That really had me concerned."

"Why?"

"Innocent civilians."

"Then what happened?"

"The Monte Carlo turns left and heads north through the streets of the High Pointe subdivision. We're still doing over sixty. The Monte Carlo makes a sharp right hand turn. That street dead ends into a cul-de-sac, so I knew the chase was coming to an end."

"Is this when the Monte Carlo wrecked?"

"Yes, sir. He took the turn too quick and started fishtailing. He jumped the sidewalk and hit dead on into a concrete light pole."

"You made the turn okay?" Tate asked.

"Yes. As I said, I knew the area. They smacked the pole hard. The front end of the Monte Carlo crumpled up like an accordion."

"Then what happened?"

"I stopped my unit ten yards to the rear of the Monte Carlo. About that time I see the front driver's door open and a fat Hispanic kid with a buzz cut jumps out and hauls ass."

"What was he wearing?"

"Looked like blue jeans and a black sweatshirt."

"Where did he run to?"

"Just off into the darkness."

"What were you thinking?"

"Honestly, Sarge, I'm thinking this is the kind of shit you only see on TV. You know, when the helicopters of the Los Angeles news stations cover a police chase live. This just doesn't happen here in Highland."

"How would you describe what you were feeling at that moment?"

"Not scared—but pretty close. I was also a little pissed off. At that moment it was almost like a scene out of a movie."

"Why do you say that?"

"I'm in a high speed vehicle pursuit with armed robbery suspects. They fire shots at me. The car wrecks and the driver takes off on foot. I know I've still got the passenger to deal with."

"Could you see him in the Monte Carlo?"

"Yes, between the light from the streetlight and my unit's headlights I could see his silhouette."

"What did you do?"

"I got out of my unit and drew my service weapon."

"A 9mm Glock?" Tate asked.

"Yes, sir."

"Describe what you were seeing at that moment."

"It was kind of weird. I mean, the Monte Carlo was totaled. There was broken glass and fluids everywhere. Steam from the engine was rising into the air, along with the dirt that my unit and the Monte Carlo had kicked up. It had just started to drizzle."

"What did you do after getting out of your unit and drawing your service weapon?"

"I yelled at the suspect *don't move* and to *show me your hands*."

"Did he comply?"

"No, sir."

"What did he do?"

"He kicked open the door with his feet."

"What were you thinking?"

"That I might have to shoot him."

"What happened next?"

"The door opens all the way and the suspect takes off running."

"Did you get a good look at him?"

"Yeah, I told you about the lighting conditions. He matched the description put out by dispatch. He was about five feet, nine inches, one hundred fifty pounds, wearing blue jeans and a white Los Angeles Dodgers jersey."

"Did you see a gun?"

"Absolutely, he had a silver handgun in his right hand."

"What did you do?"

"I fired two rounds at him."

"Did you hit him?"

"No, sir."

"When you fired, was he running away from you?"

"Yes, sir."

"Why did you fire those two rounds?"

"Because he was a fleeing felon who still posed a threat to me and innocent civilians."

"Explain that to me," Tate said.

"The suspect was armed and running into a heavily populated residential neighborhood. They had just robbed a convenience store. They had no problem engaging in a high-speed chase, and they took shots at me. If they were capable of doing that to a cop—imagine what they could do to an innocent unarmed civilian. The suspect had a gun, he was getting away, and I couldn't take that chance."

"So, you took off running after him?"

"Yes, sir. Walking trails run behind all the houses in that subdivision. The suspect took off down the trails and I gave chase."

"How'd the foot chase go?"

"Not so well for me. I was kind of surprised. I run six miles every day and I couldn't make up any ground on the little bastard—he was quick."

"How far did you chase him?"

"My best guess, about a quarter of a mile."

"What happened next?"

"He just disappears. He must have made a sharp turn into the bushes and trees lining the walking trails."

"What did you do?"

"I stopped, I was winded. My lungs felt like they were going to explode and my adrenaline was way jacked up."

As Michelle Baxter recounted the events of that night, Tate could see that she was breathing more rapidly and at times would blankly gaze at the wall while talking.

"You need a break, Michelle?" he asked.

"No," she lied, "Let's just get this over with."

Tate had interviewed enough cops, who had shot people, to know that Baxter needed a few moments to collect her thoughts. He picked up his mug, got out of his chair, and walked towards the coffee pots.

"You sure I can't get you anything?" Tate asked.

"A cup of coffee sounds good," she said, welcoming the short break.

"How do you take it?"

"Black's fine, Sarge."

Tate poured two cups of coffee. Next to the coffee maker was a red tin of Christmas cookies. He took one and set it on a paper plate.

"Scooter's wife makes a wicked Christmas cookie, care for one?"

"No thanks," she answered, accepting the cup of coffee from Tate.

"Okay, you lose sight of the suspect?" Tate said as he took a bite of the Christmas tree shaped sugar cookie. "What happened next?"

Baxter took a slow sip of coffee, thinking about her answer.

"I knew I had to quickly assess the situation. One of two things is going on. Either the suspect is gone. Or, he's hiding in the bushes, with a gun, and he's going to shoot me."

"Alright," Tate said. "You think through your options, what do you do?"

"At that moment, I believed the suspect had made a successful get away. I decided to go back to my unit. My logic was that we'd eventually find and arrest the kid. I'm guessing that we had the clerk's statement and the store's surveillance tape."

"Did you start to go back towards your unit?"

"No."

"Why?"

"I heard something. I could sense that someone was near and moving."

"What did you hear?"

"The sound of feet walking through wet grass. You know that squishing sound. It was coming from a backyard about forty feet away. I started walking towards the sound."

"Was your weapon drawn?"

"Yes, sir, I had never holstered it."

"What were the lighting conditions?

"None."

"Could you see?"

"Barely, it was real dark back there. No lights, the clouds were covering the moon. A misty rain was falling."

"Had any other deputies arrived at your location?'

"I had called in my position and that I was engaged in a foot pursuit. I knew other deputies would be there at any time, but not yet."

"What happened next?"

"I looked into a backyard, forty feet away, and there he was."

"Who?"

"It was the Hispanic kid wearing denim pants and a white Dodgers jersey—the suspect. From my vantage point, it was the kid I had been chasing."

"What did you do?"

"I yelled *Sheriff's Department, put your hands up, Sheriff's Department put your hands up.*"

"Did he comply?"

"No—Christ, it all just happened so quick, Sarge. I didn't have time to think, I could only react."

"Tell me," Tate said.

"As I'm shouting my command, the kid turns towards me—I see silver in his right hand. I fired one round into his chest."

"Why did you fire?"

"Because I wanted to see my son again and I didn't want to die on that walking trail."

"Why did you think you were going to die?"

"Fuck, Sarge, it's not that hard to figure out."

"Michelle, I understand this is emotional for you. I've got to ask."

"The kid had just robbed the Circle K. They had already fired shots at me during the vehicle pursuit. When the kid jumped out of the car, I saw the gun. It was either him or me and it wasn't going to be me. It's that simple—it's called survival."

Tate could see that Michelle Baxter might lose it at any minute. She wouldn't make eye contact with him. As she told her story she held her head down, fixated on the Styrofoam coffee cup in front of her. She picked at the rim of the cup and a small pile of the white material was building on the table. Tate continued his questions in a relaxed conversational tone. He had to get her through the interview.

"What happened after you fired the one shot?"

"After I disabled the suspect, I approached and yelled, *don't move, let me see your hands.*

"Did he move?"

"No, he never moved. When I was ten feet away, I saw the red stain growing on the Dodgers jersey. His left hand was tucked underneath his left leg. I could see his right hand. There was nothing in his hand."

"Then what happened?"

"Forty King started flying overhead. The helicopter's searchlight really lit up the backyard. That's when I saw it."

"Saw what?" he asked.

"The cell phone, five feet from his right hand. There was no gun, just the damned cell phone. When it became clear to me that this kid had no gun and the silver I saw must have been the cell phone; that's when I first had that *oh shit* feeling."

"Was the kid still alive?"

Baxter closed her eyes, squeezing them shut. She put her left hand over her mouth. Tate could see that she was trying hard not to cry.

"Yeah, he was still alive," she said. "It haunts me every night."

"What haunts you every night, Michelle?'

"His breathing was slow and labored. I could see that he was urgently fighting for each breath of life. The sound—it was horrible. I still hear it. He was just gasping. The chest wound was gurgling."

"What happened next?" he asked, trying to move along. He didn't want to lose her this late in the interview.

"I thought I heard what sounded like a dog whimpering. So I'm thinking to myself, *No that can't be*. Then, a white and tan Jack Russell Terrier walks up and just stands there, whimpering. That's when I knew."

"Knew what?"

"That something wasn't right about this scene. Things just weren't adding up. I couldn't make sense of it, I started fearing the worst."

"Why?"

"I thought I had shot the suspect from the Circle K robbery. But this kid, who is bleeding out, has no gun, just a cell phone. Then, the dog seemed to know him. It just wasn't right. When the transmission came in over my walkie-talkie—it confirmed my worst fear." Her tan colored face turned ashen.

"Do you need a break?" Tate asked.

"Yeah."

Tate left the conference room and gave her some time alone. He went back to his office and called his wife. He told her that he'd be able to pick up the honey-baked ham on his way home. After fifteen minutes, he went back into the conference room. Michelle Baxter's eyes were red and puffy.

"Tell me about the radio transmission, Michelle."

"Foster, another deputy from our station broadcast that he just took into custody the kid who robbed the Circle K. He says the Hispanic kid is wearing a white Los Angeles Dodgers jersey and blue jeans. He says he took a gun off the kid. His location was about a half mile from where I was at."

"After you received the transmission what were you thinking?"

"I'm thinking—*if Foster has the kid who robbed the Circle K—who in the hell did I just shoot?* Then it hit me—*I shot the wrong kid!* I was paralyzed. I'm watching this kid die and the only thing running through my brain is that he's about the same age as Nate."

"What did you do?"

"My entire body started shaking uncontrollably and I put my gun back in its holster. About that time, two other deputies came running into the backyard. They started giving CPR to the boy. He wasn't breathing and he had no pulse."

"What did you do while they gave him CPR?"

"I fell to the ground, on my knees, and started throwing up. I'm praying that they are able save him. *Don't let him die, please don't let him die.*"

# 13

The Sheriff's Department had set up a roadblock one quarter of a mile away from the church. Three television news vans and sixty members of *Stop Police Abuse* were on the outside, looking in. Each member of *SPA* wore a black armband with the initials M.C. in white. John Tate drove his unmarked car up to the sheriff's vehicle blockading the street. Sergeant Sue Kemp got out of the car and approached Tate's car.

"We've got to stop meeting like this," Kemp smiled while Tate rolled down his window.

"What's up with the roadblock?" Tate asked.

"Our friends from *SPA* and the media are not allowed anywhere near the services. That's a direct order from the Sheriff. What brings you down here, John?"

Tate paused, glanced over at the demonstrators, and started tapping his fingers on the steering wheel, "The kid's memorial services."

"Why?" Kemp asked. "Is something going on at the service that's part of the investigation?"

"No—I just need to go. Something I've got to do for myself."

"Yeah, I guess I can see that," Kemp said.

"Any brass here?" Tate asked.

"No, and rumor has it there's quite a story behind that."

"Like what? I hadn't heard," Tate said.

"Apparently the Sheriff called the Costa family and asked if he could pay his respects by attending the memorial services. Vincent Costa lit him up with a string of four letter words. The basic gist was that after one of his deputies had murdered his son, the Sheriff had big balls by even thinking about showing up."

"If I was in the Costa's shoes I probably would have said the same thing. Why the roadblock?"

"After Costa got done chewing on the Sheriff's ass, the boss asked if there was anything the department could do. Costa said yes, he didn't want to see his son's memorial service turned into a three-ringed circus. So, here I am."

"Guess that explains it. Well, have a good Christmas, Sue," Tate said. He rolled up his window, put the car into drive, and headed for the church parking lot.

Tate's interview with Michelle Baxter had finished at noon. While he ate lunch, alone in his office, he debated with himself on whether to attend the memorial services for Mario Costa. He didn't know how he would be received by the Costas at the services—but he had to go.

Tate found a parking spot and checked himself over in the rearview mirror. He buttoned the top button of his dress shirt and pulled tight the knot of his tie. He got out of the car and reached into the backseat for his suit jacket; putting it on while he walked towards the church.

It was mid afternoon and the sun shined bright in the cloudless sky; the type of weather that Southern California Chambers of Commerce advertised, Christmas Eve and a clear sixty-five degrees.

Parked along the side of the curb, just outside the church, Tate saw two yellow school buses. The black lettering on the side of the buses read— *East Valley High School*. Mario Costa had been in his junior year at the school. Though the students were on Christmas break, the school had provided transportation for the grieving students. Ten yards behind the school buses, Tate saw the black hearse and two black limousines. He grimaced and thought about his girls.

Inside the lobby to the auditorium Tate stopped and stared at the wood framed photograph perched on an easel. Tate guessed that Mario must have been around fourteen when the picture was made. The boy had hazel eyes, sparkling with life. He had just a hint of acne and braces on his teeth. The bangs of his jet-black hair stopped just above the eyebrows. The face smiled at Tate—and it sent chills through his body.

Tate followed the crowd into the auditorium. At the door, he took an obituary from the young male usher dressed in black. He glanced down at the cover. It was a photograph of Mario, the same as the one in the lobby. Underneath it read—*Mario Christopher Costa, December 2, 1993-December 19, 2009.*

The services would start in five minutes and there were few chairs left in the three hundred-seat auditorium. Tate spotted an empty one midway through the last row. He shuffled through the aisle, bumping the knees of others, and excusing himself until he reached the seat.

The mahogany casket was closed. A spray of yellow roses sat atop the casket, other sprays of flowers, in all colors and types, shared the altar with the casket. Tate had been to his fair share of funerals, some big, some small, but never had he seen this many flower arrangements.

Tate looked around the auditorium. The mourner's were evenly split between teenagers and adults. He presumed that the teenagers went to school with Mario and the adults must have known Mario or his family in some fashion. Most of the teenage girls were openly sobbing and hugging one another. Tate had worked enough homicides to know that death was a stranger to kids this age.

A steady hum of voices filled the air of the auditorium. Some people were whispering while others talked in a subdued conversational tone. Tate couldn't help but to hear some of the conversations taking place around him; and what he overheard cut through him like a searing hot knife. One row in front of him, and to his left, two teenage boys were talking.

"Man, can you believe that? Mario got wasted by a cop."

"I know, he wasn't even doing anything wrong. He was just taking his dog out to pee."

"How can the Five-0 just go around wasting people?"

"I don't know bro', cops suck."

Three rows in front of Tate, and to the right, two women in their thirties whispered to one another.

"I just can't get over how senseless Mario's death was."

"It's scary, Tammy, how something like this could happen. Our houses aren't that far from Vincent and Carmen's house."

"I know, Lisa, it just as easily could have been one of our kids."

"I wonder what's going to happen to the deputy."

"He needs to go to prison."

The auditorium turned quiet. Tate saw four people, all dressed in black, slowly walk down the aisle towards the front row. Vincent and Joseph Costa wore matching tailored black suits with a white shirt and silver silk tie. A black veil covered the face of Carmen Costa. She showed no emotion, staring straight ahead, with an uncomprehending look in her eyes. It was a combination of mental exhaustion and the doctor's prescription medication.

Vincent's left hand and arm helped to support his unsteady wife as they walked. With his right hand, he reached out to the people sitting in the aisle seats—touching their shoulders and giving each a nod of his head. Behind Vincent and Carmen were Joseph and his grandmother. They reached the front row and sat in the four chairs directly facing Mario's casket.

A screen came down from the ceiling of the auditorium. Mario's face filled the screen. The same face as the portrait in the lobby and on the obituary. Recorded music started playing from the auditorium's sound system—Avril Lavigne's, *"Slipped Away"*.

For the next four minutes, the song was accompanied by a photographic narrative of Mario's life. Included were photographs at holidays, on vacations, or just everyday life. Always in the photographs was Mario's lifelong companion—his dog, Payaso.

When the music stopped playing the screen went back up into the auditorium's ceiling. Tate heard the sound of sobbing throughout the room, blending with the sounds of mourners blowing their noses into facial tissues. Tate didn't have any Kleenex; he wiped away the tears with his forefinger.

A red haired teenage boy got up from the second row and made his way to the podium. Uncomfortable wearing a coat and tie, he ran his right index finger around his neck and shirt collar. The boy reached into his suit jacket and took out several sheets of folded paper. He unfolded the sheets of paper, cleared his throat, and began talking.

"My name is Archie Reed, Mario was my best friend. I don't do real good talking in front of people, but I have to tell you what a wonderful person Mario was and how much I'm going to miss him.

"I first met Mario when we were both eight years old. We played on the same Little League baseball team. I didn't really want to be there, but my dad said I needed to play some kind of sport. I don't think Mario wanted to be there either. He tried playing just because his older brother, Joseph, was a good baseball player. We played the outfield positions. We were horrible and that's where they put all the lousy kids—in the outfield. We didn't care. We'd be out there talking while balls flew over our heads. That was the last year Mario and I played baseball, or any other sport.

"We became good friends and through the years it seemed like we always had classes together. We were usually the smartest two kids in class and we competed to see who would make the best grades. We both shared a passion for science and anything related to space exploration. We lived for Space Shuttle missions. Okay—I know what you all must be thinking, and you're right—we're nerds.

"Mario had a special place in his heart for animals, especially dogs. He loved his Jack Russell Terrier, Payaso. I would always tell him that his dog was crazy. It never slowed down. I guess Mario named him appropriately. In Spanish, Payaso means clown. Mario would talk about how someday he would have to be rich, so he could take care of all the homeless dogs. Three times a week, after school, Mario would volunteer at the animal shelter. I don't think many people knew that about Mario.

"We were both going to attend Cal Tech and be roommates. We just got our SAT scores back. We both nailed it, definitely good enough to get us in. I look forward to going and I just have to convince myself, that in spirit, Mario will be there with me.

"For the past couple of years the war has had a real effect on Mario. It pained him to see all the soldiers coming home from Iraq and Afghanistan missing their arms and legs. He said he was going to devote his life to designing robotic prosthetics. That's just the kind of person Mario was.

"Mario, I'll miss you, your family will miss you, Payaso will miss you, and everyone here today will miss you. The world will miss you."

Archie Reed folded the papers and put them back in his suit pocket. He left the podium and walked over to the Costa family. One by one, they each stood up and exchanged hugs.

The auditorium went silent as Joseph Costa walked up to the dais. He put a hand on each side of the podium and leaned on it for support. He stared at the casket; then closed his eyes and took a deep breath. He opened them and struggled to get the words out, "Mario was my little brother...."

The next sentence would not leave his mouth. His lips started to quiver and his body began trembling. Fighting for composure, he started over, "Mario was my little brother...."

Joseph cast a forlorn look at his brother's casket and sobbed uncontrollably. Vincent Costa took a handkerchief out of his suit pocket and rushed to his son's side. Joseph hugged his father, crying on his shoulder.

"I'm going to miss him, dad."

"We all are, Joseph."

After the services were concluded the Costa family stood by their chairs in the first row, ten feet from Mario's casket. A line of mourners formed to pay their respects to the family.

Tate shook hands with Carmen Costa and said, "I'm sorry for your loss." She gave no response, only a slight nod of the head.

Vincent Costa held out his hand to acknowledge him and tersely said, "Sergeant Tate."

Tate then offered his hand to Joseph and introduced himself, "Joseph, I'm Sergeant John Tate with the Sheriff's Department. I'm sorry for the loss of your brother."

Joseph did not hold out his hand. He looked Tate in the eyes with a steely cold glare and said, "You shouldn't be here."

* * *

In the sanctuary of his wood working shop, Tate applied a coat of clear varnish to a front porch rocking chair. A Christmas present for his father, he had been working on the chair since October. The night air was cold, and when he breathed, he could see his breath. He had a window open to keep the workshop free of varnish fumes. The old electric space heater over in the corner, its hot orange coils glowing, did little to keep out the cold mountain air.

When he finished the job, he put down the brush and tapped the lid shut on the metal can of varnish. He then reached for his coffee mug and sat down on a worn out couch that had seen better days in the Tate living room. The burn of the Scotch felt good going down. It warmed the parts of his body that a parka could not.

The events of the day had taken its toll on him; Michelle Baxter's interview and Mario Costa's memorial services. Days like this made him reach out for those familiar words and he said them out loud. *Through these eyes I've seen love and I've seen hate. I've seen the violence and the tears.*

From where he sat on the couch he didn't see or hear his wife come into the workshop. She walked up behind him and massaged his aching shoulders.

"Feels good," he said

After a few more minutes of massaging, she walked around the couch and sat down next to her husband. She took the coffee cup out of his hands, sniffed it, and took a sip, "Good coffee".

"Is it okay to go back into the house? I, uh, need some more coffee."

"No, the girls are still wrapping your Christmas presents."

"Why are they waiting for the last minute?"

"I don't know. I guess the same reason as why you're still working on your dad's rocker."

"Good point."

"You look tired," she said, running her hand through his brown hair.

"I am."

"Bad day at work?"

"I don't know if bad is the right word, but yeah, one of those days."

"Want to talk about it?"

He took another drink of Scotch, "It's like the perfect storm."

"What is?" she asked.

"This officer involved shooting we're working right now. The punk who robbed the store had a gun. During the pursuit, he tried to shoot her. When he split on foot, she saw the gun. She then sees someone, absolutely convinced it's the suspect. It's dark and misty, really can't see shit, there's something silver in his hands and she fires in self-defense. But it ain't him."

"How is she doing?"

"Michelle is a mess, going through life with the burden of knowing that she shot and killed an innocent kid. That's a heavy weight to bear. On the other hand, she's resolute that she didn't do anything wrong, just doing her job out there. She thought it was the suspect and believed the suspect had a gun and was a threat to her. Michelle wanted to live another day to see her son—so she fired.

"What would you have done?"

"Kathy, I play that scenario out in my mind all the time. I just don't know."

"John, I know you better than that. You know exactly what you would have done."

He drank the last of the Scotch from the coffee mug, "I'm coming home to my wife and girls—I would have shot."

"Do you think the DA will see it that way?"

"I don't know, babe, this one's a close call."

"How were the services?"

"Nice—if there is such a thing as calling any memorial service nice. Do you know what the kid wanted to do with his life?"

"What?"

"He wanted to design and build robotic prosthetics for amputee soldiers coming home from the war."

"Sad."

"I'm glad I went. I really wanted to know who this kid was—more than just a name and a corpse I saw at the crime scene and morgue. The family was less than warm when I paid my respects."

"C'mon, John, how do you want them to react? Look at all they are going though."

"Kathy?"

"Yes."

"How would you react?"

"What do you mean?"

"How would we react if instead of Mario that would have been one of the girls?"

"John, I don't want to think like that."

"Why? What happened that night could happen in any neighborhood to anybody."

"It's just too upsetting to think about."

Tate got up from the couch, shut the window, and turned off the space heater, "What would we do? Would we hate the cop? Would we grieve but still have an understanding of why it happened? Could we ever find forgiveness?"

Listening to him talk, she loved the man she married; the hard-edged homicide cop with a soft under belly. She got up from the couch, walked over to her husband, and brought his hand to her lips, "John, you're thinking way too hard. It's Christmas Eve; let's go back to the house. You could use another cup of coffee."

"That and I need to hug my girls."

# 14

Winter turned to spring and Michelle Baxter was in the best shape of her life. She was also in the worst shape of her life. Tate had finished the criminal investigation and during the last week of January, he submitted his case file to the District Attorney's office. The shooting death of Mario Costa had been under review for five weeks at the DA's office and a decision was expected at any time.

During that time, while on administrative leave, Michelle had settled into a routine. She spent her days building her body up and her nights tearing it down. She would wake up at eight o'clock, maybe nine o'clock, and some day's ten o'clock. Whatever time she did get out of bed, she always felt the same way, she was used to it by now. Her head would throb and her eyes burned. Her tongue felt twice its normal size and her cotton-mouth always tasted of rum.

Nate would be at school and she'd have the house to herself. She'd go downstairs into the kitchen, open up the refrigerator, and take out the gallon jug of orange juice. She drank it like water; the cold sweet nectar made the inside of her dry and pasty mouth feel almost normal. She would then read Nate's message. Every morning he left a note on the kitchen counter telling his mother about his day. Baseball season had just started and after classes, he would be at practice or a game. He always ended each note by telling his mother that he loved her.

She'd then put on her running shoes, stretch, and head off for her morning run; usually six miles. On most mornings, she would run on the sidewalks of her subdivision. Sometimes, if she wanted to be adventurous and felt like dodging the coyotes, she'd head off into the foothills of the mountains.

She had to run; it was an exercise of pleasure, pain, and punishment. Out on a run, it felt good to let her mind wander and for just a little while, every day, she forgot about the miserable existence that her life had become. Running every morning, feeling like a warmed over pile of crap, brought pain. But, she was okay with that; it was part of the experience. The physical act of running purged her body of the poisons from the previous night, preparing it for that night's dosage of toxins. From her perspective, the mornings were her punishment. If she was going to drink— and she was going to drink — this was the price she would have to pay in the morning.

By the time she showered, it would usually be around noon. After a turkey sandwich for lunch, she'd pack her gym bag and head off for the health club. Michelle loathed daytime television and other than her rose bushes, she had no hobbies; she had to do something in the afternoons. At the club, she'd lift weights, swim, and take Zumba classes— anything to pass the time.

Back home by four o'clock, she always prepared a fresh home cooked dinner for Nate. His baseball schedule determined their dinner schedule. Sometimes they ate dinner together. Sometimes she left a plate in the oven. She had her demons, but she remained resolute in being a good mother for Nate.

At seven o'clock, she would bust out the rum and diet cola. She stashed the bottles of rum in his office upstairs. Nate seldom, if ever, went into his dad's office. The ratio of rum to diet cola had increased over the past three months to where the glass now contained equal parts of each.

He had left his iPod on his desk. The night would begin with her putting on the headphones. Sitting in his leather recliner, she'd then listen to his favorite collection of country music. After a couple more of the stiff drinks, the desired numbing effects of the rum would begin to kick in.

On some nights, Michelle would go through the drawers of his desk. She swore she could still smell the scent of his cologne on the pages of his handwritten DA case file notes. Other nights she would just flip through the legal books sitting atop his credenza. Every night, she would pick up and caress the framed family photographs.

By one in the morning, the quart bottle of rum would be empty. Turning off the lights to his office, she'd be back the next night, welcoming a fresh bottle of rum. With the aid of the hallway wall, she'd stagger to their bedroom. Once in bed, the rum proved to be no match for the sights and sounds. She saw them every night, she heard them every night—the helicopter circling over the backyard, the blood gurgling from the hole in the boy's chest.

\* \* \*

Nate was awakened by the sound of breaking glass and a loud thud hitting the floor upstairs. He blinked the sleep out of his eyes, looked at the clock by his bed, and threw on the jeans that had been lying on the floor. Running out of his bedroom and up the stairs he yelled, "Mom!"

"Nate—I think I need help," he heard is mother's weak voice coming from inside his dad's office.

A small amount of blood from a gash, just above her left eye, trickled down her face. Larger amounts of blood spurted out from a deep cut on her right forearm. Nate found her sitting on the carpet with her back against the wall. He saw the shattered drink glass lying next to her. Ice cubes and a brown liquid, smelling strongly of rum, soaked the carpet. Also soaking into the carpet was his mother's blood.

Nate breathed in deep and tried to stay calm. He rushed to the hallway linen closet and grabbed a pile of bath towels. Back inside his dad's office, he wiped away the blood from his mother's head wound. It was starting to swell, but the bleeding had stopped. The deep cut on her forearm continued to bleed profusely. He kept pressure on the towel— it didn't stop the bleeding. Fearing that his mother would bleed to death, he ran into his parents' bedroom and grabbed one of his father's belts from the walk-in closet. He ran back into the office and fashioned a tourniquet around her arm with the belt. His pulse rate lessened when he saw no more red pouring out of his mother's arm.

"What did you do to yourself?"

"I didn't do anything to myself," her belligerent words were thick, slow, and slurred. Her breath stunk of alcohol.

Nate spotted the empty bottle of rum sitting on his dad's desk. He knew his mom had been drinking— she hadn't been fooling anyone. They had both been acting as if nothing was going on.

"What happened?" he asked again.

"I was sitting at his desk and the glass slipped out of my hand and broke. A piece of glass cut my arm. I started to stand up—I fell and hit my head on the side of the desk."

"We've got to get you to the emergency room."

"Just get me a band-aid."

"Mom, that cut in your arm is deep and you have a gash over your eye."

"I'm not going anywhere, I'll be fine. Just help me get into bed."

"No, we're going to the emergency room," he said, reaching down to help his mother to her feet.

Her balance was unsteady and she had to hold on to her son for support. She tried to push Nate away, yelling, "Leave me alone!"

Angry and frustrated, he yelled back, "Then I'm calling nine-one-one and you can ride to the hospital in an ambulance."

"No, no, Nate, please don't do that," she said, pleading with her son.

"We have to go—now, you've lost a lot of blood."

"Okay."

With one hand, Nate had been holding the belt tight around his mother's upper forearm. The other hand kept pressure on the blood soaked towel covering the wound. Sensing that his mother was calming, he said, "I'm going to need some help here, mom."

"Okay."

"Keep the belt tight and pressure on the cut. Can you do that for me?"

"Yes."

It took fifteen minutes to drive from their house to the hospital. The speed limit, stoplights, and stop signs meant nothing to Nate. He looked over at his mother in the passenger seat. She was curled up in a fetal position, one hand holding the belt tight, and the other keeping pressure on the towel. Her face was pressed up against the side window and the sounds of her sobbing were muted.

"Nate, please make it stop, please make it stop."

"Make what stop, mom?"

"The sounds."

"What sounds?"

"The helicopter, the gurgling."

"Hang on, we're almost there."

\* \* \*

Nate opened his eyes and watched his mother sleep. He then eased himself out of the chair and moved his head from side to side, trying to get the kinks out. Sleeping in the chair had left his body aching. He pulled apart the shade, just a little, and let some of the morning sunlight into the hospital room. He sat back down in the chair, thinking about how he would say it to his mother.

One hour later, Michelle woke up in the hospital bed. She raised her left hand and with a puzzled expression on her face looked at the IV tube. Turning her head, she looked at the bandages wrapped around her right arm. She reached up and touched the bandage over her left eye.

"Where am I?

"The hospital."

"Why?"

"You don't remember?"

"Remember what, Nate?"

"Falling down last night and getting cut in dad's office."

"No, I don't remember."

"That's probably because you were drunk."

"That's none of your business."

"Yes, it is my business. I'm partly to blame for what happened last night. I should have called you out on your drinking. I let it get too far."

"I don't drink that much."

"Mom, don't play that game with me, yes you do—way too much."

"I've got a lot of hurt inside, Nate. Your father, the shooting."

"Drinking's not going to make it all go away."

"Okay, I promise I'll cut back a little."

"No, you have to stop completely. I can't go through this again. I thought I was going to lose you last night. You're all I've got."

"Please stop crying, honey. I never meant to hurt you."

"You need to get some help, some professional help. Can't the department do something for you?"

"Come here and give your mother a hug."

Being careful not to disturb the IV tube or his mother's bandages, Nate sat down on the side of her bed and held her tight. "Please, mom, you're all I've got. I can't lose you."

# 15

"I'm going to recommend to my boss that we file on her."

John Tate glared in disbelief at Deputy District Attorney Tim Roberts. He sat across from the prosecutor's desk and watched Roberts shove another bite of the ham sandwich into his mouth. Tate felt the anger building inside and asked, "Why?"

Roberts wiped the mayo off the corner of his mouth, put his lips on the straw of the Diet Coke, washed down the sandwich and answered, "Because I think she made the wrong call. The bottom line is your gal messed everything up from the moment she stopped behind the suspect's disabled Monte Carlo."

Tate wanted to reach across the prosecutor's desk and slap him upside the head, but he didn't. "That's pretty fucking bold of you to make that kind of statement. You've never been in that kind of situation—you've never smelled the gunpowder."

"Look, Tate, don't cop an attitude with me. I'm sitting here in my office, eating my lunch, minding my own business. You pop in, unannounced, and want to know where I'm going with the Baxter OIS. So, I told you. I'm sorry it's not what you wanted to hear."

"Alright," Tate said. "Tell me where she went wrong."

"Like I said," Roberts answered. "It wasn't just one thing. It was a comedy of errors that lead to that kid's wrongful death."

Tate closed his eyes and rubbed them. "Okay, I'm tired of playing verbal judo with you. Just lay it all out for me."

Roberts took another bite of the sandwich and while chewing said, "She should have let him go."

"What do you mean?"

"I don't think she should have cranked off two rounds at the passenger who took off on foot."

"Why?"

"C'mon, Tate, it's right there in her own statement. She told you that when she fired those two rounds, the suspect was running away from her."

"So it's your opinion that Baxter should have let an armed suspect, someone who had just robbed a convenience store, run off into a residential neighborhood."

"Yes," Roberts said.

"Did you ever stop to think that maybe she didn't fire those first two rounds to protect herself? She fired them to protect the families who were asleep in those houses."

"I thought about it—but I'm not buying it. Firing those rounds was dangerous and she started a series of events that culminated with her shooting the wrong person. She should have just let him go. The suspect is on the store's security camera system. You had the statement of the clerk. Your department arrested the driver of the Monte Carlo—who promptly gave up the identity of his crime partner. Your people were eventually going to find and arrest that kid. It may not have been that night, but certainly within twenty four hours."

"Dude, you're way off base," Tate said. "Baxter had every right, under the law, to fire those shots and then engage in a foot pursuit. How about the shooting in the Costa's backyard? Are you okay with that? There's no doubt she fired in self defense."

"I'm not buying that one either," Roberts said.

"You're shitting me—right?"

"No, I'm not. She may have thought she needed to fire in self-defense, but that's not the legal standard. You know that better than anybody does. It's what would the reasonable person, what would the reasonable cop, in that position, do? I think the reasonable cop would not have fired."

"You don't get it, do you?" Tate said, looking away from Roberts, unable to stomach another minute with the prosecutor.

"Oh, no, to the contrary. I get it perfectly. Your gal made a bad choice, a mistake, a very deadly mistake."

Tate got up from his chair and started to leave the office. "What are you going to tell Garcia?"

"I'm going to tell him that based upon my review of your investigation and the applicable law, we should file criminal charges. We should let twelve members of the community decide whether or not Baxter made a good call or a bad call."

"What kind of charges?

"Voluntary manslaughter."

Walking out the door, Tate turned around and looked at Roberts. "You should really do something about your office."

"Why?"

"It stinks."

Muttering four letter words under his breath, Tate walked down the hallway, stopping at the offices of three different homicide prosecutors. He dropped off supplemental reports on pending murder cases and inquired about jury trial dates. Wrapping up his business with the trial prosecutors, he walked up a flight of stairs to the District Attorney executive offices. While the offices of the trial prosecutors were drab with metal government issue desks and file cabinets, the executive offices were on par with that of any prestigious private law firm.

Tate spent several moments looking at the framed awards and recognitions adorning the walls outside the entrance to District Attorney Anthony Garcia's office.

Garcia's secretary finished a telephone call and asked, "May I help you, sir?"

"Is Tony around?"

"You mean Mr. Garcia?"

"No, I mean Tony, is he in?" Tate asked.

Garcia's secretary frowned at Tate, clearly annoyed with his apparent lack of respect for her boss. "Do you have an appointment?"

"No," Tate answered, "but if he's in, he'll see me."

"May I have your name please?"

"Sergeant John Tate, Sheriff's Department."

"Just wait here," she said, disappearing into the District Attorney's cavernous office.

She came out of the office, followed by a Hispanic male, in his early fifties, salt and pepper hair, and carrying around just a bit more weight than he should. His white monogrammed dress shirt was heavily starched; his suit pants sharply creased to go along with a fresh shine on his black wingtip shoes.

"I'll be damned, John Tate, wuz up dog?" Anthony Garcia said, walking up to Tate, smiling and holding out his hand.

"You clean up pretty good, Tony," Tate said, returning the handshake.

"C'mon in," Garcia motioned, walking back into his office and taking a seat behind his cherry wood desk. Tate sat in a burgundy leather wingback chair, looked around the office, and remarked, "Very nice."

"It's been a long time, John. I know you were part of that conference call I had with the Sheriff on the Baxter OIS. But aside from that, when was the last time I saw you?"

"Death row—San Quentin, three years ago," Tate said.

"That's right, Virgil Mullins' execution. The world's a better place without that shit bag breathing our air."

"I just remember him dying like a coward," Tate said. "Yeah, he thought he was a tough guy when he raped and killed little Abigail Perkins. But when that blue juice cocktail began surging through his veins—he just started bawling like a little bitch."

"We've still got one more on The Row, John."

"I know, Cecil "Dog Shit" Cooper. What's going on with his appeal?"

"It's at the U.S. Supremes. I'm confident they'll affirm and we'll have a death date within the year."

"Those were some good times, Tony. We had a hell of a run back when you were a real trial prosecutor."

"How many murder cases did we work together?" Garcia asked.

"Eleven," Tate answered.

"So, what's the deal, John? I know you're not here to talk about days gone by."

Tate reached for the jar of jellybeans sitting on Garcia's desk. He poured a handful and started picking out the black jellybeans. "You like the licorice ones?" he asked.

"No."

"Me either," Tate said.

Garcia scooped the licorice jellybeans off his desk and tossed them into a trashcan. "What's the problem, John; I can see your mind working a mile a minute."

Tate ate the last jellybean and ran his tongue over his teeth, trying to clear the sugar and goo, "That prick, Roberts, is going to recommend that you file on Michelle Baxter."

"When did you talk to him?" Garcia asked.

"Just before I came up here. He was down in his office stuffing a ham sandwich into his fat pie hole like there was no tomorrow."

"Roberts is scheduled to brief me on the investigation and his recommendations tomorrow. Until you just told me, I honestly had no clue as to how he was leaning."

"He's an idiot, Tony. Don't you be an idiot by signing off on his recommendations."

"You're putting me in a real bad spot here, John. You know my policy. I have to trust in my prosecutor's to make the right decisions. If I ask them to make a decision, then pull the carpet out from under their feet, I lose all credibility with my troops."

"But he's wrong on this one."

"Ya know what, John? What if he's not? What if it is justice to file charges on her and let a jury make the call? I mean, c'mon, for crying out loud, she killed the wrong kid."

"Tony, he's not seeing the big picture, he doesn't get it."

"Big picture—you want to know what the big picture is? I've got the entire Hispanic community demanding that I file criminal charges."

"Fuck them."

"Easy for you to say. You're not up for re-election next year."

"I'll still vote for you."

"Funny, John. Does the sheriff know you came to see me?"

"No."

"Your captain?"

"No."

"Your lieutenant?"

"No."

"Don't you think they'd be pissed if they knew we were having this discussion?"

"They'll never know."

"Why is this one so important to you, John?"

"I don't know, it just is. I guess it's because she's still getting over the loss of her husband, she's trying to raise a kid, and now this. The shooting has turned her into a complete mess."

"Any other reason?"

Tate paused and looked his friend in the eye, "That was a hell of a situation for her to be in, could of been me or any other cop. You know, Tony, when the day is done, we do what we have to do to make sure we go home to our families."

Garcia nodded his head and peered out his office window at the San Bernardino Mountains. It looked like the mountain peaks had been dusted with powdered sugar. "What do you want me to do, John?"

"Just do your job. I know you have to get briefed by that jackass, Roberts. He's going to give you his spin on why you need to file on Baxter. I understand that, I get that. Just promise me you'll do one thing."

"What's that?"

"I know you're busy and shit, but just promise me that you'll read my investigation notebook—all of it. Read it for yourself; don't rely on Roberts to tell you what's in my investigation."

"Okay, I'll read it."

"Thank you."

"John, you said Roberts is missing the big picture. What did you mean by that?"

"He's all hung up on Baxter's statement that when she fired those first two shots that missed, the suspect was running away from her, and posed no threat to her safety. He thinks this was the first, of a number of bad choices, on Baxter's part, that ultimately lead to the death of the Costa kid."

"What does he think Baxter should have done?"

"Nothing. Just let the suspect run away. You know, the standard bullshit line of we would eventually catch him."

"Really?"

"Yeah."

"How is Robert's analysis faulty?" Garcia asked.

"He's just focused on that one snippet of Baxter's statement. Tony, we both know that ain't right. We have to see his thing through her eyes. We have to consider everything that was going through Baxter's mind. From the moment she got the call, we have to know what she was hearing, seeing, and feeling. Everything that she processed in her mind to conclude that she needed to shoot in self-defense. *It was either him or me—and it wasn't going to be me.*"

"No promises, John, I can see merit in both what you are saying and what Roberts will tell me tomorrow."

"I can't ask for anything more, Tony. I'm just so tired of investigating OIS's and all the game playing that goes on with you lawyers."

"We don't play games."

"Yeah, you do, and so do the union lawyers for the cops. Your office won't justify a shooting unless they have a complete statement from the cop. The cop's lawyer doesn't want them to give the DA a statement because it could add fuel to the fire for a filing of criminal charges. The damn cop is stuck in the middle with his or her head spinning."

"It's not a game, John. It's just the parameters of the business."

"Well, it sucks. Baxter gave me a statement, probably against the advice of her mouthpiece. She did the right thing. Now that prick, Roberts, wants to shove her statement up her ass."

"Calm down, John. I'll read the file and I promise I'll give her a fair shake. But not filing charges would really put me in a bad spot with a lot of folks."

"Like who?"

"Like Roberts, the family of Mario Costa, and the Hispanic community."

"Tony, I know you'll do the right thing."

"I don't know, John, it won't look good. It'll look like I'm giving her a free pass because Jordan used to work for me."

"I don't care what it looks like, Tony. If you give her a free pass—it's because she didn't do anything wrong. She's not a criminal."

# 16

"Ball three," the home plate umpire barked. Staying in his crouch position, the Cal State Fullerton catcher threw the ball back to the fatigued pitcher. Joseph Costa took off his sweat soaked cap and wiped the salty perspiration from his forehead. On the inside bill of the cap, written in black ink, were the initials M.C. Glancing into the dugout, he saw an uneasy look on the face of his head coach. The last pitch Costa had thrown was his hundred and tenth of the ball game. In the bottom of the ninth inning Cal State held a razor thin, one to nothing, lead over the visiting Bruins from UCLA.

Costa went into his stretch position and eyed the UCLA runner, who was taking a small lead off of first base. He had walked the runner, losing his bid for a perfect game. The stifling Southern California heat, and not the Bruins hitters, was now Costa's biggest adversary. He knew he was losing command of his stuff, and so did his coach; he was on a short leash. Costa wanted his no hitter, his coach just wanted to win the game.

The supportive roar of two thousand fans gave Joseph a jolt of energy. He threw a ninety-two mile an hour fastball straight down the middle of the strike zone. The UCLA batter didn't stand a chance and swung late.

*Strike one.*

In the bleachers, standing on their feet, Vincent and Carmen Costa cheered on their son. Joseph looked their way and gave them a nod of his head. He then reared back and threw another fastball as the UCLA runner broke for second base. Again, the pitch was perfect and the batter awkwardly swung at the ball.

*Strike two.*

The runner, racing for second, had the base stolen when the Cal State catcher made the ill-fated decision to attempt a throw down to second base. The ball hit the dirt in front of second base and bounced off the glove of the shortstop. Costa helplessly watched the ball skip into the green of centerfield as the UCLA runner slid head first into third base.

The loud stadium turned quiet while the umpire lobbed Costa a fresh baseball. He rubbed the slick sphere of cowhide between the palms of his hands, catching his breath and thinking about his pitch selection. He couldn't throw a third consecutive fastball; he knew the batter would be looking for that pitch.

He threw a slider and the moment it left his hand, he wished he could have a do over. The ball was well out of the strike zone, breaking down and away from the right-handed hitter. It was the worst pitch he had thrown all afternoon. The entire UCLA dugout gaped in disbelief, stunned as their teammate swung and missed.

*Strike three.*

In celebration, Costa's teammates stormed the pitcher's mound. Before he was buried underneath the pile of human bodies, Joseph's right fist pumped his heart three times and he pointed a finger up to the heavens.

After the game, Vincent and Carmen treated their son to dinner at O'Malley's Steakhouse, a popular off campus hangout spot. Joseph's teammates, and Cal State fans, made a steady flow to the Costa's table, congratulating him on the no hitter. Pitching in the heat for two hours had left Joseph with a ravenous appetite and a two-inch thick slab of prime rib filled his plate; hot juices ran from the meat, soaking the twice-baked potato.

Vincent cut through his bacon wrapped filet mignon and asked his son, "How's the arm feel?"

"It feels okay," he answered, dipping a hunk of prime rib into au jus sauce and then horseradish. "I iced it down for about an hour."

"Your brother would have been so proud," Carmen said.

Joseph stopped chewing and blinked his eyes, determined not to tear up in the restaurant. "I know he would have. I did it for him—I wanted the perfect game."

"A no-hitter is nothing to sneeze at," Vincent said.

"I wanted the perfect game."

"Your mother has been busy with the foundation," Vincent said, changing the subject. He was surprised and concerned with his son's level of anger at not attaining the perfect game.

"What's that all about?" Joseph asked.

"It's our way of keeping your brother's memory alive," Carmen answered. "I came to a difficult crossroad where I had to make some decisions. I could continue to isolate myself in the house, grieving over his death. Or, I could go on with life."

"So, what is the foundation going to do?"

"It's going to keep Mario's vision alive. We're going to raise money to provide state of the art prosthetics for disfigured soldiers," Vincent said.

"How is it going to get money?"

"We're working on a charity golf tournament with a dinner and a silent auction," Carmen answered. "The Chamber of Commerce has been very generous in donating items."

From the bar area, Joseph's teammates called out to him and motioned for him to come over. "I'll be back in a minute," he said to his parents.

"How do you think he's doing?" Carmen asked her husband.

"Hard to say. He's channeling all the emotions into his pitching. I'm not sure whether that's a healthy thing or not."

"Are we going to tell him that we're meeting with the DA next week?"

"We have to tell him," Vincent said.

"He's going to want to be there with us."

"Carmen, that would not be a good idea, he's too unpredictable."

They sipped on their coffee and watched their son get handshakes, fist-pumps, and back slaps from his teammates. Ten minutes later, he returned to his parents table.

"Sorry about that," he said as he sat down.

"Nothing to be sorry about," Vincent said. "Enjoy it, you're the man."

"Your father and I will be meeting with the DA next week."

"When?" Joseph asked.

"Wednesday afternoon," Carmen answered.

"Cool, I'll ask Coach Riley if I can be excused from practice."

"Your mother and I have discussed it. We feel we should do this alone."

"Why?"

"Honey," Carmen began, placing her hand over her sons. "We just think its best that your father and I do this alone."

"That's not fair. He was my little brother."

"Please, Joseph, don't make this any more difficult on your mother and I," Vincent said.

"What's going to happen at this meeting?" Joseph asked. The displeasure in his voice was obvious, but he wasn't going to cross the line by being disrespectful to his parents.

"We only know what Mr. Garcia's secretary told us on the phone," Carmen said to her son.

"What did she say?"

"She told us the DA's office had reached a decision on the deputy who killed Mario," Vincent answered.

"It's about time they filed charges on that guy. They need to put him in jail right away," Joseph said.

"She just said a decision had been reached. We don't know what that decision is," Vincent replied.

"Get real, dad, they have to file charges on him. He murdered Mario."

"I hope you're right, son. I hope you're right."

* * *

"When was the last time you had a drink?" Rebecca Morgan asked.

"Two days, seven hours and thirteen minutes," Michelle Baxter replied. "I'm going to AA meetings twice a day."

The grief counselor took a long look at Baxter, dressed in her usual blue jeans, Ole Miss sweatshirt, and running shoes. Her left eye was still black and a row of small stitches almost blended in with her eyebrow. The long sleeve sweatshirt hid the unsightly wound on her right forearm.

"You really did a number on yourself," the counselor said.

"It isn't like that—I didn't intentionally try to hurt myself."

"Don't be so defensive, Michelle. I never implied that you wanted to hurt yourself. Why? Have you had those thoughts?"

"Look, Doc, I just need you to help me get my mind right—I owe that much to my son. He's already lost one parent. I thought I could get through all these issues on my own—but I can't."

"How long had you two been married?" Morgan asked.

"At the time of his death—nineteen years."

"How did you meet him?"

"After I graduated from the academy he was my Field Training Officer. He taught me how to be a cop. We spent six months on patrol together in some pretty nasty areas."

"Like where?"

"Bloomington," Baxter answered.

"Isn't that the outlaw biker capital of Southern California?" Morgan asked.

"Oh yeah," a smile broke out on her face as she thought about some of the confrontations they had with the Hell's Angel's biker gang. "But no one messed with Jordan. They wanted no part of him. He was a gentle giant, but the shitheads weren't aware of that."

"What attracted you to Jordan?"

"He was just so different from the Southern California guys I had usually dated. He was this larger than life, football-playing guy from Mississippi, but he was so nice, so polite. He always answered with yes, ma'am, yes, sir. He had the most wonderful southern drawl. I had never heard anyone speak like that and I could spend hours just listening to him talk."

"Are you angry over his death?"

"Fuck yeah I'm angry. But, Jordan lived to serve and protect. He loved being a cop and a prosecutor. After Nate and me, he loved his country. Every generation of males in his family had served in the military. Jordan carried on that tradition by serving in the Army Reserves as a military policeman.

"I'll never forget the day when he got the orders that his reserve unit was being called to Afghanistan for active duty. We always knew it was a possibility, but I still had a hard time coming to grips with it. I cried, Jordan asked me to be strong, for Nate.

"I find that I am now questioning everything—mostly my faith— and that scares me. I keep asking why. *Why did it have to be Jordan who opened the door to that booby-trapped car? How could my god let this happen to my husband and the father of my child?*"

"How is your son handling the loss of his father?"

"Probably better than I am. I was just starting to pick up the pieces after Jordan's death and now this happens."

The afternoon sunlight shined brightly through the window and into the eyes of Michelle Baxter. The counselor noticed her patient's squinting, so she got up and pulled the blinds shut. "Can I get you anything to drink, while I'm up?"

"No, thank you." Baxter answered.

"When you say, *now this happens*, are you talking about the shooting death of Mario Costa?"

"Yes, what else would I be talking about?" she answered, shooting an icy glare Morgan's way.

"Is that why you started the drinking?"

"Yes."

"Why?"

"I don't know. I guess I thought the booze would make it go away."

"Make what go away?"

"The pictures in my mind; I can't escape them. They won't let me sleep."

"Tell me about the pictures."

"I see him all the time. Every breath he fights for is more difficult than the one before. He's looking up at me, his eyes are pleading with me. It's as if he's trying to tell me, *why did you shoot me? What did I do wrong?* Blood is spilling out from the wound in his chest—gurgling and sucking—gurgling and sucking. I started to throw up on myself.

"Then, like out of nowhere, the helicopter is overhead. The searchlight burns through the night. It just keeps circling, over and over and over again. The sounds of the engine and rotor blades are etched into my memory."

"Did the alcohol make these pictures go away?"

"No."

"Now that you're sober are you still seeing the pictures?"

"Yes."

"Do you feel responsible for the death of Mario Costa?"

"Of course I do. I shot him; I killed him, which makes me responsible."

"I'm sorry, bad question on my part," Morgan said. "Do you think you were wrong in pulling the trigger of your gun?"

Baxter took a moment and thought about the counselor's question. She ran her fingers through her hair, held her head back, and stared up at the ceiling tiles. "No."

"Tell me why."

"I had every belief that the person I shot was the armed robber from the convenience store. The fucking prick had already fired shots at me during the vehicle pursuit. When he took off running, I saw he had a gun. I fired in self-defense. I believed it was either him or me—and it wasn't going to be me."

"If you don't think you were wrong in firing your gun, why do you suppose you're seeing these pictures?"

"I feel guilty about it. I was not wrong in firing my weapon, but I got it wrong. I shot the wrong person. I can't shake that guilt."

"Michelle, Let me ask you this. Do you ever think about how you would feel? As a mother, how you would feel if one of your fellow deputies was in your exact situation and shot Nate?"

A large tear formed in each of Baxter's eyes. They dropped off her eyelashes and made their way down her light brown cheeks. She wiped each tear away with the index finger of her right hand. "Yes."

"Could this also be a reason why those pictures won't leave your mind?"

"Yes."

"And why you're drinking?"

"That mother must hate me. I took her baby. If someone took my baby, I would hate him or her. Now, I'm that person. It hurts me so bad to know that I am responsible for taking that mother's baby."

"Have you shared these feelings and emotions with anyone else?" Morgan asked.

"No."

"That's not healthy, Michelle."

"I know," she answered, while pulling back the right sleeve of her sweatshirt, exposing the row of metal staples on her forearm. "I know."

"What else are you feeling, Michelle?"

"I just feel like the whole world hates me. The boy's parents have to hate me. My lawyer hates me because I gave a statement to Sergeant Tate. The department, I don't know if I'm getting fired. The DA's office, I don't know if they're going to file criminal charges on me."

"Do you want to go back to work?"

"I can't answer that right now. It's too soon."

"What about the DA's office? The prospect of being charged has to weigh heavy on you. Are they close to a decision?"

"My lawyer says it can come at any time now. I'm scared. I think the court of public opinion hates me. It's been all over the media. They hate me and they don't even know me. I think that's the worst part. Everybody out there hates me—especially my own people."

"What do you mean by *your own people?*" Morgan asked.

"The Hispanic community; it's kind of funny, but it's not. I've watched the protests on TV and read about them in the papers. My identity has not been released to the public, at least not yet, anyways. My people are automatically assuming the boy was shot by a white, male deputy, and they want their pound of flesh.

"That really hurts me. They don't know me, or why I did what I did. It's not about race— it's not about gender. I was just out there doing my job and things went horribly wrong."

"Michelle, you know that when the DA announces his decision your name will be made public?"

"Yes, I know, my lawyer told me."

"Are you prepared for that?"

"No."

"I'm familiar with Garcia's protocol," Morgan continued. "He always meets first with the victim's family. Then he will notify your department and soon after that, your name will be released to the media. Let's get together again when we know Garcia's decision and before he releases your name. We'll get you through this."

"Thanks, Doc, I appreciate your time. I just wish I would have come to you sooner."

"The pride of a cop, Michelle, I see it every day. I'm glad you came in. Sometimes they totally self destruct before they make it to me."

* * *

Michelle Baxter set down the two bags of groceries and flipped through the stack of mail. That afternoon's talk with Rebecca Morgan had lifted a weight off her shoulders. While shopping for groceries at the market, it was the first time she felt that people were not staring at her.

"Nate," she called out.

"I'm in my room, mom."

She walked down the hallway and into her son's room. On the walls were posters of Derek Jeter and Albert Pujols. Sitting atop the nightstand, next to the bed, was a framed photograph of Jordan Baxter; wearing his Army Reserve dress uniform.

She found her son sitting in front of his computer; staring at the screen while rubbing a worn baseball in his hands. She knew that something was wrong. Ever since he'd been a little boy, whenever something was troubling him, he rubbed a baseball in his hands. It was his worry stone.

"What's wrong?" she asked.

"Because I'm being recruited by Cal State Fullerton, the baseball sports information people always email me stuff about what's going on with the program."

"Okay," she said.

"Well, last weekend a Cal State pitcher threw a no hitter."

"That sounds like a good thing."

"He said his inspiration and motivation was his little brother who had recently been killed."

"I think that's admirable," she said to her son.

"Mom, his little brother had been shot and killed by a cop."

She closed her eyes and saw the pictures. They were back again. Her body told her she needed a drink. She had to stay tough; she couldn't give in.

"What's the name of the pitcher who threw the no hitter?" she asked.

"Joseph Costa," he answered. "Mom, is that the boy?"

# 17

They walked, hand in hand, from the Justice Center parking lot to the District Attorney's office. Vincent Costa was dressed in a charcoal gray suit, a white shirt with gold cuff links, red tie, and black wingtip shoes. Carmen wore an Alexander Wang dress, a single strand of pearls around her neck, with matching Louis Vuitton shoes, and handbag. Up ahead they could see a group of forty people standing outside the entrance to the DA's office.

"Isn't that Bustamonte?" Vincent asked.

"I think so, it sure looks like him," Carmen answered.

"How in the hell did he know we were meeting with the DA today?" he said with his jaw clenched.

"I don't know."

"I thought I was pretty clear when I told him to back off."

After twenty-two years of marriage, Carmen could read the anger level of her husband like a book. "Please, Vince, don't say anything. Let's just ignore them."

When the Costa's were ten yards away, Martin Bustamonte stepped out from the crowd and walked over to Vincent and Carmen.

"I understand you're going to be talking with the DA about your son's murder."

"I told you to stay away. This has nothing to do with you or your group."

"And I told you we couldn't be stopped."

Vincent gave Bustamonte an intimidating look, pulled on his wife's hand, and kept walking towards the entrance of the DA's office. They stopped when they saw an enlarged photograph sitting on an easel. It was a photograph of Mario. The same photograph of their son that had been in the church lobby for the memorial services. Vincent let go of his wife's hand and charged towards Bustamonte. He grabbed him by the shoulders and threw him up against the outside wall of the DA's office.

"You son of a bitch!" Vincent shouted. "I told you my son's death was not going to be some kind of three ring media circus."

Costa had four inches on the fat little man, who was defenseless, and waited for the next blow to hit his body.

"Vince, don't hurt him!" Carmen said, pleading with her husband.

"Where did you get that photograph?" Costa said to Bustamonte, their faces only inches apart.

Winded from fear and the force of Costa's hands on his shoulders, Bustamonte struggled to get the words out, "Why don't you ask your son?"

Before Costa could say or do anything else to Bustamonte, plain clothes District Attorney Investigators sprinted out of the lobby and pulled Costa away from Bustamonte. The Costa's gave the investigators their name and were promptly escorted into the building.

In his office, District Attorney Anthony Garcia talked on the phone with Sergeant John Tate.

"Would you please tell Deputy Baxter, John? I don't want her to find out by watching the news. No, this isn't how I wanted it to go down. I was going to meet with the parents this morning and give you a call later in the afternoon."

Garcia's secretary walked in and told her boss that the Costa's were waiting in the conference room.

"I've got to go, John. They're here."

The late morning traffic on the 210 Freeway was light and Tate made the usual thirty-five minute drive from San Bernardino to Rancho Cucamonga in only twenty minutes. He turned onto Michelle Baxter's street and glanced down at the address written on the yellow Post-It note in his right hand. Slowly driving through the well-kept upper middle class neighborhood, he looked at numbers posted on the mailboxes. Tate spotted her in the front yard of a Spanish style, two story chocolate brown stucco house, trimmed in white. She was cutting roses from the bushes that bordered the front of the house.

With her back facing the street, Michelle Baxter heard a car pull into the driveway. She put the freshly cut yellow rose into the wicker basket lying next to her on the grass and turned around. Her heart stopped when she recognized John Tate driving the car. She was not expecting him, but she knew why he was there. To keep from hyperventilating, she inhaled deep controlled breaths. She felt the same dread that she did on the day when the black Department of the Army sedan pulled into the driveway, bringing news of her husband's death.

Tate got out of the car, put his sunglasses in the front pocket of his shirt, and started walking towards her. Still kneeling, Baxter took off her garden gloves and apprehensively got to her feet.

"You have bad news—don't you?"

"Can we go inside and talk?" Tate said.

"Sure."

Baxter left the garden gloves and basket of roses on the grass and walked towards the front door. Tate followed her inside. In the living room, she motioned towards a couch and Tate sat down.

"I'll be just a minute. I need to wash my hands," she said.

She went into a bathroom off the hallway and closed the door. She turned on the cold water and splashed her face. Her hands trembled as she dried her face with a hand towel.

Tate looked at the arrangement of framed family photographs sitting on top of the end table, next to the couch. One photograph captured his attention and he started to get choked up. The photograph was of a much younger Jordan and Michelle Baxter. Michelle was in a hospital bed with

Jordan sitting next to her. They were both smiling. In his massive arms and hands, he cradled a blue blanket. Peeking out from the blanket was a tiny pink face with a tuft of black hair.

Michelle Baxter came back into the living room and sat in a chair across from the couch and Tate. Sitting in the chair, her right leg nervously bounced up and down off the balls of her foot.

"The District Attorney called me about an hour ago. He's reached a decision on the criminal investigation," Tate said.

"Okay."

"He has concluded that you were legally justified in the use of deadly force. No criminal charges will be filed against you."

"Can you say that again?" She thought she heard, what she had heard, but she wanted Tate to repeat it.

"Michelle, the DA has cleared you."

Over the past several weeks, her mind had been consumed with the pending decision by the DA. She knew that when the decision was made, either way, she would cry when she found out. She didn't want to cry. Lately, she'd been crying a lot.

Baxter looked away from Tate, blinked back the tears, and said, "That's good news."

"Why hell yeah that's good news."

"Do the boy's parents know?"

"That's why District Attorney Garcia asked me to tell you right now, face to face," Tate said. "He's got one hell of a mess on his hands right now."

"What's that got to do with the boy's parents?"

The DA is meeting with Mr. and Mrs. Costa, as we speak. After the meeting his intent was to call the Sheriff and we were going to notify you. But that plan blew up in his face."

"What happened?"

"Somebody tipped off the meeting to the media and those assholes from *SPA*. They are all camped out at the DA's office. When they get word of the DA's decision to clear you—things are going to get ugly."

"Do you think it's going to be on the news?" she asked.

"I'd count on it."

"Sarge?"

"Yes, Michelle."

She paused, fighting back a second wave of tears. "My name, are they going to release my name to the media?"

"Yes."

"When?"

"Today."

"I'm not ready for that, not today. Can't the DA put it off for a few days?"

"I don't think he has much of a choice, Michelle. Not with the media staked out in front of his office."

She got up from the chair and started to pace the living room. Tate felt awkward and didn't know what to do or say, so he just remained silent.

Baxter stopped pacing, looked out the front window, and said, "But my counselor told me I'd have a few days' heads up, so I could get emotionally prepared."

"I know, Michelle, that's standard protocol. But when the DA's meeting with the parents got leaked, protocol went out the window."

She stopped staring out the window and sat back down in the chair. "Okay, I'll get through it. I really shouldn't be bitching; things could be a lot worse. At least the DA isn't filing criminal charges against me."

"Michelle, don't get so worked up over your name being released. The news cycles are short, in two days nobody will even remember you."

"Have you heard anything about the IA investigation? Am I going to get fired?"

"I have no idea," Tate said. "I'm completely removed from the admin side of things. That's done to maintain the integrity of both the criminal and administrative investigations."

"Well, I guess they'll let me know soon enough."

"The DA did tell me that his office is filing murder charges against the shitheads who robbed the Circle K," Tate said.

"Will they be seeking the Death Penalty?" she asked.

"I don't know," he answered.

"If they do, I'd like to be the one who gets to stick the needle in their veins," she said.

"I'm guessing a bunch of people would line up to have that job."

"Sarge?"

"Yeah."

"Do you think there's any way the DA can put the case on without me having to testify?"

"No, you'll have to testify."

"I can't do it. I can't relive that nightmare again."

Tate got up from the couch and made his way to the front door, annoyed at Baxter's attitude towards testifying, "You don't have a choice."

Baxter followed Tate out the door and onto the front porch. Tate walked to his car and Baxter went over to the basket of roses lying on the grass. She picked up the wicker basket and walked towards his car.

Tate was just opening the car door, he stopped and looked at Baxter, "What?"

"I'm sorry if I'm coming across as some sort of bitch."

"Hey, it's a shitty day for everybody."

She took the roses out of the basket and handed them to Tate, "Would your wife like some roses?"

Tate smiled, shook his head, and accepted the roses from her, "Of course she would—then she's gonna want to know what I did wrong."

Baxter watched Tate pull out of the driveway and then went back inside the house. Her stomach was tied in knots and it felt like she might throw up. She was relieved at not being branded as a criminal, but scared of her name being made public and terrified at the prospect of testifying.

She fought the urge; she hadn't had a drink since the hospital. But, this one was stronger than the others. It led her into the kitchen and the cabinet where she had hidden the bottle of rum. When she unscrewed the bottle's cap, the sweet sugar cane smell of the liquor filled her nostrils. She took a juice glass out of the cabinet and filled it half way with the amber colored liquid. She raised the glass to her lips and stopped. *I can't, this time it will kill me.* She took three steps to the sink and poured it down the drain.

# 18

Garcia concluded his phone call with John Tate and stared again out his third floor office window at the forty *SPA* protesters while he put on his suit jacket. He opened the door that connected his office with the conference room, introduced himself to the Costa's, and shook their hands.

"I apologize for the mob outside," Garcia said. "For the life of me; I don't know how they knew about our meeting this morning. Sergeant Tate didn't even know about it."

Tension and silence filled the room until Carmen Costa spoke up, "No, Mr. Garcia, I think we owe you the apology. Our son, Joseph, tipped them off about our coming here this morning."

"Okay," Garcia said as he thought to himself about how to deal with the crowd once the meeting was over.

"He's not handling the loss of his little brother very well," she said.

"I understand; I wouldn't expect him to."

"Mr. Garcia, can you tell us the name of the deputy who killed our son?" Vincent asked.

"Yes," Garcia said.

"What's his name?"

"The deputy who shot your son is a female. Her name is Michelle Paz Baxter," Garcia answered, letting the words hang in the air.

Vincent and Carmen just stared at one another with puzzled looks on their faces.

"I don't know why, but I think we both assumed it was a male deputy," Carmen said.

"Mr. Garcia?"

"Yes, Mr. Costa."

"You said her name is Michelle Paz Baxter."

"Correct."

"Would Paz be her maiden name?"

"Yes."

"Is she Hispanic?"

"Yes, she is, Mr. Costa."

"I hate, with all my heart, the monster that took my son from me," Carmen said. "In our minds, my husband and I have been leveling that hate on a white male deputy."

"I can certainly understand the perception, Mrs. Costa, but that's not the case here."

Vincent Costa fidgeted with the gold cuff link on his left sleeve, thinking about what to say next. "Male, female, white, black, brown; it really doesn't matter, they shot our son. He was an innocent boy, minding his own business."

"I'm sorry for your loss," Garcia said.

"What crimes will you charge her with?" Vincent asked.

"Mr. Costa, let me first explain to you the law, it might better help you and your wife understand my decision."

"I don't like the sound of that, Mr. Garcia."

"Please, Mr. Costa, it's important to understand the law in this area."

Costa looked Garcia in the eyes. His wife stared at the clock on the wall. In the uneasy quiet of the conference room, the ticking second hand of the clock was as loud as a jackhammer.

"What crimes will you charge her with?" Vincent asked again in a calm but rigid voice.

Garcia shifted in his chair, "I will not be filing any criminal charges against Deputy Baxter. I have determined that the shooting was legally justified."

"That's unacceptable," Costa said.

"I can appreciate your frustration, Mr. Costa, but my ethical obligation is to make the appropriate decision based on the facts of this shooting and the applicable law of self defense."

"I'm confused by all this," Carmen said. "What do you mean when you say this deputy had legal justification to shoot my son?"

"Under the eyes of the law, her actions were not criminal. When she pulled the trigger of her gun, she reasonably believed that her life was in danger, and she acted in self defense."

Still confused by Garcia's explanation, Carmen shook her head from side to side. Tears were mixing with her mascara and a tiny streak of black trickled down from her brown eyes. "But, but, that deputy shot the wrong person," she said, her voice thick with disbelief.

"I can understand why you are confused, Mrs. Costa, but just because Deputy Baxter shot the wrong person— your son, does not in and of itself make her actions a crime. When she pulled the trigger of her gun, she absolutely believed she was shooting the robber of the convenience store."

"But she got it wrong!" Vincent shouted, no longer able to control his anger.

"Yes, Mr. Costa, she got it horribly wrong. I can assure you Deputy Baxter is devastated over what happened."

"Fuck her and how she feels. She murdered my son."

"Mr. Garcia?"

"Yes, Mrs. Costa."

"Okay, this deputy thought she was shooting the robber; but my son was unarmed, he posed no threat to her. Why did she have to shoot him?"

"She believed the cell phone in your son's hand was a gun."

"That's bullshit," Vincent said. "Do you really expect us to accept that explanation?"

"Vincent," Carmen begged. "Enough with the language, please."

"It was dark back there. No lights, clouds covered the moon, a misty rain was falling," Garcia said.

"If she wasn't sure about who she was shooting, maybe she shouldn't have shot," Carmen said.

"In her mind, she was one hundred percent certain that she was shooting the robber."

"I can't believe you have the gall to sit here and defend her actions," Vincent said.

"This is why I first wanted to talk about the law with you," Garcia replied. "Can I explain the laws to you now and hopefully dispel a lot of this confusion?"

"No, I've heard more than I want to hear," Vincent said, standing up and helping his wife to her feet. "Maybe that clown, Bustamonte, is right after all. You're just like the rest of them."

Carmen leaned heavily on her husband as they walked out of the conference room and into the elevator. In the lobby, they looked out the windows at the *SPA* protesters, reporters and television cameras. Mustering all the physical and emotional strength they could, they opened the door and stepped outside into the mob. They made eye contact with no one and walked towards their car. The reporters yelled out questions to the Costas:

*What did the DA say?*

*Will he be filing criminal charges?*

*What is the name of the deputy?*

They gave no answers.

The protesters sensed that things had not gone well for the Costa's in their meeting with District Attorney Garcia. Martin Bustamonte knew the flash point of his followers and sparked that fire by shouting, "We want justice, we want justice, we want justice." The activists needed little invitation from their leader and the air became filled with the mantra: *We want justice, we want justice, we want justice.*

A pair of District Attorney Investigators, wearing suits, soon came out of the lobby. One carried a light brown wooden podium; he set it down and stood by its side. The other DA Investigator pushed the chanting crowd away from the podium until a safe zone of ten feet had been established.

Five minutes later, Anthony Garcia came out of the building and walked up to the podium. He put a hand on each side and waited for the crowd to calm themselves. When the noise level settled down to a controlled buzz, Garcia began talking.

"This afternoon, my office will be filing murder charges in the death of sixteen year old Mario Costa. Charged will be Tino Rivera and Jorge Castaneda. Rivera and Castaneda are seventeen-year-old juveniles. However, they will both be prosecuted as adults.

"Defendant Rivera is the individual who, armed with a handgun, entered the Circle K convenience store, and robbed the clerk. Defendant Castaneda was the driver of the dark blue Monte Carlo used in the attempted get away.

"These defendants will be prosecuted under what we call the Provocative Murder Doctrine. The theory being that these two individuals, by robbing the Circle K convenience store, are responsible for starting a series of events that ultimately lead to the shooting death of Mario Costa.

"Additionally, we have filed gang enhancement allegations against these defendants. They are both active members in the East Side Victoria street gang. Defendant Rivera is known on the streets as "Loco" and defendant Castaneda goes by "Shaggy".

From the first row of protesters, Martin Bustamonte took a step forward, very aware that the two District Attorney Investigators were closely watching his every move. Bustamonte looked back at his mob and then turned to face Garcia.

"That's all fine and well," Bustamonte said. "What about the deputy that actually murdered Mario. What charges are you filing against him?"

The mid-day sun reflected off Garcia's watch as he took his hands off the sides of the podium, crossed one over the other, and rested them on the center of the stand.

"I have personally reviewed the criminal investigation submitted by the Sheriff's Department. It is my decision that no criminal charges will be brought against the deputy who shot Mario Costa. My review of the investigation leads me to conclude that the deputy lawfully acted in self-defense. Accordingly, her actions are legally justified."

In unison, five of the protesters began chanting, *"Conspiracy, conspiracy, conspiracy"*.

Over the clamor of the crowd, Chip Anderson, a reporter for the San Bernardino Sun, shouted out a question, "Mr. Garcia, you said *her* actions were justified. Is the deputy who shot and killed Mario Costa a female?"

"Yes."

"Can you tell us her name?" Anderson asked.

"Her name is Michelle Paz Baxter. She has been a sheriff's deputy for twenty years."

"Mr. Garcia," Dave Lyons, a reporter for the Los Angeles Times, began his question, "Recently, a great deal of criticism has been leveled at the sheriff's department by the Hispanic community. They cite the disproportionate number of Hispanics who are shot by the sheriff's department when compared to Caucasians. Can we infer anything about this deputy when you tell us her name is Michelle Paz Baxter?"

"Yes."

"Like what?" Lyons asked.

"Baxter is her married name. Paz is her maiden name. Deputy Baxter is Hispanic.

Lyons followed up with another question. "Are we dealing with a situation where a Hispanic deputy shoots a Hispanic kid?"

"Yes," Garcia answered, "Deputy Baxter just wanted to live another day to be a mother to her son. Oh, Dave, just one more thing."

"What's that, Mr. Garcia?"

"In my seven years as the elected District Attorney, I'm sure you all have paid some attention to my skin color and my last name—race had no factor in the tragic death of Mario Costa."

Martin Bustamonte stood silent in the crowd. The revelation of the deputy's gender and race had caught him by surprise. A female Hispanic deputy did nothing to further the agenda of his radical organization and he could feel his followers looking to him for further direction.

"It's still police abuse, it's still murder," Bustamonte shouted. "She shot the wrong kid. The kid did nothing wrong. He had no gun, just a cell phone."

Garcia gave Bustamonte a contempt filled look. He would address Bustamante's allegations, but not because the extremist leader was deserving of a response. The public who would watch and read about the DA's press conference needed to know the facts of Mario Costa's death.

"Deputy Baxter fired her weapon in self defense. In her mind, she was one hundred percent certain she was firing at the Circle K robber. Tragically, it was Mario Costa.

"In determining whether Deputy Baxter was reasonable in her use of deadly force we have to know what she knew, what she saw, what she heard. We have to view the event through her eyes. When we do that, we have to conclude that if we were in her exact situation, we also would have made the decision to fire in self-defense."

The reporter, Chip Anderson, raised his hand.

"Yes, Chip?"

"Mr. Garcia, are you saying it doesn't matter that she ultimately shot the wrong person, an innocent teenager?"

"It's tragic; it's not the outcome anybody would want. However, for the purposes of me determining self-defense, it's irrelevant."

"Mr. Garcia, can you tell us the specifics of why she felt the need to act in self defense," Janet Gordon, of the Los Angeles TV station, KNBC asked. "Since the shooting, there has been an information blackout by your office and the sheriff's department. This has only fueled all the speculation and rumors."

Garcia directed his attention at the reporter and began his detailed answer. "Deputy Baxter was on patrol at the time of the robbery. Dispatch gave her the robber's physical description and told her that the robber had used a gun in the robbery. She was provided with information on the getaway vehicle. From this information, she now knows that a serious crime has occurred, and a gun is involved.

"Coming from the direction of the Circle K, she saw a dark blue Chevrolet Monte Carlo with tinted windows. All of this consistent with what dispatch told her. She now has reasonable suspicion to stop the vehicle. She tries to stop the Monte Carlo with her lights and siren. The Monte

Carlo does not pull over; it takes off at a high rate of speed. She is now involved in a high-speed pursuit and the danger level is escalating quickly.

"The Monte Carlo continues in its high speed attempt to evade Deputy Baxter, when she sees a hand coming out of the open passenger window. She sees three muzzle flashes and hears *pop- pop -pop*. The suspects are shooting at her. In her mind, things have now gone from dangerous to deadly."

"Where was her back up?" Gordon asked.

"It was on the way. Make no mistake; the sheriff's department had called out the cavalry on this one. The high-speed pursuit goes in and out of residential neighborhoods. It is crystal clear to Deputy Baxter that these suspects mean business. Now that they are in a residential area, they present not only a grave danger to her, but to other innocent civilians as well.

"The Monte Carlo then took a sharp turn too quickly, over corrected, and crashed head on into a concrete light pole. As Deputy Baxter came to a screeching stop, ten yards behind the Monte Carlo, she sees the driver open the door and bolt into the neighborhood. She can only hope that her back up deputies will apprehend him. Her full attention is now focused on the suspect in the front passenger's seat— the person who shot at her.

"She pulls her service weapon out of its holster and orders the suspect to remain still, except to show his hands. The suspect does not follow her commands. She sees the door being kicked open; the suspect leaps out and starts running. He's a Hispanic male juvenile, five feet nine inches tall and one hundred fifty pounds. He's wearing dark blue denim pants and a white Los Angeles Dodgers uniform jersey. All consistent with the information she'd received from dispatch. She clearly sees that the suspect is armed with a silver handgun. She fires two rounds at the fleeing suspect; but both shots miss."

Reporter, Dave Lyons, raised his hand and interrupted Garcia, "The suspect was running away from her. How can you call that self-defense? Also, wasn't it dangerous for her to fire shots like that?"

Garcia had been in the hot sun for almost an hour. He took a handkerchief from his suit pocket and wiped the beads of sweat from his forehead while one of his investigators brought him a bottle of water. Twisting off the plastic cap, and two long sips from the bottle, gave him a few seconds to think about his answer to Lyons' question.

"It is arguable whether or not she fired those initial shots to defend herself. But don't forget, the suspect was a fleeing felon. Deputy Baxter fired those shots to disable a suspect who she knew to be armed and not afraid to use that weapon. I don't think it was dangerous for her to fire those initial shots. Her intent was to protect the innocent civilians who lived in those nearby houses.

"Seeing that the shots did not hit the suspect, Deputy Baxter engaged in a foot pursuit with the suspect...."

Lyons interrupted Garcia a second time. He asked a follow up question with an aggressive and challenging tone of voice. "You said earlier that the sheriff's department had called in the cavalry. Why did Deputy Baxter try to play the part of the hero? Why not wait for back up? Let the kid go. They were eventually going to arrest him."

Garcia glared at the reporter for a moment and took another sip of water. "Do you have any children?" he asked the reporter.

"Two."

"What are their ages?"

"One and four."

"Close your eyes," Garcia said. "Put you and your family in a house, in that neighborhood, on that night. Would you want the police to just let that urban terrorist run loose, looking for a place of safe haven—maybe even your house?"

The reporter turned red in the face, opened his eyes, and pretended to scribble some notes on his writing pad.

Satisfied that all the other reporters understood the point he was trying to make, Garcia continued. "The foot pursuit went through backyards and walking trails, which bordered the backyards. At this point, to fully understand Deputy Baxter's actions, you have to appreciate the lighting conditions back there. It was dark, very dark. The clouds covered the moon, a misty rain was falling; very few houses had any lighting on in the backyards.

"Deputy Baxter loses sight of the armed suspect. She doesn't know if he's fled the area or if he's hiding, waiting to ambush her. In a backyard, forty feet away, she hears movement through the wet grass.

"We know that person was Mario Costa. He was out in his backyard, letting his dog outside. Mario was a sixteen-year-old Hispanic juvenile. He was five feet nine inches tall and weighed about one hundred and fifty pounds. He was dressed in blue jeans and a white Los Angeles Dodgers uniform jersey. He had a silver colored cell phone in his right hand.

"From where Deputy Baxter was located, in the lighting conditions that I've described, she absolutely believed that Mario Costa was the armed suspect she had been chasing. From her vantage point, she believed the silver object in Mario's hand was a gun. She ordered Mario to put his hands up.

"We will never know what Mario was thinking. In all likelihood, he was confused. Probably puzzled as to why a sheriff's deputy in the trail behind his yard was ordering him to put his hands up. He hadn't done anything wrong.

"He did not put his hands up. He turned his body towards Deputy Baxter. She had a split second to make her decision. Mario looked like the armed suspect she had been chasing. She knew the suspect was dangerous. He had robbed a convenience store. He had already fired shots at her during the vehicle pursuit. When he ran away from the Monte Carlo, he had a gun. Now this person had ignored her command, was turning towards her, with a silver colored object in his hand."

Garcia stopped talking. He could see it in their faces. He could sense their minds working. All the media people, all the *SPA* protesters, were putting themselves in the shoes of Michelle Baxter. They were seeing it through her eyes. As if he were delivering the final sentence in a closing argument, he looked solemnly at the crowd and said, "What would you have done?"

Back in his office, Garcia took off his sweat drenched suit jacket. The armpits of his white dress shirt were wet and the back of the shirt clung to his skin. He went into his private bathroom, took a fresh shirt off its hanger, and put it on. He made a Windsor knot with the red Brooks Brother's tie around his neck as he walked to his desk; he saw a pink message slip. Garcia picked it up— John Tate had called. He dialed Tate's cell phone.

"John, its Tony, how'd she take the news?"

"About how you'd expect," Tate answered. "And the Costa's?"

"About how you'd expect. You can watch the rest on the news this evening."

"You sound tired, Tony."

"I am; I wasn't having a lot of fun out there."

"I appreciate it, Tony, you made the right decision."

"Yeah, right, I guess when the November election comes around the voters will let me know if it was a good call."

"Who are you going to have as the trial lawyer on the murder case with the two gang bangers?" Tate asked.

"I don't know, probably someone from the Major Crimes Unit," Garcia answered.

"Just don't give it to that punk ass Roberts," Tate said.

"It won't be Roberts, he's been mother-fucking me ever since I told him I wasn't going to follow his recommendation."

"Tony, that dude needs him a little freeway therapy. You should transfer him to Barstow."

"Yeah, that'd be great, John, maybe you can sign his transfer order," Garcia said with a chuckle. "When I had my little talk with him, he wanted to know when we re-did the DA organizational chart with Sergeant John Tate at the top."

# 19

Standing in the secured parking area of sheriff's headquarters, Michelle Baxter opened her purse and reached in for the pack of cigarettes. She put one to her lips and lit the tobacco. A light wind blew the smoke back into her face. She hated the smell; all her life, she had never figured out what attracted people to the evils of nicotine. But, a promise was a promise; she told Nate that the drinking would stop. True to her word, she had stopped drinking and started smoking.

She heard the door open behind her and four deputies, two male and two female, walked out of the building. Dressed in olive colored uniforms, they were talking and laughing as they walked by. In their left hand each deputy carried a black canvas briefcase, and in their right hand, a pump-action shotgun. They looked so young, she thought to herself, probably fresh out of the academy. *That was me twenty years ago.*

Baxter glanced at her wristwatch, three p.m., shift change. She eyed the four swing shift deputies as they walked to their marked units and prepared for patrol. Observing the familiar routine sparked feelings and memories. She lit another cigarette.

An unmarked detective's car pulled into the stall next to the sidewalk where Baxter was standing. It was John Tate. He got out of the car and walked over to her.

"That's a nasty habit," he said.

"You're starting to sound like my son, Sarge."

"I thought you were like some kind of fitness guru?"

"Yeah, I am. You should see the stares I get at the gym. You know, *look at her, working out and she reeks of cigarettes.*"

"How long have you been doing the cancer sticks?" Tate asked.

"Two months."

"Most people quit late in life. You decide to start."

"I traded in drinking for smoking."

"Were you hitting the sauce pretty hard?" he asked.

"Yeah—real hard," she said, looking at the scar on her right forearm.

"Let me guess, the shooting?"

"Yup."

"You doing okay now?"

"It's a day to day thing."

"I know where you've been, Michelle."

"Hey, Sarge, I just wanted to thank you again."

"For what?"

"The burrito you brought me that morning. You were the only person that didn't treat me like a piece of shit."

"Like I said, Michelle, I've been there. It's not a good place to be."

"I got called down to the Assistant Sheriff's office this afternoon," she said, flicking the cigarette butt onto the asphalt and rubbing it out with sole of her shoe.

"Good news?" Tate asked.

"I don't know what good news or bad news is anymore," she answered.

"How'd it go?"

"They took me off Administrative Leave."

"Did they clear you to come back?"

"Yeah."

"When do you go back out on patrol?"

Baxter didn't answer the question. She nervously tapped the right toe of her shoe on the asphalt. She reached into her purse for another cigarette, but then stopped. "Sarge, could I bend your ear for a couple of minutes?"

"Sure, you want to go back to my office?"

"Yeah, that'd be great."

Baxter followed as Tate walked to the secured door, held his security card to the sensor, and the door clicked open. They walked down a hallway with interview rooms on each side. Tate stopped and looked through the one way mirrored glass. Inside, Detective Scott Kane was interrogating a middle-aged Caucasian male. The suspect had on a pair of dirty ragged blue jeans and a torn *Lynyrd Skynryd* tee shirt. His greasy hair and beard were both long and unruly. When the suspect talked, Baxter saw that he was missing most of his teeth. The hallway still smelled of his rank body odor. Tate laughed and said, "Scooter's taking one for the club with this guy."

"What'd the guy do?" Baxter asked.

"Dude's homeless and lives underneath an overpass with some other homeless freaks. He discovers he's missing a can of Spam. Another bum rats out our victim. Dude goes psycho and bashes the victim's head in with a cinder block. If you look on his shirt and pants, mixed with the dirt, are some pretty good medium energy spatter stains."

"Classic case of no human involved," Baxter said with a grin.

"Yeah, a definite two-fer," Tate said, making his way again towards his office.

Tate's small windowless office fit his personality like a glove. A wooden duck decoy and an opened box of bullets rested atop the credenza behind his desk chair. He had two chairs for visitors; on one chair was a Kevlar bulletproof vest. Framed photographs hung on the walls. Most were of Tate and Chief Medical Examiner Ken Felts, hunting and fishing in the San Bernardino Mountains. A plaque with the logo of the Sheriff's Department Homicide Unit hung on the wall behind Tate's desk. The plaque was inscribed with the homicide unit's motto: *Our Day Begins—When Your Day Ends.* Sitting on Tate's desk were two framed photographs. One was of his wife, and the other, his five girls.

Baxter looked at the photograph of Tate's children and said, "You have some beautiful girls."

"Thank you," he answered. "I'm very lucky."

"Sarge, I need some advice."

"Okay, about what?"

"I don't know if I want to come back."

Baxter's statement caught Tate by surprise. The fact that she might want to leave the department didn't surprise him. He had struggled with this himself after his own shooting, fifteen years ago. He was, however, surprised that she wanted his advice. He really didn't know her that well and it made him feel good that she respected him enough to broach the subject.

"Why?" he asked.

"This whole thing has been like going through hell. I have no regrets about pulling the trigger. But, I just can't shake the guilt over killing an innocent boy. Even though I was cleared, the criminal investigation and the IA investigation have beaten me down. Now that my name is out there, I feel like I'm getting stared at everywhere I go. I haven't had a decent night's sleep since before the shooting."

"What would you do?"

"I don't know; being a cop is all I know."

"Do you like being a cop?"

Baxter took some time, thinking about her response. "Yes," she answered.

"Are you a good cop?"

"Yes—I think so."

"Do you think what we do is important?" Tate asked.

"Absolutely."

"Baxter, don't you think quitting might be a little selfish on your part?"

"What do you mean, Sarge?"

"The department needs good cops. This is what we do—protect and serve. That night you were knee deep in a very shitty situation. You made the right call, it didn't turn out well, but you made the right call."

"Are you saying I should come back?" she asked.

"No, that's not what I'm saying. If you think it's time to walk away, then walk away. All I'm saying is to really think it through. You've got a lot going for you, don't make a rash decision."

"Sarge?"

"Yeah."

"You said that you've been where I've been, and that it's no place to be. What did you mean by that?"

"Fifteen years ago. I was in your shoes."

"An OIS?"

"Yeah."

"What happened?" Baxter asked.

"It was back in the day when I was still pushing a sled. I got called to a house in the shitty part of town.

"The wife had dialed nine-one-one, said her husband had been drinking all day because he lost the rent money in a poker game. He was despondent and talking suicidal shit. He went into the kitchen and grabbed a steak knife. Well, wifey's seen about enough of this, so she calls the cops.

"I'm in the kitchen; he's got the knife in his hand. I try to de-escalate things, try to talk him into putting down the knife. He's not buying into the program. He starts yelling, *Do it, do it, do it!* He charges me; I fired one round, dead center."

"Suicide by cop?" Baxter asked.

"Yeah."

"Did you get all fucked up in the head, like I am now?"

"I was dealing with demons for a good chunk of time," he answered.

"Did you think about walking away?"

"I gave it some thought."

"But you didn't?"

Tate picked up the framed photograph of his girls. "I just knew that this is the work I was meant to do. And when the day is done—I'm going home to my girls."

\* \* \*

Sitting on the steps of her front porch, Michelle Baxter tied the shoe-laces of her running shoes. She then stood up and leaned against the house's stucco wall, stretching her leg muscles. The department's clearing her to go back on patrol weighed heavily on her mind and she needed a hearty run through the foothills to help clear the fog.

Coming from the street, not far from her house, she heard a George Strait country song being played loudly. She looked in the direction of the noise and saw Nate maneuver the Ford Expedition into the driveway. Major League baseball had held its amateur draft during the first week of June and the Atlanta Braves drafted Nate in the eighteenth round. Undecided about his baseball opportunities, he'd spent the afternoon at an informal practice session with some of his ex-high school teammates.

Nate got out of the SUV and walked to the rear cargo area; taking out a bulky nylon bag that held his bats, balls, glove and spikes. His white tee shirt was stained with grass and dirt. He walked over to his mother and gave her a kiss on the cheek.

"Whew," she said, wrinkling her nose. "You need to get cleaned up."

"Me? How about you," he answered. "Have you smelled your hair lately—cigarette smoke."

"Okay, I deserved that."

"You really need to quit."

"Yeah, yeah, yeah."

"What are you doing?" he asked.

"I'm going to take a run. I've got to clear my head. The department gave me the okay to come back."

"That's great news, mom."

"Nate, I don't know if it is or isn't. That's what I've got to work through."

"Mind if I run with you?" he asked.

"You sure you want to be seen with me? I've got smelly hair."

"I'll stay upwind from you. Let me just put my stuff in the garage and grab my running shoes."

After fifteen minutes of running through their sprawling subdivision, they veered off the sidewalk and onto a trail that took them up through the gently sloping mountain foothills. The trail was sandy and strewn with small pebbles and rocks. Behind every stride, they left a small cloud of debris.

Both Michelle and Nate were accomplished runners. At a comfortable nine minute per mile pace, conversation was easy.

"Cal State Fullerton called today," Nate said.

"And."

"They offered me the scholarship."

"Get out of here," she said, playfully hitting her son's shoulder and bursting inside with a mother's pride. "I thought they gave it to the kid from Bishop Amat."

"They did, but the kid backed out at the last minute. He signed with the Yankees."

"It's a good thing that you haven't signed yet with the Braves. You're going to accept the scholarship. Right?"

Nate didn't answer. They ran in silence for five minutes. "I don't know. It's complicated."

"What do you mean, it's complicated?" she asked.

"Well, with Joe Costa being on the team."

"Nate, son, this is what you've wanted. This is what you've worked so hard for. It's your dream."

"I don't know, mom, it just doesn't feel right."

They ran without talking for another nine minutes, one mile. Nate broke the uncomfortable silence.

"Mom?"

"Yeah."

"It kind of looks like both of us are sort of at a crossroad. You have to make a decision about going back on patrol; me, with this whole scholarship deal."

"That's a fair assessment of things," she answered.

"Let's go visit him," Nate said.

"Who?"

"Dad."

In his will, Jordan Baxter had directed that he be laid to rest in his hometown of Oxford, Mississippi. Five generations of Baxter's were buried at the family plot on the grounds of a small rural church. After his death, his remains had been flown to Dover Air Force Base, and then to Memphis. A hearse carried him on his final sixty-mile trip home to Oxford. His wake, services, and burial were closed casket.

A lump formed in her throat. "Why?" she asked.

"We need to talk to him."

"Yes, we do."

# 20

*We would like to begin boarding for our First Class passengers on American Airlines flight three sixteen; non-stop service from Los Angeles to Memphis.*

"C'mon, Nate, grab your backpack, it's time to board."

"That's just the call for First Class, mom."

"I know, let's go."

"No way," Nate said, stuffing his Baseball Weekly magazine into his backpack.

"Yes, way," she answered with a smile.

Walking down the boarding ramp, smelling the fumes of jet fuel and over the high-pitched whine of engines, Nate asked his mother, "Is this the surprise you were teasing me with?"

"Yes," she answered. "Not bad, huh?"

On board the plane, Nate arranged his backpack and his mother's carry-on into the overhead storage compartment and sat down on the wide leather seat. He looked at the other passengers sharing the First Class cabin; most were dressed in business attire. He then glanced down at the blue jeans he was wearing.

"Gosh, mom, I wish you could have given me some heads up. I would have worn a pair of khaki slacks. I'm kind of embarrassed."

"You look just fine," she said to her son.

A flight attendant walked up to their seats and asked, "May I get you two something to drink before we take off?"

"Orange juice," Nate answered.

"Coffee, for me, please," Michelle said.

Nate buckled his seat belt and looked out the window; fascinated at the bustle of activity on the tarmac, readying the airliner for its departure.

"These tickets must have set you back a fortune," he said.

"Nope, didn't cost anything, frequent flier miles," Michelle answered. She cleared her voice and then said, "Your dad and I had been saving them up for years. We were going to use them to celebrate our twentieth anniversary. Your father was going to take me to Paris."

Nate took his mother's hand, "Are you okay?"

"Yes, I'll be fine," she lied.

"I'm looking forward to seeing where dad grew up," Nate said. "Our last trip to Mississippi wasn't under the best of circumstances."

Michelle and Nate's only trip from California to Mississippi had been to bury Jordan. It was a short and painful three-day trip. Jordan's death had sent Michelle and Nate into a tailspin of emotions— denial, anger, and finally grief. The last thing they wanted to do was travel cross-country to bury their husband and father.

Jordon loved to tell Michelle and Nate stories about growing up in Mississippi. He had fond memories of his Dixie upbringing and upon retirement talked of moving back to Oxford. Every year he vowed to Michelle and Nate this would be the year they would all go to Mississippi on vacation. Every year, something would come up, pushing those plans to the side.

Twenty minutes after takeoff, the flight attendant took their breakfast orders and offered them each a hot, moist, facial towel.

"What's this for?" Nate whispered.

"Your face," Michelle whispered back.

Trying to act as if he flew First Class all the time, Nate unfolded the hot towel and dabbed at his face. He gazed out the window at the passing clouds, turned back towards his mother, and said, "I miss me-maw."

"She was certainly quite a lady," Michelle answered with a chuckle.

Me-maw was Arledia Baxter, Jordan's mother. Arledia had been married to Charles Baxter, a prominent Oxford banker. During Jordan's first year at Ole Miss, his father suffered a massive and fatal heart attack, leaving her a widow.

Arledia Baxter personified everything that a time honored Southern woman should be. Prim and proper; she never missed a Sunday church service. She also stayed active with the Daughters of the American Revolution and the Republican Women's Federation. As Michelle could attest to, her mother in law was also very headstrong and set in her ways.

Arledia came out to California to visit her son, grandson, and daughter in law four times a year: Thanksgiving, Christmas, Easter and the Fourth of July. Nate was her only grandson and she spoiled him rotten—a constant topic of discussion and debate between Jordan and Michelle. Arledia tolerated Michelle; no woman would really ever be good enough for her little boy. Michelle knew that her husband loved his mother, so she in turn, tolerated Arledia.

After a short, painful battle with cancer, Arledia Baxter joined her husband, one year before Jordan's reserve unity was deployed to Afghanistan. Jordan went by himself to Oxford to bury his mother because Nate had been in the hospital recovering from emergency appendectomy surgery.

"I still feel bad about not going to me-maws funeral," Nate said. "I was good enough to travel."

"Not by a long shot, young man. The doctor's made that very clear."

Michelle spent the rest of the flight reading a book. Nate stayed glued to the window, watching the United States pass by from 35,000 feet in the air. The headphones from his iPod played the songs of Kenny Chesney, George Strait and Keith Urban.

After four hours, and two thousand miles, the plane began its gentle descent. Nate's ears started to pop, so he stuck a piece of chewing gum into his mouth. Looking out the window, he saw a blue ribbon of water snaking back and forth between the green checkerboard patches of delta farmland. "There it is, mom, the Mississippi River."

Before heading down to Oxford, Michelle and Nate spent the next day exploring Memphis. At 4:45 p.m., they walked into the lobby of their hotel, The Peabody. The grand downtown hotel sat four blocks from the banks of the Mississippi River and dated back to the early 1900's. Two hundred people, most of them tourists, took up every square foot of the ornate lobby. Michelle and Nate were lucky and found a vacant hunter green velvet sofa along the cherry-wood paneled back wall. They sat down and rested their tired feet.

"What did you think of Graceland?" Michelle asked her son.

"The Jungle Room was pretty cool," he answered. "But my favorite was the old indoor racquetball court where they displayed every jumpsuit Elvis had ever worn."

"Yeah, that was pretty neat," she said.

"Did you notice anything weird about those jumpsuits?" Nate asked.

"Not really, I mean, they were the jumpsuits Elvis wore."

"Mom, didn't Elvis start wearing the jumpsuits only after he got all fat and stuff? The whole purpose of a jumpsuit is to make you look less fat."

"I guess," Michelle said. She was not quite sure where her son was going with the question.

"Mom, the waist on those jumpsuits was like twenty eight inches. No way could Fat Elvis fit into them. I bet they altered them for the display. You know, keep people from thinking about how fat he got."

Michelle was about to answer her son when the recorded sound of trumpets began playing throughout the lobby. Nate got up from the sofa and said, "C'mon let's get closer to the ducks."

They made their way to where the crowd of tourists had gathered around a fountain. The black marble base of the fountain stood one and a half feet high. Mosaic patterned rainbow tiles, the size of Chiclets chewing gum pieces, lined the inside of the fountain. Variegated marble figurines adorned the sculptured fountain, which sat like an island, in the center of the duck pond. Atop was a lavish orchid floral arrangement. Five mallard ducks swam contently in the fountain's clear water.

A distinguished looking middle-aged man rolled out a red carpet from the base of the fountain to the lobby's elevator. He wore a bright red suit jacket with gold trim on the sleeves and shoulder epaulettes. The red jacket radiated when contrasted with his black slacks, white shirt and black tie. He was the Duck Master.

The Duck Master held a black cane, trimmed at the handle in silver. He surveyed the crowd, looking for an Honorary Leader. A nine-year old girl with long brown hair giggled and held her hands to her face when the Duck Master asked if she would like to volunteer. Filled with excitement, she shook her head up and down. She officially became the Honorary Leader when the Duck Master gently tapped her on the shoulder with the cane. The Duck Master and the Honorary Leader walked over to the five swimming ducks. They gave the command and the five ducks jumped out of the fountain and onto the red carpet.

Sparkling camera flashes filled the lobby. The five ducks shook their wings and small droplets of water went flying everywhere. The waddling ducks followed the Duck Master and the Honorary Leader to the open elevator. Marching to the tune of "King Cotton March", by John Philip Sousa, they all got in the elevator and the door closed. After a day of swimming in the lobby fountain, the ducks returned to their penthouse cage on the rooftop of the Peabody Hotel. Since 1932, the ducks had made their daily 8:00 a.m. walk from the penthouse to the fountain and the return trip at 5:00 p.m.

With the tourists starting to leave the lobby, Nate said to his mother, "Geez, mom, you took so many pictures, were you really able to see anything?"

"Oh, yes," she said, letting out a joyful sigh. "That was all so cute. Did you see the expression on that little girl's face?" For the first time in months, she didn't hurt inside, she felt alive again.

"I'm hungry, let's get some dinner," Nate said.

"What do you feel like having?"

"Mom, we're in Memphis—ribs."

They left the lobby for the downtown streets; hectic with both vehicle and foot traffic. Pedestrians did their best to avoid the puddles of water on the concrete sidewalk. Steam rose up from the asphalt street and a clammy humidity hung in the air.

"Must have rained while we were in the lobby," Michelle said.

"Ya think," Nate answered, dripping with sarcasm.

"Alright, smartass, where do you want to go? The guide book says The Rendezvous has the best ribs in town and its right across the street."

"Nope," Nate said. "Follow me."

They started walking and two blocks south of The Peabody they heard loud music— rhythm and blues—Beale Street. Each side of the world-renowned street was lined with red brick bars and restaurants. Live blues music boomed from inside the establishments and carried into the street. People walked from bar to bar, openly carrying their beer, wine, or liquor.

"I guess they don't have any open container laws here in Memphis," Michelle said.

Nate pointed to a sign on the outside wall of a bar. In bold letters, it read— *Big Ass Beer to Go*. As they walked by B.B. Kings' Blues Club, Nate looked across the street and said, "There it is."

They crossed the street and went into the Blues City Cafe. The restaurant had a concrete floor; its metal chairs and tables had seen better days. Hungry diners filled the restaurant and only a handful of tables were empty. Nate spotted the empty table he wanted and said, "There it is, this must be our lucky day."

After looking over the laminated menu, that was smudged with barbeque sauce and a film of pork grease, Michelle said, "Hon, why this restaurant and why this table?"

"What was dad's favorite book?"

"I don't know. I suppose anything by John Grisham."

"Yeah, he liked them all," Nate said. "But *The Firm* was his favorite."

"Okay," she answered.

"Do you remember the movie?" Nate asked.

"A little, that's an old movie."

"Well, it's on cable a lot at night, and we'd watch it every time it came on, usually while you were at work."

"Okay," she said again.

"Do you remember the scene where Tom Cruise's character, Mitch, is at a restaurant, studying for the bar exam?"

"Yeah, that's when the two FBI goons confront him."

"Very good, mom, that's this restaurant and Tom Cruise was sitting right here at this table."

"You're kidding?"

"Nope."

"How'd you know that?"

"Dad."

"He would know," she said with a smile. She looked around the crowded restaurant. Years of dried up spilled beer made the floor sticky and a cloud of cigarette smoke drifted up towards the ceiling. She had no craving for a drink. She had no craving for a cigarette.

"How would your father say it? Let's eat us some ribs. Now that's what I'm talking about."

# 21

"What street are we on?" Nate asked his mother as he studied the University of Mississippi map that was folded over on his lap. "Jackson Avenue," she answered.

"Okay, I'm pretty sure we take a right at the next stoplight," he said, glancing up from the map and out the window of the rental car.

Michelle drove at a snail's pace, thankful that no cars were behind her. As they approached the intersection, Nate saw the white concrete and stucco sign, bordered on all four sides by brick. In deep red lettering, the sign announced, *The University of Mississippi, 1848*. "That's it, mom, turn here."

Michelle turned right, onto Fraternity Row, a street that went up a gentle hill. Pine and magnolia trees lined each side of the roadway. On both sides of the street, they saw fraternity houses. Their yards were emerald green and perfectly manicured. Each of the brick structures were two or three stories in height and sat well back from the street. White columns rose up from the front porches that were lined with wooden rocking chairs. Because it was summer break, the houses looked empty.

The road took them to the center of the campus. During the Civil War, the Yankees set fire to the university and only a handful of buildings had survived the rampage. The campus had been rebuilt and most of the stately brick academic buildings dated back to the late 1800's and early 1900's. Over the years, the university had taken great pride in preserving the Antebellum feel and flavor of the campus.

"This is the most beautiful campus I've ever seen," Michelle said. "I can't wait to take a run."

Many of the university's academic buildings sat clustered around a square shaped, ten-acre green space. At most colleges it would be called "The Quad". At Ole Miss, they called it The Grove. Elm trees, hundreds of years old, spread their branches to where the entire grassy area was bathed in shade.

"Look, mom, The Grove."

"Your father could sure tell some stories about The Grove."

"Oh yeah," Nate said. "His favorite saying was, *Ole Miss might not win every football game, but we've never lost a party.*"

College football and tailgating go hand in hand. But, at Ole Miss, tailgating is taken to such levels that one had to see it to believe it. The football venue, Vaught-Hemmingway Stadium, seats 60,000 people. On a football Saturday, 70,000 Ole Miss Fans party in The Grove.

Red, white, and blue party tents dot The Grove for as far as the eye can see. Pork meat is cooked over open flames; its smell and smoke fills the air. These pre-game feasts are dished up on linen covered banquet tables and eaten off fine china with silver utensils. Little boys, all wearing their prized Ole Miss jerseys, and helmets that are far too big for their heads, toss footballs. Little girls, dressed in Ole Miss Cheerleader's outfits, dream of someday growing up and going to the university. Sorority girls and fraternity boys wear their Sunday best. In the hand of every adult is the always present—sixteen-ounce red plastic Solo cup. Ole Miss Football is not just a game— it's a social experience.

Driving past The Grove, Michelle spotted the on campus hotel—The Inn at Ole Miss. "That's our hotel," she said. "It's probably still too early to check in."

"Cool, let's drive around some more. I want to see all the athletic facilities."

Michelle peeked at her rear view mirror and had a look of surprise on her face when she saw the vehicle behind her; a dark blue, University of Mississippi Police Department cruiser, with its light bar flashing.

"What the hell," Michelle said, trying to figure out why she was being pulled over. She turned into a parking stall just off the roadway. The police cruiser followed and stopped.

A tall, white, male officer got out of the police car and strolled up to Michelle's rental car. The officer looked to be in his early thirties and sported a crew cut. His pants were dark blue and his short sleeve shirt, light blue.

Michelle rolled down her window and said, "What did I do wrong?"

"Speeding, ma'am."

"I was only going twenty five."

"Y'all aren't from around here, are you?" The officer asked. He talked slow with a pronounced Southern drawl.

"No, we're not," Michelle answered.

"The speed limit on campus is eighteen miles an hour."

"You're kidding," she said, trying to remain calm. "Why not some round number, like twenty or twenty five?"

"Eighteen was Archie's number, ma'am."

"Archie who?" Michelle asked, now thoroughly confused.

"Archie Manning, mom, he used to be a quarterback here at Ole Miss," Nate said, jumping into the conversation.

"Officer, let me get this straight. The campus speed limit is based upon the number of an old football player?"

"Yes, ma'am. May I please see your license?"

"Nate, hand me my purse."

Nate leaned back and stretched his left hand behind his mother's seat, grabbing her purse off the floorboard. He gave it to his mother and she opened it up, looking for her wallet. Lying next to the wallet was her badge.

"Are you law enforcement, ma'am?"

"I'm a deputy sheriff," Michelle said, handing the officer her driver's license.

"California, y'all are a long way from home," the officer said, inspecting Michelle's driver's license. "Your son visiting campus?"

"No," Michelle answered, trying to find the right words to explain their visit to Oxford. "We sort of have family here. My husband played football for Ole Miss."

"What years?" the officer asked.

Michelle looked at her son and asked, "Nate, what years did your father play ball?"

"Nineteen eighty two through nineteen eighty six," Nate said to the cop.

"What position did he play?"

"Tight end," Nate answered.

The officer looked again at the driver's license in his hand. "Ma'am, was Jordan Baxter your husband?"

"Yes," Michelle responded. "Have you heard of him?"

"Have I heard of him?" the officer said, his face breaking out with a big grin. "Why, Jordan Baxter is legend in these parts."

"The game with Alabama, his senior year?" Nate asked— his insides bursting with pride.

"Damn straight," the officer said. "I remember that game like it was yesterday. I was ten years old and my daddy took me to the game.

"Everything was on the line that day. Winner of the game takes the SEC Championship and goes to the Sugar Bowl. The game was tied up at ten all and the Rebs were at Alabama's thirty-yard line, time left for one play, too far for a field goal attempt.

"Your daddy runs a post pattern into the end zone; he's got two Bama defenders mugging him. The quarterback throws the ball, right into the hands of the Alabama safety, an interception for sure. Your daddy just muscles the ball out of his hands for the touchdown."

"I've got the game ball in my room," Nate said. He never tired of hearing his father talk about the play. To hear the officer tell about the exploits of his father was something special.

The officer handed the driver's license back to Michelle. The joy and happiness of recounting one of his childhood memories left his face, and his look became more solemn.

"I'm sorry about your loss, Mrs. Baxter."

"Thank you, officer...."

"Harwell, Clay Harwell," he answered.

"We miss him. My son and I are here in Oxford to pay our respects to him and his parents."

"He was a true hero, Mrs. Baxter. His death really shook up this community. You know, him and his family being from Oxford and all. Nate, you should be very proud of your daddy."

"I am, sir."

"Heck," Harwell said. "Maybe they should change the speed limit from Archie's number to your daddy's number."

"I don't know if that's such a good idea," Nate chuckled. "His number was eighty five."

After checking into the hotel and unpacking, Michelle and Nate walked the half mile from campus to the old downtown area of Oxford; or as the locals called it, "The Square". The perfumed smell of magnolia flowers did little to take their minds off the oppressive late afternoon humidity and beads of perspiration broke out on both of their foreheads. One block from The Square, Nate stumbled, but caught his balance before he fell to the ground. A lesson learned to exercise caution while walking on the aged concrete sidewalks. An ankle could easily be sprained by tripping over the portions of sidewalk that were cracked and protruded up. Generations of tree roots growing beneath the sidewalk had won the battle with time.

The old county courthouse, located in the center of The Square, captured their attention and they walked over to a historical marker that gave facts of the building's history. Built in the 1880's, and recently refurbished, the three-story courthouse evoked memories of a simpler time in the old south. A waist high, black wrought iron fence formed a perimeter around the courthouse and its green lawn and shade trees. Just outside the fence, a statue dedicated to the memory of Confederate soldiers killed in the war, stood watch over the courthouse and square.

They spent the next thirty minutes checking out the rest of The Square; City Hall, upscale clothing boutiques, bars and restaurants. Nielson's, the oldest department store in the south called The Square home, as did Oxford

Square Books, a nationally renowned independent bookstore. Similar to the architecture of New Orleans and Bourbon Street, most of the bars had a second floor with an outdoor balcony area. In good weather, a popular spot for Ole Miss students to drink and smoke.

They escaped the heat and went into Ajax's Diner. While it wasn't the fanciest place in Oxford, the clerk at the hotel's front desk told them that Ajax's served up the best southern home-style cooking in town. They slid into a red Naugahyde booth that in more than one spot had duct tape covering up holes in the worn fabric.

Nate looked up at the ceiling tiles, pointed to them and said to his mother, "Mom, check out the ceiling."

Michelle looked up and saw hundreds of toothpicks piercing the ceiling's surface. They were the kind that had the frizzy things on the end and held sandwiches together. She laughed, shook her head and said, "I guess the ceiling doubles as a dartboard. I wonder how they get them to stick like that."

The server brought over their orders of iced tea. Thirsty from the hot walk, they both took long sips. The first taste of the cold brown liquid brought a grimace to their faces.

"This is way too sweet," Michelle said, pushing the large plastic tumbler to the center of the table.

"We may as well be drinking honey," Nate said.

The server came back to the table to take their dinner order. Michelle pointed to the tumbler and asked, "What is this?"

"Iced tea."

"Is it supposed to be this sweet?"

"Yes, ma'am."

"How much sugar is in there?'

"Oh no, we don't use sugar. We use cane syrup, ma'am."

"Do you have any ice tea that is unsweetened?"

"Yes, ma'am, you have to ask for that special."

Nate dared his mother to start dinner with an order of fried pickles. She took him up on the dare and the server soon delivered a plate heaping with pickle chips that had been battered and deep-fried. On the side of the plate was a bowl of dipping sauce that looked like a hybrid of Ranch and Thousand Island dressing.

"These are awesome," Nate said. "Who would have thought fried pickles would taste this good."

"They are good," Michelle answered while wiping the grease off her fingertips with a napkin. "I'm glad we're not getting blood work done any time soon."

"Thanks, mom."

"For what?"

"The trip, it's been so cool."

"I think we both needed to get away."

"Yeah," Nate said. "From the time we got on the plane, I've just sort of been working through my mind what to do about this baseball thing."

"Me too," she answered. "Do I go back to the department? If not, what am I going to do with my life? We got some big decisions to make, Nate."

"Mom?"

"Yes, Nate."

"I hope you don't think I'm crazy, but ever since we arrived in Oxford, I've had this feeling like dad is here with us. I sense that he's watching over us, helping us work through all this stuff."

"You're not crazy, Nate, I feel him too."

The server interrupted them and in front of Nate she set down a plate of fried catfish, fried okra, and collard greens. In front of Michelle, she placed meatloaf, fried green tomatoes, and cheesy grits. In the center of the table, she left a basket of steaming hot cornbread.

The next morning, after a breakfast of white sausage gravy and biscuits at the Beacon Diner, they headed west on Highway 6. The semi-rural road had two lanes of travel for each direction and connected Oxford with Tupelo, forty miles to the west.

Five miles out from Oxford, Michelle pointed to a church and said, "There it is, Nate."

"I hardly remember," Nate answered. "My mind was a jumbled mess."

Michelle turned off the main road and onto a dirt driveway that led up to the church; a cloud of dust trailed from behind the car. There were no other cars around and she parked on the church's gravel lot. When they got out of the car, the sound of the gravel crunched underneath their shoes.

The small, single story church had red brick walls and a roof made of tar shingles. A white steeple rose up from the roof of the church. On a plot of land behind the church, they saw the cemetery.

Michelle shielded her eyes from the bright morning sunlight with her hand and reached into her purse for a pair of sunglasses. They walked in silence towards the cemetery. Nate reached for his mother's hand.

The old cemetery was small, probably about half the size of a football field. Just behind the cemetery, the pine forest began. Coming out from the brush-covered forest, they could hear the clicking sound of cicadas. A white picket fence ran around the entire length of the cemetery. When they got to the fence, Nate opened the gate for his mother. The fence appeared to be freshly painted, but the gate hinges were rusted and squeaked with age.

Two hundred grave markers were evenly spaced throughout the cemetery. The grass was cut low and someone had taken great pains to insure that no grass or weeds intruded upon the base of the headstones. The only blemish was the cotton like head of dandelions— a good gust of wind sent them dancing skyward.

The gravestones were simple, and weathered from generations of exposure to the elements. A handful of the markers predated the Civil War. In the far right hand corner of the cemetery were the Baxter family plots.

Michelle and Nate found Jordan's headstone. Next to him were his mother and father. Each headstone identical— a four-foot-by-four-foot slab of gray granite and the engravings simply read, *Baxter*, with dates of birth and death.

"I love you, Jordan," Michelle whispered, the dark sunglasses shrouded the pain in her eyes. She started crying, her body shaking and quivering. Nate took his mother into his arms and with his voice choked from emotion said, "We're going to be okay, mom, we're going to make it. He's watching out for us."

Her tears flowed from under the sunglasses and onto her son's shirt. She took a deep breath, sniffled, and said, "I know."

She sat on the grass and stared at her husband's headstone. Nate took a handkerchief out of his pocket and started cleaning the markers of his father, grandfather, and grandmother.

After thirty minutes, Michelle said, "It's okay to go home now, Nate."

# 22

Vincent Costa took the small brass nail out of his mouth and gently hammered it into the freshly painted wall.

"Okay, hon," he said to his wife. "Pass it up to me."

Being careful not to upset the stepladder that her husband was standing on, Carmen handed him the dark oak framed Thomas Kinkade painting. Vincent hung the painting on the wall and straightened it.

"How's that look?" he asked.

"Looks perfect," she answered.

They had been in their new house for one week. The Southern California housing market was at an all time low and they had taken a beating on the sale of their house in Highland. The upside was that in a buyer's market, they had gotten an excellent deal on their new house in the neighboring city of Redlands.

The Costa's wanted to keep on living in their longtime family home, and they tried to make it work, but they couldn't. They had to get out. The memories of Mario, both good and bad, were too overwhelming. The house that welcomed him home from the hospital as a baby, also said goodbye to him when they slid his body bag into the back of the coroner's van.

Since the night of their son's death, the backyard had become their own personal hell. They couldn't shake the haunting memory; grass covered with the blood of their son and the vomit of the deputy who had shot him.

The phone rang and Vincent picked it up. On the other end of the line was Greg Smith, a fellow member of the country club.

"Hey, Greg, how are you doing?" Vincent asked.

"Did I catch you at a bad time?" Smith said.

"No, not at all, why?"

"I, uh," Smith paused. "I know this is probably going to be uncomfortable for you, but I think you should know."

"Know what?" Costa said with a puzzled look on his face.

"The sheriff's deputy who shot Mario, was her last name Baxter?"

"Yes."

"Hispanic gal?"

"Yes."

"Maybe in her early forties?" Smith asked.

"Probably," Costa answered. He could feel his heart beating faster and his palms were starting to sweat. "Why?"

"I was driving home from the club and she pulled me over—speeding. I was good for it, but she let me go with only a warning. Did you and Carmen know she was back on the streets?"

"No, Greg, we didn't. Hey, buddy, I appreciate the call. I really need to go now."

Vincent put down the phone, rubbed the bridge of his nose, and stared hard at the Kinkade painting he had just hung on the wall.

"What's wrong, Vince?"

"I don't believe it. I can't fucking believe what is happening to us. How many times are they going to beat us down?"

"What?" Carmen asked again.

"The sheriff's department let her come back to work."

* * *

The next afternoon, Sheriff Larry Covington agreed to meet with Vincent and Carmen.

"Mr. Costa, Mrs. Costa, I don't know how many more times I can apologize for the death of your son. Every member of this department feels horrible over the tragic events of that night." Covington's apology was sincere and heartfelt.

"Sheriff, my son's death is no tragedy—it's murder."

"Mr. Costa, we are not here this afternoon to argue about the decision of the District Attorney."

"No, Sheriff, we're not. We are here to argue about your decision to let her come back to work. Why didn't you tell us? We had to find out from a friend."

"With all due respect, Mr. Costa, I don't believe I have a duty or obligation to let you know what I do with my people."

"She wasn't just another one of your employees; she's responsible for the death of our son."

"Yes, she is, and again, I can't apologize enough."

"Why did you allow her to come back to work?"

"Because, Mr. Costa, she did not violate any of our department's procedures or policies."

"You've got to be shitting me, Sheriff, she shot the wrong person. So what are you telling us? No harm, no foul?"

"Mr. Costa, I have no intention of engaging in a confrontation with you. I fully appreciate your frustration. If we can just ratchet the tone of this conversation down a notch, I will fully explain to you why I let her come back to work."

Carmen Costa spoke up for the first time and said, "Sheriff, you have no idea how devastated we are from all that has happened. Your deputy shoots and kills our son, the DA gives her a free pass, and now she's allowed to come back to work."

"I understand that, ma'am."

"Sheriff, what if she does something like that again? No mother should have to go through this kind of hell."

"C'mon, Sheriff, throw us some kind of bone here," Vincent said. The tone of his voice telegraphed to Covington his displeasure with the way the meeting was going. "Tell us that she was given time off with no pay, a letter of reprimand in her personnel file, something, anything."

"I'm sorry, Mr. Costa, the Peace Officer Bill of Rights precludes me from telling you if and what type of discipline I took against Deputy Baxter. That information is privileged and confidential."

"Forget it, Sheriff, it really doesn't matter. You guys didn't do anything to her," Vincent said.

"Sheriff, I'm confused, you said this deputy didn't violate any of your policies." Carmen said, nervously fidgeting with the diamond and white gold bracelet around her left wrist. "She shot the wrong person; my son was not the person that robbed the convenience store."

Covington leaned back in his leather chair and thought carefully about the wording of his response. The sounds of the leather crunching and the chair squeaking were the only sounds to be heard. After several moments of icy silence, the Sheriff looked at Vincent and then Carmen.

"Did Deputy Baxter make a mistake?" Covington asked rhetorically. "Yes, clearly she did, she shot your son. Was she wrong for firing her weapon in the situation she found herself? No, she was not. She believed her life was in danger and she fired in self defense."

"Save your breath, Sheriff," Vincent said, interrupting Covington. "We already know how this movie is going to end. You and Garcia are like peas in a pod. How in the hell do you two sleep at night?"

"Sheriff, you never answered my question."

"Which question was that, Mrs. Costa?" Covington asked, sneaking a glance at his wristwatch. He was tired of being the punching bag.

"How do you know that this deputy, or for that matter, any of your deputies, won't do something like this again?"

"Mrs. Costa," Covington answered, rubbing his left eye with the open palm of his left hand, "I don't."

Vincent and Carmen had half expected the responses from the Sheriff and already had an appointment scheduled with the lawyer who handled Vincent's business affairs. After the meeting with Covington, they drove straight from the sheriff's department to the Law Offices of Christopher Sanchez.

A secretary brought the Costa's into his office and the Hispanic lawyer, with pre-mature gray hair, got up from his desk. He put down his reading glasses and walked over to them, giving each a warm embracing hug.

"I'm sorry we didn't get a chance to talk more at the dinner," Sanchez said to them. "That was a wonderful turn out."

"Yes, it was," Vincent said. "Thank you so much for the donation to the foundation. It was more than generous."

"It was the least I could do. How much did you raise for Mario's foundation?" Sanchez asked.

Vincent looked at Carmen with a questioning look on his face. "Between the golf tournament and the silent auction at the dinner, we raised seventy five thousand dollars," Carmen answered.

"Wow, that's fantastic," Sanchez said, whistling out loud.

"It's a start," Carmen said. "We still have a long way to go. Robotic prosthesis are a little on the expensive side."

"Mario would be proud of you," Vincent said to his wife, lovingly patting the top of her hand.

"So," Sanchez said. "You two have some questions about a civil lawsuit?"

"Yes," Vincent answered.

"Tort law isn't my area of expertise, but I think I can help you out."

"Vince and I have given this a lot of thought. We really don't want to sue anybody, but some degree retribution has to come out of Mario's death. It's just been so frustrating. First, the District Attorney does nothing. Now, we find out that the Sheriff has put her back on the streets."

"It has to be frustrating, Carmen," Sanchez said, opening a file that had been sitting on his desk. "I've had a chance to look at the investigative reports prepared by Sergeant John Tate."

"What do you think?" Vincent asked.

"I think if you and Carmen elect to file a civil lawsuit in Federal Court, it's a slam-dunk winner."

"What about the fact that the District Attorney justified the actions of the deputy?" Vincent asked.

"Doesn't matter," Sanchez answered.

"Or, that the Sheriff says the deputy didn't violate any of their department's policies?"

"Again, Vincent, it doesn't matter. A civil lawsuit in Federal Court means a new playing field with a new set of rules and standards of proof. The bottom line is that deputy shot the wrong person—and somebody has to pay."

"How much?" Vincent asked.

"Well," Sanchez began his answer, writing down some figures on a yellow legal pad.

"There will be damages from Mario's loss of future earnings. That one will be tough to put a dollar amount on because Mario was still in school. We really can't speculate on what he would have done with his life and how much he would have made.

"The big enchilada will be the damages associated with you and Carmen's pain and suffering because of the sheriff's department's negligent infliction of emotional distress."

"How much?" Vincent asked again.

"That check will have a whole bunch of zeros on it. My ballpark guess, five to ten million dollars."

Carmen took a tissue out of her purse, wiped the tears from her eyes, and looked at Sanchez. "It's not about the money. You can't put a price tag on my baby's life."

"Hell, Chris," Vincent said. "We don't even want the damn money. It's tainted money. We'd give it away to Mario's foundation and some other worthy charities. It's just the fact that something, anything, has to come out of Mario's death. There has to be some punishment against that deputy and the sheriff's department."

"I understand," Sanchez said.

"If we file a civil lawsuit would there be a trial?" Carmen asked. "At least a public forum where this deputy would have to sit everyday and be confronted with what she did to my baby?"

Sanchez laughed, "Excuse me; there is nothing funny about this. It's just that there is no way the sheriff's department would let a jury anywhere near this thing. That five to ten million dollars is my best guess at a settlement value. A jury could return an amount ten times that figure."

"So, that's what it all boils down to," Vincent said. "The sheriff's department writes a check for ten million dollars and says, *here, sorry for the loss of your son, now take this and go away?*

"Yes. Except they won't say they are sorry."

"Where will the money come from?" Carmen asked. "Will the deputy have to pay for her legal fees? Will she have to sell her house? Can we garnish her paycheck and retirement?"

"No," Sanchez answered. "The deputy is only personally liable if there is a finding of punitive damages and we don't have that here. When the dust settles, the deputy who killed Mario will not be out a dime."

"Then who writes this check for ten million dollars?" Vincent asked.

"You, me, and all the taxpayers of San Bernardino County," Sanchez answered. "My best guess is that the money will come out of the general operating budget of the sheriff's department. I'm sure their risk management people have some money stashed away for occasions like this."

"Let me get this straight," Vincent said and then paused for several moments. "Is it possible that some residents of San Bernardino County could get fewer services from the Sheriff because they have to cut back, here and there, to pay for the settlement? Could it even be our neighborhood, our neighbors?"

"In theory, yes," Sanchez answered.

The lawyer had a brass Lady Scale of Justice sitting on the corner of his desk. Vincent reached for the scale and held it in his hands. "Chris, I don't know what justice is anymore."

On the drive home, Carmen broke the silence, "Vince, I'm not sure about filing a civil lawsuit. We have nothing to gain. It's not as if they are getting punished. I don't want the devil's money."

"You're right," he answered. "We can't sue. The wrong people get hurt. They win again."

# 23

Sitting in front of his locker, Joseph Costa stripped off the Ace Bandage and ice pack from around his left elbow. His throwing arm felt fine, but he always iced his elbow after every practice. He headed for the showers and noticed that there were only a handful of players in the locker room. It was the second week of August and fall practice had just started; pitchers and catchers had been working out for three days, with the position players reporting in two days.

Costa shook the water from his hair and came out of the showers with a white towel wrapped around his waist. In front of his locker, one of the baseball team's student equipment managers sat, texting on his cell phone.

"Coach Riley wants to see you in his office," the manager said, matter-of-factly, looking up from his phone.

"Did he say why?" Joseph asked.

"No, and I didn't ask."

Costa pointed to a bunched up pile of clothes on the floor; the jersey, pants, and socks he had worn at practice.

"Hey, since you're here, would you take my stuff over to the laundry bin?" he asked the trainer.

"You've got two legs, take it over there yourself. I'm not touching your smelly stuff," the trainer answered. "New season, but the same old Joe Costa— Mr. My Shit Don't Stink."

"Fuck you," Costa said, reaching into the cubicle for his jeans and polo shirt.

He finished dressing, picked up his gym bag, and strolled down to the office of Stan Riley; head baseball coach for Cal State Fullerton. Costa glimpsed in the open door and saw the coach, absorbed in a game tape on his computer. Costa tapped on the door, Riley looked up and gestured him in. The team's number one starting pitcher took a seat in front of his coach's desk.

"How's the arm doing?" Riley asked.

"It feels great, Coach."

"Joseph, I think we have a situation here that we need to talk about."

"Okay."

"We offered a scholarship to Brad Wallace, the third baseman out of Bishop Amat."

"Right," Joseph said. "He was also drafted by the Yankees in the second round."

"Yes, and they offered him a ridiculous signing bonus. The kid couldn't pass up that kind of money, he signed with them."

"So, what does that have to do with me, Coach?"

"We offered that scholarship to a kid from your area, out in Rancho Cucamonga."

"Okay."

"The kid really wanted to accept the scholarship and play ball for us, but he had some concerns."

"Like what?"

"He didn't think you would want him to be on the team."

"Why would I think that?"

Riley shifted in his chair and searched for the words on how to break the news to Costa. He had attended the memorial services and witnessed Joseph's anguish over the shooting death of his brother. On his first day back at practice, after his brother's death, Joseph sat in this very same office, sobbing like a baby in Riley's arms.

From the moment Joseph Costa had thrown his first pitch for Cal State Fullerton, Riley recognized he had something special in Costa. He knew that with time, Joseph would pitch in the major leagues. Then, Riley saw a change in his pitcher after the brother's death. His pitching rose to an even higher level, he became driven. Joseph Costa was pitching for his little brother.

"The young man's name is Nate Baxter," Riley said.

The name didn't register in Joseph's brain. He gave a blank look to his coach.

"Joseph, his mother is the sheriff's deputy who shot your brother."

Joseph kept on staring at Riley, his mouth open, but no words came out. He felt like he had been hit by a scorching line drive in the chest, and spiked by a sliding base runner, all at the same time.

After several more moments of awkward silence, Costa said, "Are you sure?"

"Yes."

"How do you know?"

"He told me."

"What did he say?"

"He told me about what happened, with his mother, and the impact it was having on his decision with our scholarship offer. He said it was probably best if he not join our program.

"I asked him why. He said he didn't want to put you in a bad spot, or do anything that might make you feel uncomfortable."

"Well, it would," Joseph said. "I don't want him here."

"It's not your decision to make, Joseph."

"I don't care if it is or not. He's got no business coming here."

Riley could feel himself starting to lose patience with his pitcher. "C'mon, Joseph, he's got just as much right to be here as you do."

"No, Coach, he doesn't."

"Why?"

"His mother murdered my little brother."

"Joseph, I know this is stressful for you, and emotions are high right now, but this kid had nothing to do with your brother's death."

"No, Coach, you don't understand."

"You're right, I can never understand what happened to you and your family, but I've still got a baseball program to run. I have to do what's best for the team as a whole."

"What did you tell him?"

"I told him that it took a man of character to think about your feelings at the expense of his own personal aspirations."

"Damn, Coach; you make it sound like he's some kind of fucking hero."

Riley's face and eyes turned a fiery shade of red. "If you ever drop the F bomb on me again, you are out of here. I don't care if you are our number one pitcher. Do you follow me, son?"

"Yes, sir."

Riley didn't want to escalate an already bad situation, so he lifted himself out of the chair and walked to the far corner of his office. He gazed out a window that overlooked the baseball field. Grounds keepers were watering the outfield and dragging the infield dirt with a piece of chain link fence.

"Coach," Joseph said, still sitting at his chair, in front of the now empty desk.

"What?"

"Is he going to be on the team?"

"Yes."

"Okay."

"I know it's okay," Riley said, fighting to keep the disdain he felt, out of his voice. "And you're the captain of this team-so you're going to make it work."

\* \* \*

Nate's locker and dressing cubicle was at the far end of the locker room, the greatest distance possible from the locker of Joseph Costa. It wasn't planned; it just worked out that way. Upperclassmen were entitled to the best locker locations. Freshman weren't entitled to anything.

Nate unpacked his equipment bag and arranged his spikes, mitt, and batting gloves in his dressing cubicle. With care, he pulled a small framed photograph out of the bag. His mother had taken the picture when he was ten, and playing Little League baseball. Jordan coached his son's team and they were dressed in their baseball uniforms. Father and son were kneeling on the grass, smiling; Jordan had his arm around Nate's shoulder. In the cubicle, he put the photograph on a small shelf, next to his shampoo and deodorant.

Nate reflected on the talk he had with his mother that morning, before leaving for his first day of college. They discussed how to best handle the situation, and they agreed that Nate should introduce himself to Costa. Whatever was going to happen was going to happen; but that first encounter would set the tone for the relationship between the two.

From his locker, Nate could see Costa's dressing area. He put on his practice uniform, took a seat on the bench, and waited for Costa. Five minutes later, Costa entered the locker room and started to dress. While Costa was bent over, tying the laces on his spikes, Nate approached. Joseph peeked up and saw Nate.

"Joseph Costa?" Nate asked.

"Yes," Joseph answered, as he rose and turned his back to Nate, so he could close his locker.

Costa stood six feet, three inches tall; Baxter, six feet, one inch. They were both muscular, but Costa was three years older and had his man body.

"My name is Nate Baxter."

A chill went down Joseph's spine. He turned around, glared Nate in the eye, and said, "So."

"Look, I, uh, just wanted to introduce myself," Nate said, holding out his right hand.

"Put that away," Joseph gestured at Nate's hand. "You don't really think that I'm going to shake your hand?"

"Honestly, I don't know what to think—this isn't easy for me."

"Oh, and you think this is a walk in the park for me? Your fucking mother murdered my little brother."

"Look," Nate said, then paused, before he said or did anything that he might regret. "You're entitled to think whatever you want about my mother, but don't use that kind of language—it's offensive."

"Baxter, what do you want from me? What do you want me to say?"

"I don't want you to say or do anything."

"Then why did you come over here and introduce yourself?"

"Because we needed to have this moment; it was going to happen, might as well get it over with."

"Okay, you've introduced yourself. I hope you're not expecting me to say: *welcome to the team, buddy, let's hang out after practice.*"

"No, I know that will never happen."

"Why in the hell did you choose to come to this school?" Costa asked.

"Probably the same reason you did—to play baseball for one of the best college programs in the nation," Nate answered.

"I know you and Coach Riley talked about how this whole thing would play out," Costa said.

"How what would play out?"

"You, me, on the same team—bad blood."

"We did. I told him it might be best for me to go somewhere else."

"That would have been a wise move on your part," Costa said.

"Okay, Costa, this is going nowhere. I came over, extended my hand; I did what I had to do. I can see how this is going to work, and I'm cool with it. You don't have to like me; you don't have to talk to me. You're the senior and I'm the freshman. I don't care. I'm going to play my ass off for you and the team."

Nate turned and started to walk away.

"Hey, Baxter," Costa said.

"What?"

"You know, I'm the team captain."

"Yeah, I know."

"I'm not the only one who will be giving you the cold shoulder."

Later that night, Nate Baxter sat at the desk in his dorm room, eating an In-N-Out Double-Double hamburger. His roommate, Brian Crafton, was out on his own late night food run at the Taco Bell. Crafton was also a freshman and played for the baseball team.

Nate ate the little bits of melted cheese off the burger wrapper, finished the last of his greasy french fries, and tossed the wrappings in a trashcan. He picked up his cell phone and hit auto dial for the number to his mother's house in Rancho Cucamonga.

"Hey, mom."

"How'd you're first day of practice go?"

"The actual baseball part was fine. Everything else sucked."

"Did you speak to Joseph Costa?"

"Yeah, just like we had talked about."

"How'd it go?"

"Not good."

"That's to be expected, son, he's gone through a lot."

"I know, I can understand that, but he's turned the rest of the team against me."

"What do you mean?"

"Well, he's the team captain, a senior, the number one pitcher, and the most popular guy on the team. He's got it so that the whole team is giving me the silent treatment."

"What about your roommate?"

"Brian? Oh, no, he's a real cool dude. We get along great. He's the only one talking to me."

"You've just got to hang in there. You knew it would be tough."

"I don't know, mom, I think I've made a big mistake by coming here."

# 24

Vincent Costa's tee shot travelled two hundred yards and came to a rest in the center of the fairway. He bent down to pick up the wooden tee and said to his son, "Now, what were we betting on this hole? Loser puts up the Christmas lights?"

"Watch this, old man," Joseph said, teeing up his ball and taking a practice swing. "I'm not one of your geezer buddies who you beat out of their lunch money."

His tee shot went forty yards beyond his father's, but sliced to the left and into a thicket of pine trees. Vincent laughed when he heard his son's golf ball bouncing off one tree after another.

"Son of a bitch," Joseph said as he walked back to the cart and threw the club into his golf bag.

"Let me drive," Vincent said, still laughing. "I think I have a pretty good idea where your ball might have landed."

"I'll put up the Christmas lights tomorrow," Joseph said with a scowl.

Vincent released the parking brake on the golf cart and pushed down on the accelerator. The whirr of the electric motor mixed with the sound of jostling golf clubs as they drove down the bumpy asphalt golf path.

"Now that fall practice is over, how's the team looking?" Vincent asked.

"Good," Joseph answered. "I think we can make it back to Omaha again."

"Who is Riley going to start at third base?"

"Baxter."

"He's a freshman—is he that good?"

"Yeah, his glove is like a vacuum cleaner."

"Are you still giving him a hard time?"

"Every day."

The father gave his son a stern look. "Joseph, it's not his fault."

"I don't care."

Vincent maneuvered the golf cart off the path and into the thick grass surrounding the trees where Joseph's ball had settled. "Son, the season starts right after the holidays and the games will start counting in the won-loss column. I think your attitude is a little counterproductive and detrimental to the team."

"No, it's not. I throw the pitch to the catcher. If the batter hits the ball towards third base, that bag of shit better field it and throw the guy out. I don't have to like him; I don't have to talk to him. There's my ball."

Joseph pointed to the little white sphere, peeking out from the tall grass. Vincent stopped the cart while Joseph got out and snatched a five iron from his bag.

Before he drove off to find his own ball, Vincent said, "Think it over, son. It's not his fault."

They played the next two holes in silence—Vincent irked at his son's bad attitude and Joseph pissed that his father had brought up the Nate Baxter issue. Joseph broke the silence while they were putting on the sixteenth green. "How's mom doing?"

Vincent lined up the easy three-foot putt. The ball went in the hole and he marked the bogey on his scorecard. "For the most part, pretty good; but she's not doing so hot right now. You know, with Christmas and the anniversary of Mario's death coming up."

"How about you; how are you doing, pop?"

"Not much better than your mother."

After their round of golf they had drinks in the lounge of the club-house. Vincent nursed a scotch and water while Joseph chewed on the ice from his Coke.

Vincent stirred the drink with his right index finger and took a small sip. He put the glass down and said to his son, "I don't remember if we've told you, but your brother's murder trial is starting right after the holidays."

"Yeah, I know, mom told me."

"In talking with the DA who is prosecuting the case, it sounds like the trial will drag on into the start of the baseball season. I hope we don't have to miss any of your games, this being your senior year and all."

"Why would you guys miss any games because of the trial?" Joseph asked.

"Because we'll be at the trial."

"Every day?"

"Yes."

"Why?"

Vincent took the last swallow of scotch. The melting ice cubes had caused condensation to form on the outside of the glass; he dried his wet fingers on the front of his golf shirt. "It's just something we have to do."

"Can you guys handle that kind of stress?"

"We don't have a choice."

"Why?"

"Your mother and I need to be there for your brother."

Joseph didn't want his father to see the tears in his eyes. He held the glass to his mouth, took in some ice, and started chewing.

While her husband and son were out playing golf, Carmen stayed at home to decorate the Christmas tree. The living room smelled of vanilla candles and the scent of the freshly cut Douglas-fir Christmas tree. Payaso was fast asleep in the dog bed. His snoring almost drowned out the Christmas carols from the CD player. His front paws twitched involun-tarily—he was having a dog dream.

Carmen stepped back from the tree, took a sip of hot cocoa, and looked to see if any of the multi-colored miniature lights were burnt out. Satisfied that all the lights were working and blinking, she opened up a banker's box that contained the tree ornaments.  One of Vincent's old faded cigar boxes sat atop of the ornaments.  Her heart skipped a beat.  She knew the contents of the cigar box, but didn't know it would be the first set of ornaments she would come across.  Laura Grogan, Carmen's friend and former next-door neighbor, had taken down and boxed last year's Christmas ornaments.  With the death of her son, Carmen had neither the focus nor strength to take down the Christmas tree.

She sat down on the couch and rested the cigar box on her lap.  Her hands became clammy and trembled when she opened the lid.  Inside, an ornament was wrapped in red tissue paper and another ornament in white tissue paper.  A fragile smile formed on her face as she unwrapped the ornament in the red tissue.  The ornament bore a photograph of her son, Joseph, when he was ten years old.  She placed the ornament on the coffee table and began unwrapping the ornament in the white tissue paper. While unwrapping the ornament she would stop and caress the soft tissue.  She stared at Mario's face on the ornament— he was six.  She reminisced how the photograph ornaments had been Mario's idea.  He had see them in a mail order catalogue and insisted that a pair be ordered with a picture of him and his brother.

Carmen brought the ornament to her lips and gave it a tender kiss.  She picked up Joseph's ornament and walked over to the Christmas tree.  She hung both ornaments, eye level, in the center of the tree.  The blinking white, red, and green lights shimmered off the faces of Joseph and Mario.

* * *

At 8:17 p.m., Michelle Baxter got the call of shots fired and in three minutes pulled up in front of the apartment complex.  It was in the low rent part of Highland, not far from the Circle K convenience store.  The black gangs controlled this section of town, and in particular, this apartment complex.  She was the first sheriff's unit on scene; from the inside of her car, she assessed the situation.

A slumlord out of Los Angeles owned the rundown two-story complex. Many of the windows were busted out and had been patched over with plywood. Gang graffiti covered the exterior walls. Streetlights lit up the complex, allowing Baxter to see several of the residents loitering outside their open doors, looking and pointing to one of the complex's units. In front of that unit, a group of five African-Americans stood outside.

She grabbed her Mag-lite, opened the door, and started walking to the apartment where the crowd had gathered. From ten yards away, she saw the bullet holes. She knew right away that they had been made by an automatic or semi-automatic assault rifle. Four bullets had splintered the wooden front door. Multiple other bullets had shattered the apartment's front window that looked to the street.

The African-American's were young, in their early to mid twenties. Two were male and three were female. The females were crying.

"What happened?" Baxter asked.

"Mother fucking drive by, they shot Reisha," answered one of the males. He wore a blue doo-rag on his head and had gold front teeth. His blue jeans hung down around his ass, exposing his white boxer shorts.

"Where's Reisha now?" Baxter asked.

"The kitchen," he said, pointing towards the inside of the apartment.

Baxter walked through the front door. Broken glass crunched beneath her boots. Off to her right, she saw a small bathroom, the door was open. Inside, she made out two figures sitting in the bathtub—one, a young girl, who looked to be about ten or eleven. In her arm's she held a little boy, dressed only in diapers, who was no more than two years old.

"Are you okay?" Baxter asked the scared girl.

"We're okay, because momma said that whenever there's a drive by, we should get in the tub," she answered.

Baxter heard the sound of the approaching sirens getting louder. Coming from the kitchen, she heard a female voice crying. Between sobs, the voice hysterically screamed out, *Why my baby? Why my baby, oh God, why my baby?*

She went into the kitchen and saw blood on the wall, just above a small dining table. She recognized the blood to be in a high-energy impact pattern. The blood drops were small and grouped closely together; like a red mist, shot out of an aerosol spray can. Mixed in with the blood were small sections of grey and white. On top of the table, parallel to the bloodstains on the wall, she noticed a bowl of melting strawberry ice cream.

Baxter glanced down and saw the crying female, crumpled up on the floor next to the table. She wore a white t-shirt covered with blood and cradled her six-year-old daughter, Reisha. Baxter knelt down and touched the little girl's throat, looking for a pulse. She couldn't find one.

Baxter wanted to throw up. The little girl had long braided hair with pink ribbons. The braids were now matted with sticky blood. A stray bullet had blown out a good portion of her skull; propelling blood, brain, and bone onto the wall. Two paramedics came into the kitchen. Baxter looked up at them and shook her head in the negative. The paramedics tried to take Reisha from her mother's arm, but she wouldn't let go of her child.

"Ma'am, you have to let the paramedics try to help your daughter," Baxter said to her.

The mother reluctantly let go of the little girl and said to Baxter with a confused look in her eyes, "Why? She was just eating her ice cream."

Baxter held out her hand and assisted the woman to her feet. She was unsteady and leaned on Baxter for support as they walked out of the kitchen. The mother turned around and looked one more time at her daughter.

Baxter helped the woman walk towards the bathroom. The young girl and the male toddler were still cowering in the bathtub.

"Ma'am, are those your children?"

"Yes."

"What are their names?"

"Shanice and Marcellus."

Standing at the doorway to the small bathroom, Baxter said to the young girl, "Shanice, hon, can you help me and your mother out?"

"Yes."

"Okay, here's what I want you to do. You're in charge of your little brother. You carry him and follow your mother and me outside to my police car. Can you do that for me?"

"Yes," she answered, as she stood up in the tub, took her little brother in her hands, and carefully stepped over the white porcelain tub ledge and onto the bathroom floor.

At the front door of the apartment, Baxter met up with her watch commander, Sgt. Sue Kemp, and briefed her on the situation in the kitchen. "One victim, six year old girl, single gunshot wound to the head. The paramedics are doing what they can." Baxter said.

"Do we need to roll out homicide?" Kemp asked.

Baxter didn't want to give a verbal response with the little girl's mother standing right there. Instead, she gave her sergeant a look that answered the question.

"Okay," Kemp said. "Who do we have here?"

"Victim's mother, brother, and sister," Baxter answered.

"You know the protocol; take them back to the station."

"Will do, Sarge."

The dead little girl's mother continued to lean on Baxter for support. Blood from the mother's t-shirt now covered Baxter's light olive colored uniform shirt.

"C'mon, Shanice, you and Marcellus follow me and your mother," Baxter said.

Five other uniformed deputies from the Highland Station were now at the crime scene. Three were securing the area, rolling out the yellow crime scene tape. The other two deputies were rounding up possible witnesses to be interviewed by homicide detectives.

Baxter helped the mother and her two children into the back seat of the sheriff's car and drove away. She looked in the rear view mirror at Reisha's mother.

"Ma'am, my name is Michelle. What's your name?"

The mother didn't respond right away, she just stared out the window, her weary eyes transfixed on the now distant apartment complex. "Jemel," she finally answered.

"Hey, Police Lady," Shanice said.

"Yes, Shanice."

"Is Reisha gonna be okay?"

Baxter guessed Shanice to be no more than ten years old; she didn't know how to answer the young girl's question. *Did Nate understand death at that age?* She asked herself.

"I don't know, hon. The doctors are going to do all they can for your little sister," Baxter lied. She knew that sometime during the night a homicide detective would explain to Shanice what had happened to Reisha.

At the station, Baxter brought them into the briefing room. She went to a storage closet where donated clothing and other items for crime victims were kept. She gave Jemel a clean shirt, placed the bloodied t-shirt in a plastic bag, and marked it as evidence.

Marcellus's diaper was soiled, confirming what she had smelled in the car on the drive to the station. Baxter thanked whoever had the foresight to keep diapers and baby clothes at the station as she changed Marcellus's diaper and dressed him in pajamas. From the refrigerator in the briefing room she grabbed a Coke and a bottle of water. She gave the Coke to Shanice; then put some water in a Sippy cup and gave it to Marcellus, who eagerly reached for the cup.

At 11:00 p.m., a homicide detective came into the briefing room and took Jemel to one of the station's interview rooms. At 12:30 a.m., Jemel and the homicide detective came back into the briefing room. Marcellus squealed with joy when he saw his mother come through the door. Two and a half hours after her shift had ended; Baxter gathered up her gear and got ready to go home.

In the restroom, she looked at the mirror. Her eyes were red and lined with dark circles. She pulled down a paper towel from the dispenser, got it wet, and dabbed at the bloodstains on her uniform. She splashed cold water on her face and thought about the last time she had been in this restroom, looking like this and feeling like this. She let her head hang over the sink; almost one year to the day.

Before leaving the station, she went to the area where deputies received inter-office and inter-department mail. A single white envelope stood alone in her mail slot. Baxter looked at it and saw the seal of the District Attorney's office. Her hands shook as she opened the envelope and unfolded the official looking document. It was a subpoena, ordering her to testify in Mario Costa's murder trial.

*I'm not ready for this.*

# 25

Jury selection in the murder trial of Tino Rivera and Jorge Castaneda started during the third week of January. In a typical two-defendant murder trial, the process of selecting a jury takes one week. In the case of *People of the State of California v. Rivera and Castaneda*, it took three weeks to seat twelve impartial jurors. Many prospective jurors had to be excused because of their exposure to the media attention over the death of Mario Costa. Other prospective jurors were unable to accept the legal concept that Rivera and Castaneda could actually be charged with murder. After all, a police officer had shot and killed Mario Costa.

Judge Wayne Norwood presided over the trial. He had been on the bench for twenty-five years, and before that, a prosecutor for seventeen. His white hair and beard gave him a little bit of a Kris Kringle appearance. For most of Norwood's judicial career, he had presided over murder trials. A first rate trial judge, Norwood had earned the respect of prosecutors, defense lawyers, cops, victims, witnesses, and jurors.

Judge Norwood's courtroom dated back to 1926. The grand old courtroom conjured up images of the courtroom scenes in *To Kill a Mockingbird*. Frosted glass and brass handles bedecked the door to the courtroom. Porcelain tiles covered the floor and the walls were adorned with cornice molding. Everything in the courtroom was wood—tables, chairs, witness stand, jury box, and spectator benches. When you looked up, you could see the painstakingly preserved ceiling paintings.

"Is there anything else we need to take up before we adjourn for the day?" Norwood asked the attorneys.

In response to the judge's question, Deputy Public Defender Nicole Blanco got up from her chair and said to Norwood, "Yes, Your Honor, on behalf of my client, Mr. Rivera, we do have one issue we'd like to discuss."

Nicole Blanco had been with the Public Defender's office for fifteen years. She had received both her undergraduate and law degree from Berkeley. A true believer, Blanco proudly carried her ACLU membership card.

"And what would that be, Ms. Blanco?" Norwood asked.

"I would request that the court unshackle my client for the remainder of the trial," Blanco said.

Franklin Parker, the court appointed attorney for Jorge Castaneda, rose out of his chair and addressed the court, "Your Honor, on behalf of my client, I would also make that request."

Parker was one of the most respected defense attorneys in San Bernardino County. A reputation he had earned over the thirty-five years of practicing law. Parker was African-American and could be described as a gentle giant. He stood six feet, five inches tall, dressed immaculately, and carried about him an aura of success. Most people thought he looked and talked like the actor, James Earl Jones. Parker was not a true believer. He knew that many, if not all, of his clients were guilty, and his job was to insure that the prosecutors and cops played by the rules of the game.

"But, Ms. Blanco, Mr. Parker," Norwood said. "Your clients have been here in court everyday for jury selection, I don't think the prospective jurors are paying any attention to whether or not your clients are shackled."

Vincent and Carmen Costa were sitting on the left side of the courtroom, in the first row of spectator benches, directly behind the table where Deputy District Attorney Drew Logan and John Tate sat. They followed the exchange between Judge Norwood and the defense attorneys and then glared at the two thugs who were charged with murdering their son.

When they glanced at the feet of both defendants, under the defense counsel table, they could see metal shackles binding their ankles. For the entire three weeks of jury selection, both Rivera and Castaneda had always kept their hands resting on their laps. When the Costa's looked closer at their hands, partially hidden under the table, they could see the shackles around their wrists. In addition to Judge Norwood's armed bailiff, an armed sheriff's deputy sat in a chair behind Rivera, and another behind Castaneda.

Castaneda, the driver of the blue Monte Carlo, was big for a seventeen year old. He stood six feet three inches tall and obese. The starch-laden food served at Juvenile Hall didn't help his weight problem. Castaneda's gang name was "Shaggy". His fellow urban terrorists in the East Side Victoria street gang were always giving him a hard time about his facial hair. Castaneda had a goatee, or more aptly, a poor excuse for a goatee. A sparse collection of black whiskers jutted out from his chin. His homies said it made him look like the character "Shaggy" from the Scooby-Doo cartoon.

Franklin Parker made sure his client wore a long sleeve shirt to court; it hid the gang tattoos which coated the entire lengths of both arms. Castaneda's head was clean-shaven and Parker had no solution for the tattoo on the back of his client's head, inscribed with the letters "ESV".

Physically, Tino Rivera was the complete opposite of his crime partner—on the short side at five feet eight inches and thin. When the deputies brought Castaneda and Rivera into court, it was quite a contrast, like someone out on the sidewalk, walking a Rottweiler and a Chihuahua.

Rivera wore whatever clothes Nicole Blanco could find in the Public Defender's indigent clothing closet. Because he was on the scrawny side from doing crystal meth, they always hung loosely on him; like a little kid wearing his big brother's hand me downs. Rivera had a severe case of facial acne and when he became a resident of Juvenile Hall, he shaved his head. Rivera's gang name was "Loco", because he was one crazy little fucking bastard. Proud of his reputation, he had the gang moniker tattooed on the outside of his right knuckle. When Vincent and Carmen Costa looked at Rivera, they didn't think he bore much resemblance to their son.

"Your Honor," Parker said. "It's not an issue of how the jurors perceive our clients. I mean, let's be real here, they are both flanked by armed deputies. I think the jurors have already figured out why."

Norwood took a good hard look at the defendants and said, "Under no circumstances am I going to remove the ankle shackles. What is your argument as to why I should remove the wrist shackles?"

"With all due respect, Your Honor," Blanco said. "Those wrist shackles deny our clients the constitutional right to assist in their own defense."

"How so?" Norwood asked.

"With the shackles on, our clients are unable to take notes and communicate in writing with Mr. Parker and me during the testimony of witnesses."

At the prosecution table, Tate leaned over and whispered into Logan's ear, "You gotta be kidding me; those shitheads don't know how to read and write." Logan smiled and nodded his head in agreement.

Still looking at Loco and Shaggy, Norwood asked, "Mr. Logan, what is the people's position on the wrist shackles?"

Drew Logan stood up and addressed the court, "Those two defendants are dangerous gang members. For the security of the courtroom, the wrist shackles should stay."

Norwood stopped writing on his yellow legal pad and tapped his pen up and down. He looked over to the desk of his bailiff, Jack Hall, and said, "Jack, how have the defendant's been behaving in Juvenile Hall?"

"Well, they are not what you would call model citizens," Hall answered. "On two occasions defendant Castaneda was found with a shank on his person and Defendant Rivera gassed a guard."

Norwood let out a deep breath, took a disgusted look at Loco, and said to Nicole Blanco, "Ms. Blanco, why didn't you tell me your client threw feces on a guard?"

Blanco's face turned red when she answered the court, "I, uh, didn't know, Your Honor."

Drew Logan entered the discussion and said, "Your Honor, Sergeant John Tate has some information that might assist the court in its decision."

"Okay," Norwood said. "Let's hear it."

John Tate stood up and addressed the court, "Your Honor, on the day after Mario Costa's death, I went to Juvenile Hall and interviewed defendant Rivera. I advised him of his Miranda rights and he said he would talk to me.

"He came across as a pretty cool customer, a lot on the cocky side. He said he didn't have a problem doing some time for the robbery of the Circle K. He said because he was a juvenile, he'd be back on the streets by his twenty- third birthday. He knew the system.

"I told him I was booking him on a murder charge and he was looking at twenty five years to life. He shot out of his chair and started to get into my face. He screamed that it was fucking bullshit. Why should he go down for murder, it was a fucking cop who shot and killed the kid? I, um, had to give him a little bit of an attitude adjustment."

Norwood interrupted Tate and said, "Alright, I've heard enough, there is no way I'm taking any chances with courtroom security. The shackles stay on. Mr. Logan, after opening statements, who will be your first witness?"

"Deputy Michelle Baxter," Logan answered.

"Very well," Norwood said as he got up and strolled back to his chambers. "See everybody on Monday, have a safe weekend."

Loco and Shaggy glared at John Tate as the deputies ushered them out of the courtroom. They shuffled their way out, with the sound of metal on metal coming from their ankles and wrists.

* * *

A capacity crowd filled Goodwin Field for the Cal State Fullerton Titan's first home Saturday game with their cross county rivals, the Anteaters from the University of California Irvine. Both teams were out on the field, doing pregame warm-ups. Some players did their stretching routines, while others played long toss. The *pop-pop-pop* sound of the ball striking leather mitts' filled the air.

Off by himself in right field, Nate Baxter twisted his hips and leaned from side to side, loosening up his thigh muscles. In the starting lineup, at third base, he was nervous, excited, and proud. For the fourth time he stopped and looked at his uniform, to make certain that it was just right.

The Titan's wore their home white uniforms with navy blue pin stripping. The *Titan* moniker was sewn across the uniform chest in navy blue with orange trim. Their caps were navy blue with an orange "F" just above the bill. Nate bent over and pulled up his navy blue stockings until they almost touched the bottom of his kneecaps. Nate liked the "old school" style and could never understand why players would want their uniform pants to be baggy and down around the ankles.

He went on with his stretching exercises until he saw Head Coach Riley walking towards him.

"How are you doing, Nate?" Riley asked.

"Nervous," Nate said.

"Good answer. If you told me anything different, I would have scratched you from the starting lineup."

"I appreciate you putting me in the starting lineup, Coach."

"You earned it. Say, Nate, how are you doing with that other stuff?"

"What other stuff?"

"You know, that whole deal with Costa. I've been trying to keep an eye on how Costa and his buddies have been treating you. There are things I can do, but I can't make them be your friend."

"I understand, Coach. Sure, I'd like for him and the other guys to accept me into their group, but that's not going to happen, and I'm cool with it. On the field they treat me like a teammate; off the field they treat me like I have leprosy."

"You're a strong kid, Nate."

"I don't know about that, Coach. I'm doing my best to not let those articles in the newspaper get me down."

Riley took off his cap, rubbed his forehead, and gazed into the jam packed bleachers. "I'm sorry about that, Nate. Our people over at the Sports Information Department did all they could to downplay the story. The situation between your mom and the Costa family trickled out into the media and unfortunately, it is a story. You're just gonna have to develop a tough skin."

"I will. Hey, Coach, you know all about the black rubber bracelets the team is wearing today?"

"Yeah, Costa had them made as a tribute to his little brother. Something about the murder trial starting on Monday."

Nate glanced at his left wrist. "I don't have one, only guy on the team that doesn't. Joe didn't give me a bracelet and I didn't feel it was my place to ask."

"Would you like one?" Riley asked.

Nate looked down and kicked his left cleat back and forth over the freshly cut outfield grass. "Yeah, I would."

The coach slapped his player on the buttocks, turned to trot back towards the dugout, and said, "Let me see what I can do."

In the bottom of the eighth inning, the Titan's held a commanding 6-1 lead over the Anteaters. Joseph Costa was well on his way to pitching a complete game and picking up the first victory of his senior season.

In the parking lot of Goodwin Field, Michelle Baxter listened to the game on the radio in her Toyota Camry. With her windows down, she could hear the crowd yell every time Cal State scored a run or made a good play in the field.

She wanted so badly to see her son play his first college game. However, she told Nate that it would be best if she not go into the stadium. They would get together afterwards and go out to dinner. She tortured herself over what to do about the game. She believed that her presence in the ball field would not be welcome. Surely, the Costa family didn't want her to be there, and now with the articles in the sports section of the local papers, neither would the spectators. She was playing mind games with herself. In reality, with such a large crowd, no one would notice her presence.

She turned up the volume on the radio when the announcer broadcast Nate coming up to bat.

*This is the fourth plate appearance for the freshman third baseman from Rancho Cucamonga, and Baxter is still looking for his first hit as a Titan. He grounded out in the second, flied out in the fourth and drew a walk in the sixth.*

Coming from inside the stadium, Michelle heard the sound of an aluminum bat striking the baseball and then the roar of the crowd.

*There it is folks, Nate Baxter's first base hit as a Titan-a single over the head of the leaping UC Irvine second baseman.*

*Baxter is being congratulated by the Titan's first base coach and as he takes his lead off the bag, he's rubbing the black bracelet he's wearing around his left wrist.*

*The entire Titan team is wearing those black bracelets this afternoon. There's an interesting story about those bracelets and the relationship between Baxter and his teammate, Joe Costa.*

Michelle Baxter knew the story and she didn't want to hear it again. She turned off the radio.

# 26

The courtroom became silent when Deputy District Attorney Drew Logan called his first witness to the stand. John Tate turned around in his chair and watched Michelle Baxter enter the courtroom. She wore a light blue wool skirt, a matching wool jacket, and a white blouse. Tate could tell that she was nervous. She walked with purpose down the center aisle of the courtroom; looking straight ahead and making eye contact with no one. Sitting in the old wooden chair on the witness stand, she pulled the microphone closer, and the courtroom clerk swore her in as a witness.

Tate had also been keeping an eye on Vincent and Carmen Costa, sitting in their usual front row seats, right behind the prosecution table. When Baxter walked towards the witness stand, Tate noticed Vincent's face turn red and his neck muscles clench the inside collar of his dress shirt. The Costa's held hands and Tate could see Carmen squeezing her grip on the hand of her husband.

During a jury trial, these were the situations that Tate hated the most. It was awkward, and no matter how many times he did them, it never got any easier. As the lead investigator on the case, he had to preserve a cordial relationship with all the parties. Tate appreciated the feelings that the Costa's harbored towards Michelle Baxter. But, whether he truly felt that way or not, he had to uphold an air of neutrality. At times like this, he felt like a referee in a battle between the Hatfield and McCoy's.

Prosecutor Logan questioned Michelle Baxter about what happened after she received the call from dispatch on the Circle K armed robbery, almost duplicating the way John Tate had done his interview with Baxter. She answered the prosecutor's questions, showed no emotions, and paid no attention to the newspaper reporters furiously writing in their notepads.

When Logan had navigated his questioning of Baxter to the point where the blue Monte Carlo had wrecked into the concrete light pole, Michelle Baxter felt her emotions starting to boil.

"Deputy Baxter, after the Monte Carlo crashed into the concrete light pole, when did you first get a look at the driver?"

"Just as I was getting out of my unit and drawing my service weapon."

"What did you see?"

"I saw the driver's door open quickly; a figure leaped out and started running away."

"Did you get a good look at the driver?"

"No, I did not."

"Why?"

"It all happened too fast."

"Can you give us any description of the driver?"

"The driver was a juvenile male, taller than average, and overweight."

"Do you see the driver of the dark blue Monte Carlo in the courtroom today?"

Michelle Baxter crooked her head towards the defense counsel table and took a long hard look at "Shaggy" Castaneda. He glared back at Baxter with a shit-eating grin on his face.

"Mr. Logan, the male sitting at the defense table," Baxter said, pointing to Castaneda. "The one with the smirk on his face."

"Your Honor," Logan interrupted. "Let the record reflect that the witness is referring to Defendant Castaneda. Go ahead, continue, Deputy Baxter."

"Defendant Castaneda has the general height and build as the driver of the Monte Carlo, but I cannot make a positive identification."

"Fair enough," Logan said. "Let's talk about the passenger in the Monte Carlo. What happened after the driver ran off into the night?"

"Well, my first thought was that the backup deputies would apprehend the driver and now my full attention was on the passenger still inside the Monte Carlo."

"Did you issue some commands to the passenger?"

"Yes."

"Did the passenger follow your commands?"

"No."

"What happened?

"The passenger kicked open the door and took off running."

"Did you get a look at the passenger?"

"Yes."

"Better than the look you got of the driver?"

"Yes."

"Why?"

"The lighting conditions. The way the light was shining down from the street lamp and the way my unit's headlights were shining on the Monte Carlo."

"Deputy Baxter, do you see the passenger of the Monte Carlo in the courtroom today?"

Michelle Baxter looked at Tino Rivera. "Loco" made a kissing gesture with his lips and then a slight licking motion with his tongue. She bit her lip to control her anger.

*Kiss my ass punk, you tried to kill me. I'd like nothing more than to cut your nuts off and shove them down your fucking throat.*

"Yes," she answered, pointing to Tino Rivera. "That's him, sitting at the defense table."

"Your Honor, let the record reflect that Deputy Baxter has identified Defendant Rivera."

"Mr. Logan?"

"Yes, ma'am."

"Today, Defendant Rivera has a shaved head. That night, he had a full head of black hair."

Under his breath, Loco muttered, "You're fucking crazy, bitch."

"Deputy Baxter, when Defendant Rivera jumped out of the car and started running away, did he have a gun?"

"Yes."

"Are you sure?"

"Positive."

"You told us earlier, that during the vehicle chase, the passenger of the Monte Carlo fired shots at your marked unit."

*Yeah, and it pissed me off.*

"That is correct," Baxter answered Logan.

"When Defendant Rivera was running away, did you discharge your service weapon?"

*Discharge my service weapon? Do you mean, did I try to kill the prick? My only regret is that I missed.*

"Yes," Baxter said.

"Why?"

"He was a threat to me, every man, woman, and child in the surrounding houses. And, he was a fleeing felon."

Carmen and Vincent were staring down at the courtroom's porcelain floor tiles, unable to make eye contact with the woman who had killed their son. They absorbed every word of her testimony. Carmen and Vincent exchanged glances; each thinking the same thing. They hated this woman and they wanted to keep hating her. However, they had never heard this side of the story and it got them thinking.

"Deputy Baxter, what did you do after you fired those shots at Defendant Rivera?"

"He was trying to get away, so I took off running after him."

"Did you catch him?"

"No."

"What happened?"

"I don't know. Unlike the street, the lighting conditions were very poor back there. He just disappeared. My best guess was that he ran off the walking trails and into the trees and shrubs that surrounded the backyards."

"What were you thinking?"

"I was thinking that he might be in the bushes, waiting to ambush me—and he had a gun."

"You stupid bitch, I was long gone," Loco muttered again under his breath.

"What did you then decide to do?" Logan asked.

"I decided to go back to my unit."

"Did you make it back to your unit?"

"No."

"What happened?"

"I heard the sound of someone, something, walking on the wet grass."

"Where was the sound coming from?"

"About forty feet away from where I was on the walking trail, it came from the backyard of a house."

"What did you do?"

"I walked towards the sound?"

"Where was your service weapon?"

"In my hand, drawn, and ready to fire."

"How were the lighting conditions?"

"Bad, very bad."

"Did you see anything in this backyard?"

"Yes."

"What?"

"I saw a Hispanic male, probably sixteen or seventeen years old. He was approximately five feet eight inches tall and looked to weigh about one hundred and fifty pounds. He had on blue jeans and a white Los Angeles Dodgers jersey."

"How did this person compare to the suspect you had been chasing, but lost sight of?"

"With the lighting conditions being what they were—identical. I believed this was the suspect in the Circle K robbery."

"What happened next?" Logan asked.

"I aimed my gun at him and yelled; *Sheriff's Department put your hands up! Sheriff's Department put your hands up!*"

John Tate heard the sound of muffled sobs behind him. He turned around in his chair and saw Carmen Costa crying, her head buried against her husband's shoulder. With his free left hand, Vincent Costa signaled for Tate to come over. From the witness stand, Michelle Baxter watched Tate walk towards the crying woman. She knew who the woman was and why she was crying. Baxter closed her eyes, and for the first time in months, the sound of the circling helicopter took over her mind.

"Sergeant Tate, this is too much for my wife to handle," Vincent Costa whispered to Tate. "Could you please take her outside for some fresh air?"

"Yes, sir," Tate answered. "How about you?"

"I don't want to, but I have to stay here. I need to hear what she says."

Tate helped Carmen Costa to her feet and led her out of the courtroom. Logan stopped his questioning of Baxter as all eyes in the courtroom were riveted on the sights and sounds of the grieving woman. Loco and Shaggy looked at each other and smiled.

The emotion of the moment caught Logan off guard and he didn't know whether to go on with his questioning or ask the court for a brief recess. Judge Norwood sensed the prosecutor's unease and came to his rescue. "Mr. Logan, ask your next question, please."

"Deputy Baxter, after you shouted these commands, did this person put their hands up?"

"No."

"What did he do?"

"When I shouted the command, I had an almost sideways profile view of the suspect. After I shouted the command, he began turning his body towards me."

"When he made the turn towards you, were you able to see anything in his hands?"

Baxter felt the icy glare of Vincent Costa. She closed her eyes for a moment before she answered the question. "Yes, I saw something silver in his right hand." She stopped, took a deep breath and fought back the tears. She wanted to ask the judge for a time out so that she could run to the restroom and throw up. "I believed the silver object to be the gun that I knew he had."

Everyone in the courtroom was engrossed on watching Michelle Baxter, knowing what the next question and answer would be. Had anyone been paying attention to Loco, they would have seen him grinding his teeth and forming fists with his shackled hands under the defense counsel table.

"What happened next?" Logan asked. His voice trailed off, almost into a whisper.

Baxter couldn't hold back any longer and the tears flowed freely. She took a tissue from the Kleenex box sitting in front of her; she wiped her eyes and blew her nose. "I fired one round into his chest."

For the first time since taking the witness stand, she looked over at Vincent Costa. He sat all alone in the first row, hunched over with his head in his hands.

"I am so sorry," she said between sobs. "God, I am so sorry for shooting your son."

With one swift burst of pent up anger and energy, Loco Rivera pushed over the defense counsel table with his shackled hands. Papers went flying off the table, along with Nicole Blanco's briefcase. Water spilled all over from the carafe and glasses. Loco shot up out of his chair, spat at Michelle Baxter, and started yelling, "Why are you fucking crying, bitch? You ain't the one who's going to prison and you're the one who shot that fucking punk."

Franklin Parker, being as big as his client, took "Shaggy" to the ground and restrained him until the sheriff's deputies removed Castaneda from the courtroom and back to the secured lock up. Within seconds, two other deputies took Loco to the ground. He put up a fight and the deputies got their shots in on the wiry gang-banger. Until he was taken away from the courtroom, Loco kept on yelling; "Man, this is fucking bullshit! I didn't shoot that punk!"

The jurors watched in stunned silence as a screaming Loco was led out of the courtroom. Using a Kleenex, Michelle Baxter wiped Loco's spit from her blue jacket; Vincent Costa continued to cry. Judge Norwood let the jury go home for the day.

* * *

The trial of Loco and Shaggy went on for another three weeks. After only four hours of deliberation, the jury found them both guilty of First Degree Murder in the death of Mario Costa. Judge Wayne Norwood sentenced them to twenty-five years to life in prison.

# 27

Nate Baxter got into his defensive stance, three feet to the left of the white third base bag. With a right-handed batter at the plate, he positioned himself more towards third base, guarding against any ball that might be hit just inside the foul line. Hunched over, and up on the balls of his feet, the mitt on his left hand was ready for action. Chewing on a fresh hunk of bubble gum, he blew a pink bubble, and when it popped, the fruity smell filled his nostrils.

The feel in the air, both on the playing surface, and in the stands of Goodwin Field was electric. The Cal State Fullerton Titans were one strike away from advancing to the College World Series in Omaha, Nebraska. Adding to the buzz and excitement, Joseph Costa needed one more strike to pitch a perfect game; no runs, no hits, no walks, no errors.

The Titans were as hot as the Southern California heat on this day in mid-June and they held a commanding 6-0 lead over the Sun Devils from Arizona State. Joseph Costa's stuff had been blazing all day, baffling the opposing hitters. With the game well in hand, Coach Stan Riley let his star pitcher stay in the game, in the pursuit of perfection.

The power hitter at the plate represented Arizona State's best and last chance to break up the perfect game. Costa was ahead in the count, two strikes to one ball. The Sun Devil hitter stepped out of the batter's box and took a couple of practice swings. Costa moved off the pitcher's mound, turned around, and studied the defensive alignments of his infielders and outfielders.

Nate Baxter's freshman season at third base had gone well. On defense, he shined, committing only three errors. Offensively, Nate had been a solid contributor, a .297 batting average, nine home runs, and forty-one runs driven in. In spite of Nate's good play, most of his teammates still gave him the cold shoulder and sided with Joseph Costa in the silent dispute.

Costa stepped back up to the rubber on the pitcher's mound and took the sign from his catcher. Nate saw that the pitch would be a fastball, Costa's best pitch. All day his fastball had been nasty, overpowering the Sun Devil batters and reaching almost one hundred miles an hour on the radar gun.

Costa reared back and threw towards home plate, a ninety-five mile an hour fastball, but the pitch was straight over the strike zone and belt high to the batter. The batter timed the pitch perfectly and a sharp *ping* from the aluminum bat making contact with the ball filled the air. The crowd went silent, Costa shook his head in disgust, and he knew he had just lost his perfect game.

The ball shot off the bat like a rocket, ten feet above the dirt infield, heading for the gap between Nate at third base and the shortstop. The shortstop had no chance of making the play and Nate's chances were not much better.

Nate had little time to react and his athletic instincts took over. He leaped into the air as high as he could, while diving to his left, and the ball. He stretched out the mitt in his left hand and the screaming ball smacked into the cowhide. With the ball nestled securely in his mitt, gravity kicked in and one hundred ninety pounds of Nate Baxter landed square on his left ankle, which had been at an awkward angle when he launched his body into the air. It snapped like a twig.

The infield umpire couldn't believe that Nate had made the headfirst catch and sprinted over to Nate. "Third baseman, show me the ball, show me the ball!" The umpire shouted.

Excruciating, white-hot searing pain shot through Nate's crumpled up body. He mustered all the strength he had left, lifted his glove inches off the dirt, and turned it for the umpire to inspect.

Seeing the ball in Nate's glove, the umpire made a fist with his right hand; held it in the air and barked, "Out!"

A roar went up from the crowd. The catcher tossed off his mask, running out to the pitcher's mound and into the arms of a screaming Joseph Costa. The Titan's bench emptied and the players formed a human mound on top of Costa and his catcher.

The coping mechanism of Nate's body took over when the pain became too much for him to bear; he lost consciousness. The umpire saw that Nate's eyes were closed and then noticed Nate's ankle, contorted in a grotesque position.

"Coach, you've got a man down!" The umpire yelled, trying to be heard above the pandemonium on the field.

By the time Coach Riley and the team trainer made it out to Nate, he had regained consciousness. His teeth were clenched and his right hand clawed at the infield dirt. Nate's left ankle was folded under the back of his leg; it almost looked like he had no ankle.

"It's broken, Coach," the trainer said as he took a walkie-talkie off his belt and radioed the injury cart personnel.

"Hang in there, Nate, we're gonna get you to the hospital," Riley said, holding Nate's head.

Nate's cap had fallen off during the play and lay on the ground, next to his dirt-covered piece of chewed up bubble gum.

When the injury cart came onto the field, the celebrating Titan's first noticed their fallen comrade. The players went over to Coach Riley and when they saw Nate's ankle they formed a circle around Nate, got on one knee, and held hands. While his teammates were at Nate's side, Joseph Costa walked off the field and into the stands, searching for his mother and father.

Coach Riley and the trainer raised Nate off the dirt and put him on the flat bed of the injury cart, careful not to touch or put any pressure on the busted ankle. The limp ankle flapped like a sock hanging from the clothesline on a windy day.

* * *

Dr. Emily Sykes knocked lightly on the door and walked into the hospital room.  Nate had the remote control in his hand, channel surfing on the small television that hung from the ceiling in front of his hospital bed.  Michelle sat in a chair by the window, reading a book.  Dr. Sykes inspected the cast on Nate's ankle and then went over his medical charts.  Nate hoped that the young attractive surgeon hadn't noticed the roses his mother brought in from her rose garden.  He had waged a losing argument with his mother over the roses; he asserted that it wasn't manly to have flowers in his hospital room.

"Considering how badly you shattered the ankle," Sykes said, "The surgery went well.  We put a bunch of metal plates and screws in there to reconstruct the ankle.  You should heal completely, but the TSA folks aren't going to like it when you go through an airport security checkpoint."

Michelle Baxter put down the book, looked at the cast on her son's left ankle, and asked the doctor, "What kind of timetable, do you suppose, for him to be back at one hundred percent?"

"One hundred percent?  We're talking about a good long while, and it depends on what you mean by one hundred percent."

"I think what we're all talking about here is when can I start playing ball again," Nate said.

The doctor let out a soft sigh, took her glasses off, and dangled them from the corner of her mouth.  "At least one year," Sykes answered.  "But more realistically, two years."

"Why so long?" Michelle asked, seeing the look of disappointment and gloom on the face of her son.

"It was a very serious break, doesn't get much worse.  It's just going to take time for the bone to regenerate and strengthen.  With all the side to side, sudden stop and go movement baseball requires, if your son tries to come back too soon and re-injures that ankle—well, that would be a bad thing, a real bad thing."

Nate chewed on his lower lip and stared out the window, "That's not the news I wanted to hear, Doc."

"No, it's not," Sykes said as she started to leave the room. "I know this is of no consolation, but that was a great catch you made."

Nate blushed at the thought of the pretty doctor knowing what had brought him into the hospital, "Yeah, it was."

After the doctor left, Michelle sat on the side of the bed, held her son's hand, and said, "I'm so sorry, honey." She didn't know what else to say and there really wasn't anything more she could say to lighten her son's spirits.

Nate hadn't cried when he was sprawled out on the infield dirt, his ankle a shattered mess, and he wasn't going to cry now. He choked back the emotion and his words were broken, "It's over, I can't believe it's over."

"Nate, you heard the doctor, it may not be for a couple of years, but you'll be able to play ball again."

"No, mom, you don't understand. In the baseball world, I'm damaged goods, an injury risk. I'm through."

Michelle struggled to think of a way to steer the conversation in a new direction, anything to get her son's mind off his injury. She glanced at her wristwatch. "Nate, its dinner time, how about I run down to the In-N-Out for a couple of Double Doubles and some fries?"

Nate picked up the remote control and started channel surfing again, "...and a shake," he said to his mother.

She knew a greasy burger would do the trick. She kissed her son on the forehead and went out for the fast food.

Ten minutes after his mother had left; Nate heard another knock on the door. He turned down the volume on the television and said, "C'mon in."

Vincent and Carmen Costa walked into the room. Carmen carried an arrangement of carnations that looked like the top half of a baseball. It had white carnations for the cowhide of the baseball and red carnations for the ball's stitching.

"Hello, Nate, my name is Vincent Costa and this is my wife, Carmen. We're Joseph's parents."

"Yes, sir, I know," Nate said. "I've seen you talking with Joe, before and after games."

"I hope you don't mind, but we brought you some flowers," Carmen said.

"No, ma'am, I don't mind at all. They're very pretty, thank you."

"Where would you like me to put them?"

Nate pointed to the shelf where his mom had placed the vase of yellow roses. "Over there is fine, ma'am."

An uncomfortable quiet permeated the room while Carmen put the flower arrangement next to the vase of roses. Vincent unconsciously tapped his right index finger up and down on his cell phone.

"I, uh, don't know where to start," Vincent said, breaking the silence. "This is kind of awkward."

"Yes, sir, it is," Nate said.

"Nate, my husband and I just felt that we needed to come here and thank you."

"Thank me for what?"

"For making that incredible catch and saving our son's perfect game," Vincent answered.

"I was just out there doing my job, Mr. Costa, making a play."

"No, Nate, it was more than that. You didn't have to go after that ball. The game was well in hand, there were two outs, and Joe would have gotten the next batter to end the game."

"Yes, sir, probably, but he would have lost his perfect game. I knew how important it was to him."

"That's why we want to thank you, Nate," Carmen said. "The way our son has been acting towards you, he really didn't deserve that kind of effort."

"We didn't raise our son to be that way," Vincent said. "We don't condone the way he's been treating you."

"I got to tell you, Mr. Costa, straight up, it's been rough the way he's turned the team on me. I understand why he's doing it, but whatever beef he has with my mom, he shouldn't take it out on me."

"We agree, Nate," Carmen said.

"When will you be able to play ball again?" Vincent asked.

"My baseball days are over, sir."

Carmen and Vincent looked at each other and they both had the same thought. *This kid gave up his baseball career for our son.*

The sound of footsteps entered the room, accompanied by the smell of hamburgers and fries. Seeing the Costa's in her son's room, Michelle Baxter froze and almost dropped the bag of food. She gathered her courage, put the bag of food on the table next to her son's bed, and acknowledged the Costas, "Mr. Costa, Mrs. Costa."

"I hope you don't mind," Carmen said. "But we just needed to thank your son for making that catch and to see how he was doing."

"No, I don't mind, "Michelle answered.

The hospital food sucked and Nate was hungry. He reached into the bag for a burger and unwrapped it. He took a big bite of the double burger loaded with cheese and all the fixings. While chewing, he looked at his mom and then the Costas, wondering how this scene was going to play out.

"Mrs. Baxter," Vincent said.

"You can call me Michelle," she said.

"Michelle, can the three of us go down to the cafeteria and get a cup of coffee?"

The request took her by surprise. Sure, she had imagined what this moment would be like, but she never actually thought it would happen. She looked at her son. In between bites of the burger, he glanced over at his mother and shook his head in the affirmative.

"Okay," she answered.

They walked down the hallway, in silence, and into the elevator. On the ride down, Carmen and Michelle made eye contact. Their eyes were the same color, hazel, and shared the same weary look. The cafeteria was almost empty; Michelle took a plastic bottle of Diet Coke out of the cooler, while Carmen and Vincent poured cups of coffee from a stainless steel urn. After he paid for the drinks, Vincent led the way to a table tucked away in a back corner. Before they sat down, Vincent took a napkin and wiped salt and water drops off the table.

Michelle looked Carmen in the eyes, then Vincent, and said, "I'm sorry."

Vincent took hold of his wife's hand on top of the table, "We know you are."

"There's not a day that goes by where I don't agonize over what happened that night. What could I have done different? Should I have done anything differently?"

"Michelle, let's get one thing straight," Vincent said. "Our family does not forgive you for taking the life of our son."

"I'm not asking you to forgive me, and I would never expect forgiveness."

Carmen cleared her throat, sniffled just a bit, and spoke up for the first time, "Like my husband said, in our hearts, we will never have forgiveness for you, but our hearts no longer harbor hatred for you."

The words struck a hard blow and Michelle's nerves were getting the best of her. From a small white ceramic bowl in the center of the table, she picked up a packet of sugar and started fidgeting with it.

"We did hate you; oh how we hated you," Vincent said. "Then we listened to your testimony, hearing from you about what happened that night. It helped us, and it hurt us. It hurt us to hear about the final moments of our son's life. It was good in that it answered the many questions we had. We now understand why you believed you had to do what you did."

"Michelle, can I ask you a question?" Carmen asked.

"Yes."

"We understand that your husband was killed in Afghanistan, by a car bomb."

"Yes, I lost my husband."

"Do you understand why those people put a bomb in that car?"

"No."

"Do you have hatred in your heart for those people?"

"Yes."

"Do you think you will always carry that hatred in your heart?

"Yes."

"That's no way to live, is it?"

"No, Carmen, it isn't."

Vincent and Carmen got up from the table. Michelle put down the sugar packet, looked up and watched them walk out of the cafeteria and down the hallway. When they were out of earshot she whispered, "I needed to hear this from you."

# 28

In front of an audience of 55,000 people, the children's choir finished singing the Star Spangled Banner. After mouthing the words to the national anthem, Vincent Costa put the Dodgers cap and radio headphones back on his head. Sitting next to him were his wife and daughter-in-law. To ease his anxiety, he cracked open a peanut shell, popped the nut into his mouth, and washed it down with a swig of draft beer. The game hadn't even started and a pile of empty shells lay on the concrete in front of his seat.

The Los Angeles Dodgers' infielders and outfielders took the field and went through their warm up routines. Five minutes later, the blue door to the bullpen opened and the Dodgers starting pitcher trotted from the outfield to the pitcher's mound. Vincent, Carmen, and Angela stood up, clapped their hands, and cheered so loudly that they almost went hoarse.

Angela pointed to the pitcher and said to her in-laws, "There he is— there's Joey. I can't believe he made it to the majors!"

Carmen took off her sunglasses, turned towards her husband, and gave him a long hug. The overjoyed parent's sat back down and watched their son take his warm up tosses. Vincent turned up the volume on his radio headphones and beamed with pride as Vin Scully talked about his boy.

*Today's starting pitcher, Joseph Costa, is making his major league debut as a Dodger. Joe is getting the mid-season call up from Triple-A, after going eight and two, with seventy-one strikeouts, for the Albuquerque Isotopes. Joe is well put together at six foot, four inches and two hundred and twenty pounds. He is now in his fourth season with the Dodger organization after being taken in the third round of the amateur draft.*

*Some of you Dodger fans might be familiar with the name Joseph Costa. He's a local boy, the pride of Highland, California. Joe played his college ball for the Titan's of Cal State Fullerton and in his senior year led the Titans to the national collegiate championship.*

*Costa is really going to have his hands full today with our rivals from the bay area. The visiting Giants lead the National League Western Division by one game over the Dodgers. So, you can only imagine the butterflies in the stomach of this young man.*

Costa's first appearance as a major league pitcher got off to a rocky start, giving up two runs in the first inning. After that, he calmed down and had his good stuff working for him. By the middle innings of the game, it was a pitcher's duel, and the score stayed steady at 2-0.

Vincent turned up the volume on the headphones to drown out the conversation between his wife and very pregnant daughter-in-law. He liked it that way; nothing annoyed him more than the girls yakking away while he was trying to concentrate on the game.

"How are you feeling?" Carmen asked Angela.

"Um, okay, I guess."

"And the baby?"

"The baby's fine, Joey and I went to the doctor yesterday before we flew out from Albuquerque."

"Too soon to know whether it's a little boy or girl?" Carmen asked.

"The doctor knows, but we don't want to know. I guess we want to do the old fashioned thing and be surprised."

The Costa's were sitting in the good seats just behind home plate and attended to by female servers wearing Dodgers jerseys and blue shorts. From the not so good seats, in the upper deck, near the left field foul pole, Michelle and Nate Baxter watched the game.

Michelle squinted through her sunglasses to follow the action on the field. The mid-afternoon sun now shined directly into their eyes, making the already hot August day even hotter. Michelle rolled the sleeves of her t-shirt up to her shoulders and rubbed a cold bottle of water against her sweaty forehead. The heat didn't stop Nate from munching down on his second foot long Dodger Dog, piled high with onions, relish, and mustard.

"I'm kind of surprised that you wanted to come to the game today," she said to her son.

"Why?"

"I don't know, I guess with Joe Costa pitching, I just sort of thought."

Nate interrupted his mother, "Mom, that's exactly why I wanted to come out today. It's his major league debut. This is a big deal. I wanted to be here for that."

"You don't have any bad feelings about how things turned out, you know, with baseball?" She asked, taking a long sip from the bottle of now lukewarm water.

"Nah, not really," he answered. "I mean, I wish I hadn't gotten injured, but I went out making the play that saved a perfect game. It's kind of nice owning a little piece of history."

Two rows in front of Michelle and Nate, the peanut vendor peddled his wares. *Nuts- get your peee-nuts* he barked out in a deep voice, well practiced from years of slinging peanuts at Dodger Stadium. Michelle held up her hand and yelled out, "Peanut man." The vendor took a cellophane bag of peanuts from his satchel and tossed them up to Michelle. She made the catch, then took a five-dollar bill out of her pocket and gave it to the fan sitting in front of her. The greenback got handed from fan to fan until it found its home with the peanut man.

Later that inning, Nate cracked a peanut between his fingers, ate the nut, brushed the empty shell off of his shorts and said to his mother, "Are you really okay with me going into law enforcement?"

"Well, when you first told me you wanted to go into law enforcement, I was thinking law school and then the DA's office. I wasn't thinking that you wanted to be a cop."

"Are you okay with it?" Nate asked a second time.

"You know, you'll probably be the only person in your academy class with a Bachelor of Science Degree in Chemical Engineering."

"Mom, you're not answering my question."

They heard the crack of a wood bat and caught sight of a foul ball coming their way. The ball landed three rows behind them and bodies scurried, going after the ball, before it started rolling under the seats.

Michelle looked at her son and smiled, "I am so proud of you and I'm honored that you'd want to join your father and me in serving. I do have one concern."

"What's that?

"I'm not happy about your choice of agencies; the Los Angeles Police Department."

"What's wrong with the LAPD?"

"No, Nate, I think the question is what's wrong with the San Bernardino County Sheriff's Department?"

"Nothing's wrong with them, it's a great agency. I just didn't think you'd want me to work with you—well, in a sense."

"You should have asked me. I'm kind of hurt by your decision. It's like tradition within the department. If your kid becomes a cop, they follow your footsteps, in the department."

"I didn't know it was that big a deal."

"It is, Nate."

"Okay."

"Okay, what?" Michelle asked.

"Let's not mess with tradition. Besides, I like the green uniforms of the Sheriff's Department better than the black ones worn by the LAPD."

It was the bottom of the ninth inning and their discussion had distracted their attention away from the action on the field, until they heard the roar of the crowd. They looked up and saw the Giant's right fielder shout an obscenity while watching the ball sail over the fence and the Dodgers batter trotting around third base. The Dodgers' dugout emptied and all the players waited on the batter to cross home plate. A walk off home run, the Dodgers won, 3-2.

One hour after the game had ended; Michelle and Nate were still in the parking lot of Dodger Stadium. Thousands of cars battled to get to one of the four stadium exits that dumped traffic onto the freeways. Masses of Dodger fans walked between cars. Many of them appeared to be drunk and shouting vulgarities about the visiting team from San Francisco. Beer bottles and cans littered the emptying parking lot.

"This sucks," Nate said, impatiently tapping his fingers on the steering wheel of the SUV. He watched people walk by, who were making better progress than they were.

Michelle turned the air conditioner up to full blast and pointed all the vents so that they blew into her face. "I knew there was a reason why we stopped coming to Dodger games."

Thirty minutes later, they exited Dodger Stadium and drove through Elysian Park, which led to the 110 freeway. The park was home to the Los Angeles Police Department Training Academy and they passed by a group of new trainees jogging in formation.

"Mom?"

"Yeah."

"What do you think the odds are of me getting into the kind of situation like you got into?"

"Do you mean when I shot the boy?"

"Yes."

"I don't know, son. I hope to God you never find yourself in a situation like that."

# 29

Lieutenant John Tate walked out of his office and made his way to the asphalt parking lot of the San Bernardino County Sheriff's Department Training Academy, where a new class of deputy trainees stood in formation. After getting promoted from Sergeant to Lieutenant, he now managed the new deputy-training academy.

The academy sat fifteen hundred feet above sea level, nestled in the foothills of the San Bernardino Mountains. At nine o'clock in the morning, a combination of dense fog and low-lying clouds blanketed the academy grounds. Before he could see the new class of thirty trainees, he heard his two staff members, Sergeant Billy Grimes and Deputy Tina Smith, yelling at the top of their lungs.

*Did you bother to look in the mirror this morning?*

*I can't believe you even showed up here!*

*What the hell—did you sleep in this wrinkled ass uniform last night?*

Just by looking at Billy Grimes, you could tell he had once been in the Marine Corps; shaved head and not an ounce of body fat on his five foot eight, muscular frame. Because of Grimes' diminutive stature, he had a severe case of the Little Man's Syndrome, and getting in the faces of new trainees always gave him a woody. Tina Smith was African American and towered over Grimes. At six feet two inches, she had once played women's basketball for USC. Grimes and Smith complimented each other perfectly and every new class was scared shitless of them.

From twenty yards away, Tate saw Grimes go face to face with an overweight male Caucasian trainee whose pot bellied stomach hung over the waistline of his pants.

*What are people going to think when a blob like you shows up at their door?*

The thirty new trainees stood at attention with their eyes staring straight ahead and their chins touching their necks. They all wore light green shirts, dark green slacks, and black boots. Tate walked up to Grimes and the overweight trainee.

"What do we have here, Sergeant Grimes? Tate asked.

"Sir, this is new trainee, David Lewis. Trainee Lewis is a fat tub of lard, sir."

Tate looked up and down at David Lewis and did his best to keep from laughing. He could see Lewis trembling and on the verge tears. "Mister Lewis, how long ago were you accepted into this academy?"

"Four months, sir."

"And when you were notified of your acceptance, were you told to report in good physical shape?"

"Yes, sir."

"What's your excuse, Trainee Lewis?"

"I have no excuse, sir."

"You owe me thirty pounds, Trainee Lewis."

"Yes, sir."

"That will never happen, Lieutenant," Grimes said. "Fat turds like Lewis have no discipline or self control. He's nothing but a Pillsbury Dough Boy."

"I like that, Sergeant Grimes," Tate said, showing no emotion. "Class, say good morning to Trainee Pillsbury."

The other twenty-nine new trainees said nothing, they didn't know whether Tate was serious or not. Tate reached deep into his lungs for air and yelled out, "I said to say good morning to Trainee Pillsbury!"

Twenty-nine voices yelled back, "Good morning, Trainee Pillsbury!"

Standing in formation, to the immediate left of David "Pillsbury" Lewis, stood Nate Baxter. He had been up most of the previous night, preparing for his first day of academy training. Nate didn't consider it to be cheating when he grilled his mother on the tricks of the trade for looking sharp at inspection. His shirt and slacks were crisply pressed; a straight gig line and his black boots were spit shined.

Tate redirected his evil looking scowl from Pillsbury to Nate and looked at his nameplate. "Trainee Baxter," he said. Nate could smell the coffee on Tate's breath.

Tate knew that Michelle Baxter's son would be a member of this academy class. In light of everything his mother had gone through, he admired the kid for wanting to follow in her footsteps. Tate's natural tendency would have been to take the kid under his wing. However, in the academy setting, that wouldn't look good. To over compensate, he decided to be tougher on Nate than he would be on the other trainees.

Tate inspected Nate's uniform, looking for anything, but the uniform was damn near perfect. Then he saw it, a small thread sticking out from underneath Nate's shirt collar. Tate reached over, plucked it off Nate's shirt, and held it up to Nate's eyes. "What is this, Trainee Baxter?"

Nate wanted to crawl underneath a rock. He was mad at himself for not spotting the thread and apprehensive about what would happen next.

"It's a thread, sir," was all Nate could say.

"Drop down and give me twenty," Tate said.

Nate went down to the damp asphalt, did twenty pushups, with ease, then got back to his feet.

Tate glared at the class with a disgusted look on his face and shook his head, "I guess Sergeant Grimes or Deputy Smith hadn't told you yet. When one trainee gets dinged, you all get dinged. Now, drop down and give me twenty."

Nate and his twenty-nine classmates dropped down and gave Tate twenty push-ups. When they were finished, Tate took ten steps back and addressed his new class of trainees.

"For the next twenty-six weeks, I own you, Sergeant Grimes owns you, and Deputy Smith owns you. We are going to be on you like stink on poop and then we'll be on you some more, just for good measure. If you can't handle the stress of this academy, the streets will eat you alive.

"You will be here every morning at zero seven hundred hours — that means six-fifty, for physical conditioning. You will shower, then inspection. You will attend morning classes; you will bring your lunch, and then have afternoon classes.

"We do however; have a special treat for you today. This will be the only time where the department takes you out and pays for lunch."

Tate turned from the class to look at Grimes and Smith, who were standing off to the side. "Sergeant Grimes, Deputy Smith, these boys and girls are all yours."

The new trainees stared at Tate as he walked back towards his office and the academy classrooms. They all understood the message Tate had delivered, twenty-six weeks of hell lay ahead of them.

Deputy Tina Smith barked out the order to march and the class marched from the asphalt onto a dirt trail. Keeping his eyes staring straight ahead, Nate used his peripheral vision to look at his fellow trainees. Some had the look of fear, others, like Pillsbury, had the look of regret. They marched for one-half of a mile through desert like terrain. Deputy Smith ordered the trainees to stop when they reached the chain link, topped with barbed wire, gates of the Glen Helen jail facility.

Glen Helen housed four thousand social deviants. They had all been convicted of crimes and ordered by a judge to spend up to one year in the county jail. The resume of their criminal offenses ran the gamut: drug users, drug pushers, drunk drivers, thieves, burglars, and wife beaters. Many of the inmates had gang affiliations; the Mexican gangs, the black gangs and the white skin head gangs. Glen Helen may not have been state prison, but it wasn't Disneyland.

After clearing three different security checkpoints, Grimes and Smith led the trainees into the mess hall chow line. Inmates wearing plastic hairnets and gloves plopped a meat, potatoes, and vegetable onto the trainee's aluminum eating trays. A section of stainless steel tables with stainless steel stools, welded to the tables, had been reserved for the training class.

Nate sat down at a table with Pillsbury and trainees Monica Vargas and Jeff Price.

"It smells in here," Price said.

"Yeah," Nate said. "I don't know which is worse, the smell of this food or the stench of the inmates."

Vargas glanced around the mess hall and saw that most of the inmates were staring at her or one of the other seven female trainees. "I wish they'd stop looking at me. It's freaking me out."

"What's the big deal, Monica? These guys are in jail." Price said. "They're just having their way with you in their minds."

When all the trainees had gone through the chow line and found a seat, Tina Smith banged an aluminum tray on a table to get the attention of her class.

"You have ten minutes to eat your lunch and I don't want to see any food left on trays. Like your momma told you, kids in China are starving." Her loud voice carried throughout the entire mess hall. The inmates gawked and laughed at the trainees.

Monica Vargas poked a fork at the food on her tray. "This is disgusting; I can't even tell what it is."

Pillsbury was almost done with the food on his tray and said while chewing, "I think it's meatloaf, the gravy's kind of weak, but the mashed potatoes are okay."

Jeff Price saw that Nate had pushed his tray away, untouched. "What's the matter, Baxter, not hungry?"

"My mom's a deputy," Nate answered.

"So, what's that got to do with not eating?" Price asked.

"She never eats jail food."

"Why?" Vargas asked.

"The inmates cook it," Nate said, watching Pillsbury fork in another mouthful. "I don't like to eat food that someone's whacked off in. I guess I'm just funny that way."

Price and Vargas wrinkled their noses in disgust. Pillsbury shrugged his shoulders and kept on eating.

After lunch, and more verbal harassment from the inmates, Sergeant Grimes and Deputy Smith made the class jog in formation from the jail back to the academy. It wasn't hot and the sun had yet to completely burn off the fog. But, after the half mile jog, a winded and sweating Pillsbury threw up on the dirt trail.

Nate and his classmates settled into the daily routine of academy life; morning PT, classes, lunch, more classes. Cliques started to form within the class and Nate continued to hang out with Pillsbury, Jeff Price, and Monica Vargas. Nate took a particular liking to Pillsbury and did all he could to support him in the weight loss battle.

Midway through week two, Monica Vargas did not show up for the seven a.m. physical conditioning. She had gotten into a minor traffic accident on her way to the academy. No one was hurt, but she didn't arrive at the academy until the morning class break.

Tate told Grimes and Smith why Vargas would be coming in late. Grimes couldn't let this opportunity go by, so he went to the academy's vehicle-training center, in search of a crash helmet. He found one that looked like what NASCAR drivers wore on Sundays; except a bright hideous shade of yellow.

When Vargas arrived, he called her to the front of the class and presented her with the crash helmet. Her face turned three different shades of red. They made her wear the helmet for one week and she earned the nickname, "Bumblebee".

The trainees brought in their lunch from home and had one-half of an hour to eat in the academy's break room. Just before the lunch break, on the Monday of week three, Smith and Grimes wheeled a doctor's office style scale into the break room. Lunchtime came and the trainees made a beeline to the break room's microwave and refrigerator, making the most of what little time they had to eat.

Billy Grimes watched David Lewis take his lunch cooler out of the refrigerator and sit at a table with Nate, Jeff Price, and Monica Vargas. Just as Lewis was opening the cooler, Grimes yelled out, "Trainee Pillsbury, stand at attention!" Lewis gave a puzzled look to his tablemates and then got up from the table.

"Trainee Pillsbury, please tell the class how your diet is coming along," Grimes shouted at Lewis.

"It's coming along good, sir," Lewis answered.

"How much weight have you lost?" Grimes asked.

"I don't know, sir."

"I don't think you've lost any. You still look like a fat piece of crap. Pillsbury, get your butt up here and get on this scale."

Nate, Price, and Vargas acted as if they were eating, to keep from busting out in laughter. Lewis went to the scale, hesitated, and then did as ordered. Grimes moved the lead weight to the right, until it was balanced.

"Two hundred and forty pounds—you haven't lost a damn ounce, Pillsbury," Grimes said with a scowl. "Deputy Smith, would you please go over to Pillsbury's table, open up his Partridge Family lunch box, and tell us what the fat boy brought in for lunch."

Nate, Price, and Vargas stopped eating when Tina Smith came over and towered over their table. She unzipped the blue nylon lunch cooler and reached in.

"Ooohh child," she said, looking at Lewis as she removed the aluminum foil from three cold slices of sausage and pepperoni pizza. "You must love you some pizza."

Smith reached back into the cooler, pulled out a bag of Cool Ranch Doritos, and held it up for everyone to see. She then went into the cooler and took out three individually wrapped Little Debbie oatmeal raisin snack cakes. She tossed one each to Nate, Price, and Vargas.

The entire class just stared at Lewis, who was still standing on the scale. Grimes went face to face with the petrified trainee. "What kind of diet program is that, Pillsbury? Weight Watcher's, Jenny Craig, or South Beach?

"No, sir," Lewis answered, in a low and cracked voice.

"Trainee Pillsbury, we will try this again in one week, and if I don't see some progress, your fanny is out of here. Do you understand me? Have I made myself clear?"

"Yes, sir."

The next week, David Lewis stood on the scale. Grimes flipped the metal weight to the left until it was balanced. "Two hundred and thirty five pounds, that's a start, Pillsbury. Deputy Smith, please inspect Pillsbury's lunchbox."

Tina Smith opened Lewis's lunch cooler and pulled out a turkey breast sandwich on whole grain bread, a zip lock baggie full of celery, and a cup of sugar free Jell-O.

Over the next four weeks, Pillsbury lost ten more pounds, but Grimes and Smith were suspicious about some of Pillsbury's behavior patterns. During every break, Lewis would sneak out to his car in the trainee parking lot and sit in the passenger's seat with a newspaper covering his face. Grimes told Smith to check out Lewis's vehicle.

Tina Smith went to the parking lot and pulled on the front passenger door handle of Lewis's white Ford Fiesta. It was unlocked. She inspected the interior of the vehicle and found nothing out of the ordinary. She opened the glove box and hit pay dirt; Pillsbury's stash—one Snickers bar, two Reese's peanut butter cups, and a bag of Skittles.

When the class broke for lunch and entered the break room, they stopped in their boots when they saw Lieutenant John Tate, standing over a table, pulled away from all the other tables. A shoebox, lined with cotton balls, sat atop the table. Inside the shoebox, resting on a bed of white toilet paper lay Pillsbury's candy stash.

Tate looked solemnly at David Lewis and said, "Trainee Pillsbury, would you please take this candy out into the foothills and give it the burial it deserves. Trainee's Baxter and Vargas, you will be our gravediggers. Trainee Price, you will be the pallbearer."

Tate heard the snickers from the rest of the class.

"I would like all the other trainees to attend as well, so that this candy may have its proper send off. And when you're done with the services, everybody owes me two miles."

# 30

"You guys don't stand a chance. They're going to give it to me," Jeff Price said, between bites of his cheese enchilada, rice, and refried beans.

Nate took a drink from the bottle of Corona beer, put it down, and replied, "I don't know, Jeff, don't be getting too excited. I kind of like David's chances."

"Pillsbury? No way, not after that little candy incident," Price said with a smirk on his face as he looked across the table at David Lewis.

"I agree with Nate," Monica Vargas said, picking up her glass of red wine and taking a slow sip. "He did lose all that weight."

David Lewis finished the last bit of lettuce off his taco salad and eyed the basket of deep fried tortilla chips and the bowl of salsa. He wanted nothing more than to load up a chip with the garlic-laden salsa and plop it into his mouth; but he didn't. "Thirty pounds," Lewis said.

The server came to the table, cleared the plates, and asked if they needed more drinks. Nate ordered another bottle of Corona beer, Vargas a glass of red wine, Price a draft Miller-Lite and Lewis a Diet Coke.

Every Thursday night, after classes, the now close-knit group had dinner and drinks at Nena's Mexican Restaurant in downtown San Bernardino.

The quaint restaurant had been around forever and served the best authentic Mexican food in town. The establishment did a booming lunch business and was a favorite among the local lawyers, cops, and court staff. Nena's dinner business was usually slow and they pretty much had the whole place to themselves.

The evening's hot topic of conversation was over who would be named number one in the class and deliver the next week's academy graduation speech.

"In all fairness, Nate should be named number one," Lewis said, looking at Nate. "You've aced most of the written exams and you kick everybody's ass in physical conditioning."

Price took a sip of his draft beer, let out a belch, and said to Lewis, "Ain't going to happen, dude. Not if Lieutenant Tate has any say in the matter. I mean, he fucks with all of us, that's part of his gig. But, it's like he actually hates Nate."

"I get that feeling too," Vargas said. "Nate, what did you do in another life to piss off Tate?"

Preoccupied with peeling the label off of his beer bottle, Nate answered, "I don't know."

"Do you think it might have anything to do with that whole thing of your mom shooting the kid?" Lewis asked.

"Probably," Nate answered. "Back then, Tate was a Sergeant with homicide. He worked the case."

"How did your mom deal with it?" Vargas asked. "I can't even begin to imagine how I would feel if I killed an innocent kid."

Nate looked at the small flame burning from the candle in the center of the table. He put his right index finger into the hot wax, pulled it out, and watched the wax cool around his fingertip.

"It was a bad scene. We went through some rough times. I wouldn't wish that on anybody."

"When we get out there, it could happen to any one of us, at anytime. That's some heavy shit," Price said.

"Yeah, we'll get a taste of it in the morning with the live training scenarios," Lewis said.

"I have a hunch we will," Nate said, reaching for the check. "We better go, we've got a big day tomorrow."

"Nate, let us help out with that," Vargas protested.

"Nope, my treat."

"But you treat every week," Lewis said.

"Hey, leave the guy alone," Price said. "If he wants to pay every week, let him pay."

Nate took a wad of cash out of his pocket and threw some money on the table, including a more than generous tip for the server. It was no consolation to Nate, but with his dad's life insurance money and military death benefits, he was never short on walking around money.

* * *

After the morning inspection, the trainees were sitting outside on metal folding chairs, near the door to a classroom. The door opened and Lieutenant John Tate walked out. "Boys and girls, this morning we will be doing live scenarios. Everything you've learned in the past twenty-five weeks will be put to practical use in these exercises. You will be graded and your grade will count heavily towards your overall class ranking."

Tate turned to Deputy Tina Smith and asked, "Deputy Smith, have you inspected each trainee's service weapon to insure that they are loaded with blanks?"

"Yes, sir, I have," she answered.

Tate next turned to Sergeant Billy Grimes. "Sergeant Grimes, tell these pukes about their first scenario."

"Sir, for the first scenario this morning, the trainees will be responding to a loud music call."

"Very well," Tate said. "Trainee Vargas, you're up."

From inside the classroom, the sounds of heavy metal rock music blared. Monica Vargas stood up from her chair, it was a cool morning, but sweat started to form on the brow of her eyes. In the pit of her stomach, she could feel the Egg McMuffin from breakfast gurgling away. She looked at Nate, who nodded his head in encouragement.

While the class watched, Vargas went to the door and knocked three times. No one answered the door. After one minute had passed, she knocked on the door again; this time with more authority. An undercover sheriff's department narcotics detective, who played the role, opened the door. His long black hair was tied into a ponytail and he had a ZZ Top beard. He wore a Harley Davidson tee shirt with tattered blue jeans.

He stood in the open doorway, looked at Vargas, and with an annoyed tone in his voice said, "What?"

"Sir, I'm here because of the loud music."

"So."

"It's too loud; it's disturbing your neighbors."

"Fuck 'em."

"Sir, I'm asking you to turn the volume down on the music."

"Which one of those mother fuckers dropped dime on me?"

"That's not important. What's important is that you comply with my order."

"Damn, you've got a sweet ass."

Vargas sensed her anger and frustration building. She wanted to kick the guy right between his nuts. "Sir, if you don't turn the music down, I'm going to need to see some identification."

"Why?"

"So I can run you for warrants."

"Fuck it—I'll turn the music down."

The door closed and the music stopped. Vargas breathed a sigh of relief and started to walk back to her chair. She passed by a table where Tate, Grimes, and Smith were scribbling notes. She thought she had done an okay job.

At her seat, Nate leaned over and whispered, "Nice touch on threatening to run him for warrants."

"Thanks, I figured a douche bag like that has got to have some warrants floating around in the system. It was his choice, turn the music down, or go to jail."

The noise of hip-hop gangster rap music came from inside the class-room. It was loud enough to make the door vibrate. "Price, you're up," Tate yelled over the noise.

Before getting up from his chair, Price turned to his friends and said, "I'm going to show you how it's done and lock up number one in the class."

Price walked up to the door with a little bit of cockiness in his stride. He knocked on the door three times, banging as hard as he could to be heard over the music.

A female Caucasian with gray hair, in curlers, and wearing a bright pink moo-moo opened the door. She looked to be in her early sixties. Price didn't know it, but she was Tate's secretary. For a moment, he was con-fused. She didn't fit the music.

"Ma'am," Price said, "We've received a call about the loud music."

"I know; I'm the one that called. It's my fourteen-year-old grandson—he lives with me. His momma's in prison for dealing meth. I'm at my wit's end with the boy. He insists on listening to that god awful shit."

"Ma'am he's going to have to turn it down."

"Good, let me tell him." The woman turned her back to Price and yelled into the classroom, "Dwayne, the police are here. They say you need to turn that shit off."

The music stopped playing.

"Thank you, officer, I appreciate your help."

"Yes, ma'am, no problem. Have a good evening."

Price walked back to his chair and he could see his classmates smiling and chuckling. His face turned red.

"Ooohh, you really showed that old lady and her grandson who's the boss," David Lewis said, laughing.

"Fuck you, Pillsbury."

Loud Mexican Mariachi music started playing behind the closed door of the classroom.

"You're up, Baxter," Tate yelled out.

At the door, Nate knocked three times. There was no response, the music continued to play and Nate heard the scream of a female coming from inside. Two feet to the left of the doorway was a window with horizontal vinyl blinds. Nate saw a set of bloodshot eyes peek out from the closed blinds.

Nate's heart started to beat faster. He looked down at the gun holster on his right hip and flipped off the strip of black leather that ran from the holster over the top of his .9mm Glock. Keeping his right hand down by his holster, he knocked three more times on the door with his left hand. He yelled out, "Sheriff's Department, open the door!"

The door opened and the role was played by a different undercover narcotics detective; Hispanic and about forty years old. He was shorter than Nate was, but weighed more. He had black uncombed hair and a day's growth of stubble to go along with his Fu-Manchu mustache.

Before Nate could say anything, the man started speaking Spanish in an agitated tone of voice. Nate did not understand the man. His mother spoke Spanish, but while growing up, the language was not used at home. Even though Nate didn't understand the man, he knew the man was pissed at something.

When the man talked, Nate smelled alcohol on his breath. On the front of his dirty tee shirt, Nate saw some fresh red stains that looked like blood.

"Do you speak English?" Nate asked.

"No hablo," the man answered.

Nate heard a female voice crying from somewhere inside the classroom. It sounded like she was in pain. He made the decision to enter the classroom, but the man stood between him and the doorway entry. Nate saw the man's right hand reach around to the rear waistband of his blue jeans. In one fluid motion, Nate drew the Glock from his holster and fired one blank round into the chest of the man. The undercover detective acted like he had been shot and fell backwards to the ground. Nate continued to point his Glock and gasped for air. He felt like he had just run a marathon.

The class watched in stunned silence. David Lewis breathed in the smell of gunpowder and said to no one in particular, "Holy shit."

Tate got up from the table and started to walk to the doorway of the classroom. The undercover detective continued to lie on his back. His eyes were closed and he pretended to be dead. Nate stood over the body and watched Tate come towards him.

"Jesus Christ, Baxter, you shot him," Tate said. He sounded angry.

"Yes, sir."

"Why?"

"He was reaching for something in his rear waistband."

"Maybe he just wanted to scratch his ass."

"With all due respect, sir, I doubt it."

"Baxter, what the hell were you thinking?"

When Nate fired the shot, he knew it was the right decision. But listening to Tate berate him, he was now beginning to question his actions.

"Sir, there was no answer at the door. Inside, I heard a female screaming. When the suspect answered the door, it was clear to me that he was upset at something or somebody. His breathe smelled of alcohol. On his shirt, I saw what I believed to be blood. I then heard a female inside, crying. I decided to enter the premises to check on the welfare of the crying female. It was apparent to me that the suspect did not want me to enter. I saw him reach for something, behind his back. I made the decision to discharge my weapon."

"Nice choice of words, Baxter, *discharge my weapon*," Tate said. "Why don't you just say it? *I shot him.*"

"Yes, sir, I shot him."

"How does it feel to kill someone?" Tate asked.

"Not good, sir."

Tate reached out his hand to the undercover detective, who was still playing dead. "Detective Hernandez, let me give you a hand in getting up."

The detective got to his feet, his back still facing away from Tate, Nate, and the class.

"Detective Hernandez, what were you reaching for?" Tate asked.

Hernandez reached behind his back for the object in his waistband, still concealed by his untucked tee shirt. For the class and Tate to see, the detective held up a snub-nosed .38 caliber revolver.

"Detective Hernandez, when Trainee Baxter shot you, were you reaching for this handgun?" Tate asked.

"Yes, sir."

"Detective Hernandez, had Trainee Baxter not shot you, what would you have done?"

"I would have shot him."

"What was your intent?"

"My intent was to kill him."

Nate closed his eyes and swallowed hard.

"Good job, Baxter, it was the right call," Tate said. "You made it to the end of your watch and you'll live to see another day."

Nate walked back to his chair; all the eyes of his classmates were trained on him. Tate took the revolver from Hernandez. He clicked open the cylinder and let the six blank rounds fall to the concrete. The brass casings clinked, then bounced a few times before they rolled and came to a rest.

Tate looked at the class and said, "If you hesitate, if you think twice—you're dead."

That night, Nate stayed up late, watching television in the family room. The events of the day had stressed him; he was restless and couldn't sleep. He flipped through the channels and settled on a *Seinfeld* re-run.

Right around midnight, he heard his mother come home from work. Entering the house from the garage, she went to the kitchen and grabbed a Diet Coke from the refrigerator.

"Hey, mom, how was work?" Nate asked.

Michelle twisted off the cap, took a sip, and walked into the family room. "Not bad, how was your day?"

"We did the live training scenarios."

"What scenario did you do?" she asked.

"Loud music call," he answered.

"Which one did you get? Doper Biker Dude, Granny Lady, or Drunk Mexican? They never change them."

"Drunk Mexican."

"Did you shoot?"

"Yes."

"Is that why you can't sleep?"

"Yeah."

Michelle stood by the couch and massaged her son's shoulders. She could feel the knots and tightness.

"What did Lieutenant Tate have to say?"

"He said, *if you hesitate, if you think twice—you're dead.*"

She stopped massaging his shoulder and started to walk upstairs, to go to bed. "That's the best advice you'll ever get. In our line of work, good words to live by."

# 31

In the academy gym, Tina Smith rode a stationary bike, while John Tate and Billy Grimes lifted weights. Grimes knocked out bench press reps, with Tate spotting for him. Tate shook his head in amazement as he watched Grimes handle the weight with no problem.

"Damn, Billy, how much do you have on that bar?" Tate asked.

"Two hundred and fifty," he answered, between grunts.

"That's pretty impressive—for a little guy," Tate said.

"It's that Napoleon's, little man complex, he's got," Smith said, from the bike, four feet away. "He'll never be as tall as me, so the best he can do is maybe some six-pack abs."

"Billy, you gonna let her run that smack on you?" Tate asked, trying to stir the pot.

"I've got to Lieutenant, she *can* kick my ass."

Smith got off the bike, wiped the sweat from her face with a towel, and went over to Grimes. She snapped his ass with the towel. "That's right, Billy, you'll always be my little bitch."

Tate took three bottles of water out of an ice chest and went over to a table in the corner of the gym. Grimes and Smith followed and sat down with Tate. With the class out on a six-mile run, they were alone in the gym.

"Do we agree that it's between Lewis and Baxter?" Tate asked.

"Yes," Grimes answered.

"Agreed," Smith said.

"Billy, who do you like?" Tate asked.

"Baxter."

"Tina?"

"I'm with Billy, I like Baxter."

"How about you, LT?" Grimes asked.

"Lewis."

Smith and Grimes looked at one another; they both had a surprised expression on their faces. "You really like Pillsbury over Baxter?" Smith said.

"It's a tough call, but yeah, I do."

"Why?" Grimes asked.

"The guy's come a long way in twenty six weeks. If you had asked me after week one, I would have said there's no way he makes it to graduation. He lost all the weight, that's a big accomplishment in itself. You've got to admit, you two fucked with him something terrible during that whole ordeal."

"We did," Grimes said, with a big grin on his face.

"It shows me that he's developed a thick skin, he's not going to let anything spook him. That's the quality a new deputy has to have when they hit the streets. Academically, he graded out number one in the class. He's not the sharpest tool in the shed and he had to bust his ass studying to make those grades."

"But, Lieutenant, the class doesn't respect him," Smith said. "I agree with what you're saying, but he's not a leader."

"Baxter's the leader of the bunch. Academically, he graded out number three, behind Lewis and Price. Physical conditioning, not even close, Baxter smokes them," Grimes said.

Smith took the last sip of her water and launched the plastic bottle towards a metal trashcan, twenty feet away. It clanked against the rim and fell in. "I still got it," she said. "Lieutenant, I know it's our job to be tough on these kids. It just seems like you've been tougher on Baxter, real tough."

Tate stood up and looked at them, "I know." He left the gym and started jogging. A quarter of a mile into his run, he veered to his right and onto the trails of the foothills.

After another mile, he saw his class appear over the horizon. With each stride, they grew larger and larger. At one hundred yards, he could see the class jogging in perfect formation. Nate Baxter, without breaking a sweat, led the formation. Tate was proud of this class; they had turned out to be one of his best. Twenty-six weeks ago, they had their tongues hanging out of their mouths, panting for air and throwing up. Tate jogged in place as the class went by; he then jogged to the front of the formation and kept pace, next to Baxter. "All right, you bunch of pukes," he yelled. "Let's pick up the pace and bring it on in."

After the run, Nate, Lewis, Price, and Vargas sat on the grass in a circle, drinking water and doing cool-down stretching exercises.

Tate came up to the group and said, "Baxter, my office, ten minutes." With that, he was gone.

Monica Vargas mimicked the voice of a small child, "Uh-oh, someone is getting called down to the principal's office."

"What did you fuck up now, Baxter?" Price asked.

"Beats the hell out of me," Nate answered.

He got up off the ground, brushed the grass off his shorts, and made the two hundred yard walk from the exercise field to the classroom and office complex. He racked his mind trying to figure out why Lieutenant Tate wanted to see him. He came up with nothing, but guessed it couldn't be good.

The door to Tate's office was open. He was signing paperwork at his desk, still wearing his olive colored exercise shorts and white tee shirt. Nate knocked lightly on the door's frame. Tate looked up, saw that it was Nate, and motioned him to come in and take a seat.

Tate looked at his armpits and took a sniff. "It smells like one of us needs to shower," he said.

Nate didn't know how to respond and answered, "Yes, sir."

"How's your mother doing?"

"She's doing well, sir."

"I'm sure she told you that I worked the shooting."

"Yes, sir, she told me."

"That was a bad situation all the way around. She went through hell," Tate said.

"Yes, sir, she did go through hell," Nate answered. His mind drifted to the painful memories of his mother's drinking, driving her to the emergency room and pleading with her to stop, before she killed herself.

"I just wanted to explain myself about why I've been riding your butt for twenty six weeks," Tate said.

"I don't think you've been tougher on me than any of the other trainees. It's part of the program; it's what we signed up for."

"C'mon, Nate, you can cut out that political correctness crap. I hear your classmates talking, *Why does Tate have a hard on for Baxter?*"

"Okay, so you've been tough on me, it's no big thing."

Tate shifted his weight in the chair and the worn leather creaked. "I'm not real good at expressing my emotions, but let me see if I can explain where I'm coming from. It's like the dad who coaches his son's little league baseball team. Sometimes the dad is tougher on his own kid, to not show favoritism. Do you see where I'm coming from?"

Nate cracked a smile and answered, "Yes, sir, I understand what you're trying to say."

"Since the shooting, your mother's had a place in my thoughts. I've been where she's been and I've seen what she's seen."

"My mother thinks very highly of you, sir. She credits you as being the reason for her coming back after the shooting."

Tate stared out his window, he watched the inmates from Glen Helen picking up trash between the academy and the jail. "I guess because of her, I just wanted you to succeed. So, to keep that from showing, I've been riding your fanny."

"Thank you, sir—well, you know what I mean."

"You've got a good strong character, Nate. You've overcome a lot of obstacles; the loss of your father, your mother's ordeal, and the baseball injury."

"None of those were good things, but they made me stronger, as a person."

"You'll be a fine cop, Nate."

"I'm going to give it my all, sir."

"Well, enough of this emotional crap," Tate said. "You got big plans for the weekend?"

"No, sir, just getting ready for Monday's graduation."

Tate's left hand rubbed a day's growth of gray stubble on his face. "You might want to set some time aside to do a little bit of writing."

The statement puzzled Nate. He thought about it for a moment and asked, "What kind of writing?"

"The graduation speech."

\* \* \*

When Nate broke the news to his mother that he was number one in his class, she insisted on a celebratory dinner. Nate did not object. The restaurant was packed, with people waiting at the bar, and outside. They had been lucky to get a table on a Friday night, because Lucille's served the best ribs in Rancho Cucamonga. The air inside the restaurant smelled of cooked meat and deep-fried potatoes. No comparison to the ribs found in Memphis restaurants, but the folks in Southern California didn't know any better.

Nate put a baby back rib in his mouth, devoured the meat, and sucked the bone clean. Michelle's fork picked at her beef brisket platter; she looked at her son and her eyes glistened with pride.

"Did you have any idea, at the time, why Lieutenant Tate wanted to see you?" she asked.

"Yeah, I thought I was in trouble."

"You can't tell me you had no clue that you were going to be number one."

"No, mom, I really didn't. The way the lieutenant was riding me, I figured it was either going to be Price or Lewis."

"Well, I'm proud of you."

Nate put another rib in his mouth and picked it clean. "You have to say that, you're my mother," he said, licking his fingers.

"You know, at the luncheon, you'll be sitting at the head table with the sheriff," she said.

"Yeah, Lieutenant Tate told me. He said to make sure I was wearing clean underwear."

Michelle stirred her iced tea with a straw and watched the lemon wedge get caught up in the swirling vortex. "I wish I could be there to take pictures."

"Don't worry; I'm sure there will be plenty of picture taking. You're still going to make it to the graduation ceremony, right?"

"Absolutely, I wouldn't miss it. I swapped out a shift, that's why I can't make the luncheon."

Michelle picked up her brown leather purse that was lying on the bench of the booth. She opened the purse and took out a box that measured four inches by four inches. The box was old and at one time had been white, but it was now cream colored. Burgundy ribbon and a burgundy bow garnished the box. She handed it across the table to her son.

Nate took the box and asked, "What's this?"

"Your graduation present."

Nate untied the ribbon and opened the box. He took the men's pocket watch out of the box and held it up. The glass face was scratched; the backing of the watch was gold. He turned it in his hand and read the engraving, *CAB*.

"Wow, this is neat. Where did it come from?"

"It belonged to your grandfather; those are his initials on the back, Charles Andrew Baxter."

"How come I've never seen this watch before?"

"I don't know. Your father's had it all these years. I found it when I was going through some of your dad's stuff—after he died."

Nate gave a closer inspection to the pocket watch, turning it over several times in his hands.

"It still keeps perfect time," he said.

"I took it to a jeweler."

"This was dad's?"

"Yes."

"And before that, pa-paws?"

"Yes."

"I don't know what to say."

"You don't have to say anything, just think about your father."

"I will."

"On second thought, there is one thing you can say."

"What's that?"

She reached across the table for her son's hand. "Say, I love you, mom."

"I love you, mom."

# 32

From the kitchen, servers brought out trays of individual salads, and the hotel ballroom started to fill up with sheriff's department personnel. Sheriff Larry Covington, Assistant Sheriff Frank Peters, and the Executive Staff of Deputy Chiefs wore their dress uniforms. Dark olive wool slacks, white shirt, and a black tie. Over the shirt, they wore a dark olive wool jacket. The rich green of the jacket contrasted the gold buttons that ran down the jacket's center, along with the gold seven-pointed sheriff's badge that was pinned above the left breast. Lieutenant John Tate and his graduating class of Sheriff's Trainee's were dressed in dark olive slacks, light olive long sleeved shirts and a black tie.

A long head table for the Sheriff, his Executive Staff, and the number one class graduate took center stage in the ballroom. Smaller round tables, that sat eight people, were for the graduating trainees and their families.

Making his way to the head table, Nate Baxter stopped and took a moment to talk with his friends. David "Pillsbury" Lewis introduced Nate to his wife, Patti, and their ten month old baby girl. Monica Vargas and Jeff Price were flying solo.

"Is your mom going to be here?" Vargas asked.

"No, she's out on patrol, but she'll make it to the graduation."

The cell phone in Nate's front pants pocket was set on vibration mode and it went off. He took the phone out of his pocket and looked at the number of the incoming call. "That's her now," he said.

Nate walked out of the ballroom, into the lobby, and answered the call.

"Hey, mom, what's up?"

"I'm in my unit, out on patrol."

"Is everything okay? You're still going to make it to the graduation?"

"You're such a worrier, Nate. Yes, everything's fine, but I do need a favor from you."

"What's that?" he asked.

"Could you stop at the cleaner's, pick up the dress I'm going to be wearing tonight and drop it off at the house?"

"Sure, no problem."

While they were talking, a radio transmission from dispatch came into Michelle's car.

*Thirteen Paul One, we've got a domestic disturbance at 1793 Palm Court, Highland. The reporting party is the victim. She advises that her husband hit her. He's been drinking, is agitated and despondent.*

"Isn't that your call sign?" Nate asked.

"Yes, I've got to go."

"Alright, mom, be careful and I'll see you tonight at the graduation."

"Okay, hon, I will, love you."

Nate put the cell phone in his pocket and went back into the ballroom. When he got to the head table, the Deputy Chiefs stood up from their chairs and extended their congratulations. Embarrassed by the attention, Nate shook their hands, accepted their congratulations, and looked for his nameplate on the table. *Oh crap, I'm right between the Sheriff and Lieutenant Tate.*

In four minutes, Michelle Baxter arrived at the neat single story home in one of Highland's newer middle class subdivisions. She saw a female Caucasian, about thirty years old, sitting on the front steps with her head in her hands; it looked like she was crying. Baxter pulled into the driveway, parked the marked sheriff's car, and went over to her. When the woman looked up, Baxter observed red marks on her face and the left eye starting to swell.

"Ma'am, did you call nine-one-one?" Baxter asked.

"Yes."

"Tell me what's going on."

"It's my husband," she said, alternating between crying and talking. "I know he didn't mean to do it. It's just that things have been so tough lately. His hours got cut back; the bank is taking the house."

"Has he been drinking this morning?" Baxter asked.

"Yes."

"Do you have any children?"

"Two."

"Where are they now?"

"At school."

"Are there any guns in the house?"

"I don't know."

"Alright, ma'am, "Baxter said. "Here's what I want you to do. Go out into the front yard, another deputy should be here anytime now."

Baxter took her .9mm Glock out of its holster and held it in both hands, down by her right side. She took a deep breath and stepped inside the house.

The front door opened into a long hallway lined with framed family photos. From behind a wall to her left, the living room, she heard a voice talking.

"What should I do, mom? She called the cops on me. Yeah, I hit her, but I didn't mean to do it."

"Sheriff's department, I'm coming in!" Baxter yelled.

"Okay," the voice answered.

Baxter went into the living room with her gun pointed. She trained the gun on a male sitting in the middle of a white leather couch that abutted the living room wall. He had a white leather pillow on his lap and both of his hands were obscured under the pillow.

*This can't be happening again.*

He looked to be about the same age as his wife. His short brown hair was tousled and he had a two-day growth of stubble on his face. He wore a pair of gray dress slacks and a white dress shirt with the sleeves rolled up.

*This might not be so bad. He looks like the average Joe, who's down on his luck, and on a bender.*

"Sir, I'm going to have to take you down to the station," Baxter said, still pointing her gun at the man.

"Why?"

"It's the law in domestic dispute cases. I have no choice."

"I don't want to go. I want to stay here."

"That's not an option, sir."

*Does he have anything in his hands under that pillow?*

Baxter looked at the end table next to the couch. She saw a cell phone charger plugged into the wall, but no cell phone.

*I heard the guy talking on the phone. I see the cell phone charger. If he's got anything, it's probably the cell phone. I've seen this movie before, what in the hell am I going to do?*

She glanced again at the cell phone charger; looking for the phone. The man screamed at the top of his lungs and it took her by surprise.

"I'll see you in hell, bitch!"

In one rapid motion, the man slid a .9mm semi-automatic handgun from underneath the pillow and began shooting.

*Oh shit, he's got a gun!*

The first shot caught her in the chest. Underneath her uniform shirt, she was wearing a Kevlar vest, and the force of the bullet striking the vest knocked her backwards two feet. Before getting hit again, while falling to the floor, she fired one shot that hit him in the left shoulder.

The second bullet hit her in the throat and travelled upward through her jaw and into her skull. It exited just above her right ear. The third bullet struck her in the left thigh. The fourth bullet shattered her right kneecap.

The man stopped firing when he saw Baxter lying motionless on the cream-colored carpeting. His eyes, filled with rage, looked at the gun in his right hand. White smoke rose out of the barrel; leaving his last breath of life tasting and smelling of gunpowder. He opened his mouth, jammed the blue steel barrel of the gun up against the roof of his mouth, and pulled the trigger.

The man's wife had been waiting outside when she heard the gun battle taking place inside the house. When the firing stopped, she ran inside. She first saw Michelle Baxter, on the carpet in a spreading pool of blood. She shrieked when she saw her husband. He was missing the top half of his head. Most of his skull bone, hair, and brain matter dripped down the side of the wall.

Lying on the floor, in her own warm blood, Michelle Baxter knew that her time on earth had ended.

*Damn it! Why didn't I shoot? Why did I wait? I'm getting cold. I love you, Nate.*

She closed her eyes and surrendered to the bright white light. It gave her warmth and comfort. A hand emerged from the light and reached out for her. She recognized the hair on the knuckles and the scar on the left index finger. She recognized his white gold wedding band—it matched hers.

Feeling good about the way things were going; Nate forked the last bite of strawberry cheesecake into his mouth. So far, he hadn't said anything too stupid to the Sheriff while they were eating lunch.

Sheriff Larry Covington dumped two packets of sugar into his cup and stirred the coffee. "They tell me you're one hell of a ball player," he said to Nate.

"Used to be," Nate answered.

"I know we could use you on the department's softball team."

"I don't know, Sheriff, It's been four years since I've picked up a bat."

The entire sheriff's brass, sitting at the head table, had their cell phones on vibrate. Almost in unison, all the cell phones at the head table started buzzing. Assistant Sheriff Frank Peter's phone pulsated, followed by those of the three Deputy Chiefs. They each got up from the table, went to separate corners of the ballroom, and took the calls. Larry Covington watched the scene unfolding. He knew something was going down, and it had to be bad.

Covington saw Peters and the three Deputy Chiefs leave the ballroom for the lobby. Ten minutes later, Peters returned and stood in the doorway of the ballroom. They exchanged eye contact and Peters nodded his head, up and down. "Would you excuse me for a minute," Covington said to Nate.

"Yes, sir," Nate answered.

Covington got up from the table; all eyes were on him. Everybody in the room had figured out that there was a big problem somewhere in the county. To keep up an atmosphere of calmness, he stopped at a few tables and shook hands with some of the graduating trainees.

In the lobby, he sat down on a couch with his Assistant Sheriff and Peter's briefed him on the gruesome details of what had just happened at 1793 Palm Court. Covington took off his glasses; put the tips in his mouth and bit down, hard. He closed his eyes and rubbed his forehead with his left hand.

After three minutes, he opened his eyes, put his glasses back on, and said, "Okay, send Tate out to the scene, to get her personal items. I need to tell the kid."

Inside the ballroom, Nate sat by himself at the head table. He felt awkward and played with the rim of his water glass. He looked at the table where his friends were sitting. They looked back and he just shrugged his shoulders, as if he didn't know what was going on either.

Assistant Sheriff Frank Peters came up to the table and said, "Nate, the Sheriff would like to see you, in the lobby."

Nate followed Peters to the lobby. His mind raced through all the possibilities of why the Sheriff wanted to speak with him. It could only be one thing—his mother. He sat down in a chair next to the Sheriff's couch. Nate breathed in, deep and heavy, trying not to hyperventilate. Nate looked into the sallow eyes of the Sheriff. He'd seen that look before—when the Army Major came to the house and broke the news about his father's death.

"Is my mom okay?" he asked the Sheriff.

"No, Nate, we lost her—about an hour ago."

# 33

Parked along the street in front of 1793 Palm Court, Tate recognized Randy Bell's crime scene investigation van, Detective Scott Kane's unmarked car, and the coroner's van. A chill went through his body when he saw Michelle Baxter's marked sheriff's unit sitting by itself in the driveway. He didn't know why, but it reminded him of a loyal old dog waiting on its master.

For late February, the weather was crisp, and Tate put on his old homicide unit jacket over his uniform. He closed his car door, took in a deep breath of air, and looked at the snow-capped San Bernardino Mountains. The mountains gave him solace, especially in times like this.

*I need to see my girls.*

Tate went to the front passenger's door of Baxter's car, opened it, and sat down in the seat. In the center console cup holder, he saw a Starbuck's coffee cup. The rim of the cup had red lipstick smudge marks. The car's interior smelled of perfume—not overpowering, but just enough to know that a woman had been there. Tate didn't know much about perfumes and couldn't place the scent, but whatever the brand, it had been Michelle Baxter's calling card.

On the floorboard, by his feet, Tate saw Michelle's black canvas duty bag. The top of a Hallmark card peeked out from the bag. Tate picked it up. It was Nate's graduation card for that night's ceremony. The card was loose, not yet in its envelope. Tate debated on whether or not he should read the card. He didn't think he would be intruding upon their privacy, so he opened the card. In blue ink, with perfect penmanship, the card read:

*Nate, a mother could never love a son, more than I love you.*

The handwriting was incomplete and looked like it had been interrupted. Tate guessed that she probably had been working on the card between calls. Tate put the card in its envelope and placed it back in the canvas bag.

He picked up the bag and heard a jingle-jangle sound. Again, his curiosity got the best of him. He reached into the bag for the object making the noise; pulling out two small metal plates. The engraved plates were linked by a metal chain—Jordan Baxter's dog tags. Inside the bag, the dog tags had been lying next to a laminated newspaper excerpt—Mario Costa's obituary.

*You don't have to run from your demons anymore, Michelle.*

Tate picked up the duty bag and reached over for the Starbucks cup. He then put Michelle's personal items in the trunk of his unmarked car and went inside the house. In the hallway, he ran into Detective Scott Kane.

"Hey, LT," Kane said. "It's been awhile."

"Yeah, Scooter," Tate answered. "But not long enough. Is it bad in there?"

"Yes, sir."

"How bad?"

"Have you ever seen the movie *Scarface*? The one with Al Pacino." Kane asked.

"Yeah," Tate answered.

"Do you remember the chainsaw in the shower scene?"

"Yeah."

"Well, it's that kind of bad."

Tate turned left and walked into the living room, the crime scene. He looked around the room.

*Son of a bitch, the chainsaw shower scene was tame, compared to this.*

"Hey, Scooter."

"Yes, LT."

"I was briefed that the shithead over there on the couch, the one missing the top half of his skull, had a wife."

"Yes, sir," Kane answered.

"Where is she now?" Tate asked.

"They had to take her to the nut house. Apparently, she walked in on this little mess and went fucking loony tunes."

The dead guy on the couch and his wife had spared no expense in decorating the living room. Top of the line cream colored carpeting covered the floor. The couch, love seat, and chair were white leather. After the melee between Baxter and the dead guy, it looked like someone had dipped a paintbrush in red paint and then flicked their wrist; sending the red paint everywhere. An expensive wall painting that hung above the couch was now covered with blood, hair, bone, and brain. On the end table, next to the phone charger, sat a silver framed family photograph—the man, the wife, and twin nine-year-old girls. Like the painting on the wall, the photograph was spattered with human tissue.

In addition to the white of the furnishings, and the red of blood, a third color shared the room—yellow. The numbered plastic evidence placards were everywhere. The living room floor looked like a campground of yellow pup tents. A flash of light went off every couple of seconds as crime scene technician, Randy Bell, took his crime scene photographs.

"Hey, LT," Bell said to Tate.

"Hey, Photo Boy, how have you been?" Tate asked.

"I've had better days," Bell answered, pointing his camera at the body of Michelle Baxter.

Tate glanced at what was left of Michelle Baxter's jaw and said, "Looks like it's going to be closed casket."

"That's my guess," Bell answered.

"I saw the coroner's van outside. Who did they send out?" Tate asked.

"Vicky Jennings," Bell answered.

"Where is she?"

From the hallway, Tate heard a female voice, "I'm out here, LT."

Tate looked up and saw a heavyset middle age woman, with short blonde hair, come into the living room. She wore blue jeans and a polo shirt with the logo of the coroner's office. In her left hand, she carried a plastic box that looked like something Tate would take when he went fishing.

"Photo Boy, are you almost done with Michelle?" Tate asked.

"Yeah, I'm done."

"Good, let's get her to the morgue. This isn't dignified, she deserves better. But that piece of shit over there can rot, for all I care."

Jennings wheeled a collapsible gurney into the living room, next to the body of Michelle Baxter. On top of the gurney was a yellow body bag.

"Vicky, can you do me a favor?" Tate asked.

"Sure, LT."

"The Sheriff asked me to bring back all of Michelle's personal effects. Could you bag her badge and name plate."

The deputy coroner took a pair of latex gloves out of her supply kit, put them on, and kneeled by the body. Michelle's black hair was matted with congealing blood. Her eyes still had the death stare. Next to her torso sat a yellow evidence placard with the number "1".

Because of the Kevlar vest, there was little blood on Michelle's chest area. Jennings unbuttoned Michelle's shirt and unpinned the badge on the left side of the chest and the nameplate on the right side. Traces of blood spatter were on both the badge and nameplate. Jennings took a plastic spray bottle of anti-septic solution out of her kit and wiped them down. She placed them in a clear plastic bag and handed it to Tate.

Tate and Scott Kane watched as Jennings and Bell placed Michelle's body into the yellow body bag. The bag was zipped shut and Jennings wheeled the body outside to her van. Both Tate and Kane said a silent prayer.

Tate walked outside, with Kane not too far behind.

"Do you have any idea how it went down?" Kane asked.

Tate shielded his eyes from the sun and answered, "Yeah, she was still a little spooked from shooting the kid."

"What do you mean?"

"I bet she might have been second guessing herself, not wanting to make the same mistake twice."

"What is it we always preach to the Trainees at the academy?" Kane asked, even though he knew the answer.

"If you hesitate, if you think twice—you're dead," Tate answered.

* * *

The academy graduation ceremonies were always held at the historic California Theatre in downtown San Bernardino. Amidst the glitz and glamour of the times, the ornate theater opened in 1928 and had premiered classic films such as "King Kong" and "The Wizard of Oz". The theater's other claim to fame was that Will Rogers gave his last performance there, before his death in a 1935 plane crash.

The sheriff's department graduated two classes a year and the graduation ceremonies served as an important rite of passage for the trainees. They no longer wore the badge of a Sheriff's Trainee, in its stead, the seven star badge of a Deputy Sheriff. It marked the first day of their lives as sworn peace officers. It was also a night to honor the family and friends of the graduating trainees. The grueling twenty-six week academy could be just as trying on the loved ones at home.

Emotions in the theater were confused and conflicting. It had been five years since the department lost a deputy in the line of duty; let alone the night of graduation ceremonies. The ceremonies presented the first chance to grieve their fallen comrade and a somber mood permeated the packed auditorium. Badges on uniforms were draped with black mourning bands and most of the people in attendance had a distraught look of disbelief on their faces. The Sheriff and his Executive Staff sat in the first row. The two seats to the right of the sheriff remained empty; the only empty chairs in the theater. They were the seats traditionally reserved for the parents of the top graduate.

The graduating class sat on the elevated stage; their chairs arranged in neat rows on the wood flooring.  Seated in front of the class were Lieutenant John Tate, Sergeant Billy Grimes, and Deputy Tina Smith.  After the invocation, a video screen made a soft humming noise as it came down from the ceiling of the theater.  Michelle Baxter's image appeared on the screen.  She wore her sheriff's dress uniform.  Underneath her likeness were the words:

*Michelle Paz Baxter*
*End of Watch—February 17, 2010*

From the left side of the stage, the sheriff's department's bagpipe detail marched out.  Their footsteps on the wood stage echoed like thunder throughout the quiet auditorium.  The lonely wail of the bagpipes sent the audience over the edge of emotions.  Some cried openly, others fought back tears as the bagpipes played *Amazing Grace*.

John Tate blinked back tears, turned around in his chair, and gave a nod to Nate Baxter. Nate walked to the podium in the center of the stage and looked out into the audience.  Seven hundred sets of crying eyes returned his look.  Nate didn't fancy himself as a public speaker and he'd been worrying about the speech all weekend.  He feared that he would be nervous and an embarrassment to himself, his mother, and the memory of his father.  Standing at the podium, he wasn't nervous, he felt numb.

In the six hours since his mother's death, Nate had been living in a fog.  He felt everything, and yet he felt nothing.  The Sheriff told him that it would be okay to pass on giving the graduation speech.  Nate said he would consider it.  At least it gave him something other than his mother's death to think about.

Like any athlete, his gut instinct told him to think about the decision from a sports perspective.  He remembered Brett Favre playing in a Monday Night Football game, the day after his father's unexpected death.  It turned out to be the best game of his season, maybe even his career.  Nate thought about what his mother would want him to do.  What his father would want him to do.  He felt their presence, telling him to get up to that podium and give the speech.

Nate cleared his throat and before he started the speech, he put his hands in the pockets of his dark olive uniform slacks. In the right pocket, he wrapped his fingers around his father's dog tags and his pa-paws pocket watch. In the left pocket, he wrapped his fingers around his mother's badge and nameplate. He took his hands out of his pockets, looked up at his mother's image on the video screen, and began his speech.

"This morning, my mother's watch came to an end. Tonight, my class-mates and I will embark on our watch..."

# 34

The black hearse maintained a steady sixty miles per hour, in the center lane of the 10 Freeway, as it made the twenty minute drive from the mortuary to the Arrowhead Credit Union Baseball Park in downtown San Bernardino. The morning rush hour traffic had lightened up and passing motorists gawked at the three sheriff's department motorcycle units in front of the hearse and the two that trailed behind. Many of the drivers' had a look of curiosity when they saw the American flag draped casket resting in the rear of the hearse.

The hearse turned off the freeway, onto "E" Street. It was met by a sea of law enforcement officers who lined both sides of the road. Sheriff's deputies in their green uniforms, police officers wearing black uniforms, and California Highway Patrol officers dressed in tan uniforms. They numbered in the hundreds and came from the neighboring counties of Riverside, Los Angeles, Orange, and Kern. Some came from as far away as Wyoming and Texas to pay their respects to a fallen comrade. In unison, they crisply saluted as the hearse passed by.

The Arrowhead Credit Union Baseball Park served as the home field for the Inland Empire 66'ers, a minor league baseball team. On this morning, it would be the site of Deputy Michelle Paz Baxter's memorial services. The stadium had seating for five thousand people, and fifteen minutes before the start of the services, all the seats were taken. The mourners were a mix of law enforcement officers, elected officials, and local citizens. Vincent and Carmen Costa had come to pay their respects to Michelle Baxter and sat in seats behind third base.

Picturesque weather conditions shared the stadium with the mourners. The Santa Ana winds had blown out the smog, leaving a rare pristine blue sky. Rising above the outfield fence, the five thousand foot high mountains towered over the San Bernardino Valley. The caps of the mountains were white with a fresh dusting of snow.

Brown plastic tarps had been laid over the dirt infield and rows of white plastic folding chairs stretched from home plate to the edge of the grass outfield. Nate Baxter sat in the center of the first row of chairs. Seated to his left were Monica Vargas, David Lewis, and Jeff Price. Seated to his right were John Tate, Sheriff Larry Covington, and District Attorney Anthony Garcia.

Twenty feet in front of the first row of chairs, a casket stand and a podium bearing the sheriff's department shield awaited the hearse. Hundreds of floral sprays stood alone in the grass. One of the largest, and most ornate arrangements, came with a condolence card to Nate, signed by Vincent and Carmen Costa. From his chair, Nate breathed in the scent of the carnations and roses. He thought about how much his mother loved flowers.

Between the podium and the casket stand there was a framed photograph of Michelle Baxter. An official department photograph and she was wearing her Class A uniform. Her light brown skin, black hair, and hazel eyes stood out against the uniform's dark green jacket. She was smiling for the photographer.

In left field, a gate had been opened to allow vehicles to enter the grass outfield from the parking lot. On each side of the gate, a fire engine guarded the entry. Their ladders reached skyward and intersected over the entry gate. An American flag hung down from the intersected ladders and waved peacefully in the gentle wind.

People stopped talking when the three motorcycle units passed through the gate and underneath the American flag. The black hearse and two more motorcycle units followed close behind. A flock of birds were feeding on the outfield grass and scattered when the funeral procession passed by.

Nate watched the black hearse and motorcycles travel, at a walk like pace, through the outfield and stop ten yards from his mother's photograph. He wore dark aviator sunglasses and a single tear rolled down his right cheek. Vargas, Lewis, Price, Tate, Covington, and Garcia got up from their chairs and walked to the back of the hearse.

It came as a surprise to Tate when Nate asked him to be a pallbearer, and he answered that it would be an honor. On the day of Michelle Baxter's murder, Tate turned over her personal belongings to Nate. He also volunteered to help Nate with the arrangements. Without hesitation, Nate took him up on the offer. Over the past days, Tate spent countless hours with Nate, helping him cope with the trauma over the sudden and violent death of his mother.

Two nights after Michelle's murder, Tate busted out a bottle of Jack Daniels and they talked until the sun came up. Nate repeated several times how appreciative his mother had been over everything Tate had done for her. His mother had told him about the story of Tate going to bat for her with District Attorney Garcia. This caught Tate a little off guard; He'd never told Michelle about his meeting with Garcia, and going to bat for her.

The pallbearers walked the flag draped mahogany casket to the pedestal and returned to their chairs. Nate stood up and gave a hug to Vargas, Lewis, and Price.

During Sheriff Covington's eulogy, Tate looked over at Nate.

*What a kid, he's doing a great job of keeping it together. Last night he was in my arms crying like a baby.*

After the Sheriff's eulogy, Sheriff's Chaplain Robert Parks went up to the podium and read from the Book of Mathew; Chapter 5, verse nine. "Blessed are the peacemakers, for they shall be called the children of god."

A lump formed in Tate's throat and he closed his eyes. For twenty-five years he'd kept a laminated copy of this verse in the pocket of his leather notebook.

*I've heard this verse at too many cop funerals—please let this be the last one.*

Two deputies from the sheriff's honor guard approached the casket and went to opposite ends. Their white gloved hands lifted the American flag and they went through the military flag folding ceremony. The mourners watched in silence as the honor guards presented the tight, crisp, perfect triangle flag to Nate. He ran his hand over the flag, feeling the stitching between the white stars and blue background.

Two days earlier, at the Baxter house, Tate saw Jordan Baxter's flag, displayed atop a bookcase in a wood and glass flag holder.

*That's it, that's all this kid's got left of his mom and dad—a pair of flags.*

In right field, seven deputies stood at attention with the butt of their rifles on the grass. Coming from the west, the mourners heard the sound of approaching helicopter engines and rotor blades. They looked to the sky as the sound grew louder and louder. Not quite hovering, but flying slow, three sheriff's department helicopters came over the stadium— in the missing man formation.

Just as the helicopters cleared the stadium, the seven deputies in right field raised their rifles to the air and fired. They fired a second time and then a third time. The sound of the shots reverberated against the outfield scoreboard and the acrid smell of gunpowder filled the air. Twenty-one expended brass shell casings littered the outfield grass. The dark sunglasses kept his friends from seeing Nate cringe with every fired shot.

A solo bugler in center field started playing *Taps*. The lonesome notes mixed with the sound of five thousand people sobbing and sniffling.

Nate took off his sunglasses and handed them to Monica Vargas. His eyes were streaked with red and the sockets were dark from the lack of sleep. He walked the twenty feet to his mother's casket. He touched the casket, went to one knee, bowed his head, and made the sign of the cross.

After what seemed like minutes, but was only seconds, Nate got to his feet and walked towards his mother's photograph. He looked at her face and smiled, she smiled back. From his right pants pocket he reached in and took out his mother's badge. He then reached into his left pants pocket and took out a black elastic mourning band. Everyone in the stadium felt the love in his fingers as he placed the mourning band around his mother's badge and rested it up against her photograph.

\* \* \*

Driving up the steep and twisting two-lane mountain road, John Tate was halfway to his home in Big Bear when his hands started to tremble on the steering wheel. He couldn't expunge from his mind the words Nate Baxter said to him when he told him that he was number one in the class:

*My mother thinks very highly of you. She credits you as being the reason for her coming back after the shooting.*

He pulled onto a turn out, a parking area just off the side of the road, where tourists liked to park and take photographs of the majestic mountain scenery. He reached into the glove box for a CD and slid it into the car's CD player. The sounds of hard-core punk rock music blared from the car's speakers. Tate rolled down the windows and breathed in the cold mountain air. It smelled like pine.

The name of the band was Social Distortion—a Southern California band that had been around since 1978 and at the forefront of the 1980's hardcore punk rock explosion.

He'd listened to the band's music in high school and college. He continued to listen to the band into his thirties and now his forties. The name of the song was *Through These Eyes*. A single song can stay with someone forever and become the song that defines his or her life. *Through These Eyes* was the song that defined John Tate's life. He'd listened to this song for thirty years and would probably listen to it for another thirty.

John Tate looked out over the San Bernardino Mountains and silently mouthed the lyrics to the song, in perfect sync with the music.

*Through these eyes, I've seen love and I've seen hate*
*I've seen the violence and the tears*
*Through these eyes*
*I got my schooling on the streets*
*I've seen the things in life*
*You don't' wanna see.*

*Through these eyes, I've looked the devil in the face*
*And I've seen God's holy grace*
*Through these eyes*
*I've tried to walk the straighter line*
*I found myself again*
*But nearly lost my mind*

# 35

Nate Baxter opened the door to his hotel room. He was greeted with a blast of frigid morning air. Putting his hands in the pockets of his suit pants, he hurried to the rental car parked just outside the door to his room. After starting the car's engine, he turned the heat up to full blast. Exhaust vapors streamed out of the car's tailpipe as he dashed back into the warmth of the hotel room. He finished getting ready, buttoning the sleeves of his dress shirt and making a knot in his tie. The tan wool overcoat and brown leather gloves, lying on top of the unmade bed, still had their store tags. He picked up his pocketknife from the nightstand, along with his wallet and badge. He cut off the tags, turned off the television, and went back out into the cold.

Clothing wise, the cold front had caught Nate by surprise. Luckily, the day before, after flying into Memphis, he made it to Oxford before Nielson's clothing store closed. The sales clerk at Nielson's was blonde and attractive looking. She was also a full time student at Ole Miss and almost fell over herself when Nate walked into the store. By all standards, at twenty-two years of age, handsome, and with a muscular build, Nate would make quite the catch for any self respecting Ole Miss Sorority girl.

Nate opened the front passenger's door; warm air poured out and it felt good on his cold face. He tossed the overcoat and gloves onto the passenger seat and closed the door. Walking back in front of the car, he noticed a layer of ice on the windshield. He reached into his rear pants pocket for his wallet and took out a credit card. Jumping up and down, trying to stay warm, he scraped as much ice as he could off the front windshield.

Before he drove away from the hotel, Nate held his hands inches from the car's heater vents and flexed his fingers. Confident that he had at least enough feeling in his fingers to drive, Nate put the car in gear and pulled out of the parking lot. The hotel was just off The Square and at eight o'clock on a cold and blustery morning; there was not a soul around.

Nate turned onto Highway 6 and headed west for five miles. The morning sky was overcast with a foggy visibility of maybe half a mile. It took his best driving efforts to steer clear of the random patches of black ice.

Because of the poor visibility, Nate started to think that maybe he had missed the turn. Then, just up ahead and coming into view, he saw the small brick church. He turned left off the paved road and onto the church's dirt driveway. A white Ford F150 four-wheel drive pickup truck was idling on the gravel parking area. Red clay mud covered the truck and smoke billowed out of its exhaust pipes.

Nate pulled up alongside the pickup and parked the car. He reached over to the passenger seat and grabbed the wool overcoat and leather gloves. Standing outside, Nate put on the coat and gloves. A white male opened the driver's door and got out of the truck. He looked to be in his fifties and he wore dirty blue jeans and a denim jacket. His work boots were caked with red mud and the faded green John Deere cap on his head had seen better days.

Another white male got out of the passenger's side of the truck. He looked a whole lot like the driver, only twenty years younger. His work boots were also covered with mud and the blue Ole Miss cap on his head was stained with sweat. As he walked around the tailgate of the truck, he took a can of Copenhagen snuff from the front pocket of his North Face parka and loaded the pungent smelling smokeless tobacco into his lower lip.

"Nate Baxter?" the older man asked.

"Yes, sir," Nate answered.

"My name's James Fauntleroy, you can call me Jimmy," the man said, with a thick Mississippi drawl. "That's my boy, James, Jr. You can just call him Junior."

Jimmy held out his right hand to Nate. The calloused hand had dirt underneath the fingernails. Nate extended his leather-gloved right hand and shook Jimmy's.

"You two are with the local funeral home?" Nate asked.

"Yes, sir," Jimmy answered. "I've been digging graves with them now for thirty years; Junior's just now learning the business."

"Okay, let's go," Nate, said.

They walked the thirty yards from the church's parking area to the small cemetery just behind the church. The only sound breaking the rhythm of boots and shoes on gravel was the noise of Junior spitting his dip.

Junior opened the creaking white picket fence gate and waved through Nate and Jimmy. In the far right corner of the small cemetery, Nate saw the mahogany casket and a mound of red clay dirt with two shovels stuck into the ground.

At the gravesite, his mother's casket sat on a funeral gurney draped with purple velvet. Nate let out a long sigh and touched the casket with his right hand.

"A relative?" Jimmy asked in a reverent tone, breaking the uneasy silence.

"My mother."

"I'm sorry."

"Thank you."

"These are family plots. Who else do you have out here?" Junior asked.

Nate should have been perturbed by Junior's question, but he wasn't. Nate pointed to the three neighboring headstones and answered, "My father, my grandfather, and my grandmother."

"Damn," Junior said.

"Jimmy?"

"Yes, Mr. Baxter."

"Could you please lower my mother's casket into the grave?"

"Yes, sir."

Jimmy looked at Junior and nodded his head. Thinking it was the respectful thing to do, Junior took the dip of Copenhagen out of his mouth. Jimmy began turning a crank under the grave apron and the casket inched its way into the cold dirt grave. A steady freezing rain started to fall. When the casket touched the bottom of the grave, Junior removed the belts, apron, and crank.

"Would you two mind going back to your truck for a little while?" Nate asked.

"Absolutely, Mr. Baxter," Jimmy said. "Whatever you want."

Before going back to their truck, Jimmy and Junior embraced Nate. They may have been strangers, but they felt Nate's loss. While Jimmy and Junior were walking back to their truck, Nate went to his grandmother's headstone and paused for a moment. He continued on to his grandfather's and then to his father's plot.

Lying on the iced over grass, next to the mound of dirt, Nate saw a folding metal chair. He guessed that it must have belonged to Jimmy and Junior. He reached down for the chair, opened it up, and placed it by the side of his mother's open grave.

Nate sat down on the chair. He rested his hands on his knees and started talking to his mother. "We got you here, mom. It was a long flight, but we made it. It was sad, sitting on the plane while we were still on the ground in Los Angeles; I looked out the window and saw them loading your casket. Well, at least I knew you were on the plane.

"Since you've been gone, I don't know what I would have done without Lieutenant Tate. I was such a mess—still am. The lieutenant asked me about burial arrangements. I didn't have a clue. He helped me find your will. It was right where you left it, in dad's office.

"You wanted to be here with dad, pa-paw and me-maw. That's what we did.

"I'll take care of things with the Costa's—just like you want. I did call them from the airport, on my cell phone. I told them about your donation to The Mario Costa Foundation. I'm proud of you for doing that with your life insurance money. You knew I'd be just fine, between my job and the money from when dad was killed."

Nate stopped for a moment and wiped the tears away with the sleeve of his wool overcoat. The freezing rain continued to fall and crunched under the soles of his shoes.

"When I spoke with the Costa's, they mentioned that they were at your memorial services. They also sent a beautiful floral arrangement; you would have really liked it.

"It was a very special memorial service, mom. You're a hero.

"Everybody keeps telling me that you're in a better place—that you're with dad. I don't know whether to believe that or not, but I sure hope so. I don't know what I'm going to do without you. You're all I had left. I love you, mom."

Nate got up from the metal chair and walked over to the mound of dirt and red clay. A one-inch thick layer of sleet covered the mound. He took off his gloves and put them in the pockets of his overcoat. Nate grabbed one of the shovels and the cold metal handle stuck to his warm naked palm. He wanted this to hurt; it should hurt.

He scooped up a shovel full of dirt and tossed it into his mother's grave. The frozen dirt made a hollow sound on the top of her wood casket. For twenty minutes, he shoveled dirt into the grave. His muscles ached and sweat soaked through his overcoat. He started to walk away and gave one last look at his mother's grave and the headstones of his father, grandfather, and grandmother.

After a hot shower, Nate spent most of the afternoon sleeping in his hotel room. He woke up at six o'clock to pangs in his stomach. He then realized that he'd not eaten all day. He threw on a pair of blue jeans, with a sweater and his overcoat, and walked across the street to the Boure' restaurant.

Nate sat at the bar and ordered a Jack Daniels, straight up. The bartender was a little younger than Nate was and wore a white cotton long sleeve shirt with a black tie. He had the standard Ole Miss haircut; longish hair with bangs that swept down to his eyebrows.

The bartender set a cocktail napkin in front of Nate, put the Jack Daniels on the napkin, and introduced himself.

"My name is Max."

"Nate," he answered the bartender, taking a sip of the Jack Daniels.

"Will you be having dinner with us tonight, sir?"

"Can I eat here at the bar?"

"Absolutely."

"What do have that's good, Max?"

"The shrimp and grits."

"I'll try it."

After fifteen minutes, the bartender brought out Nate's dinner and a third Jack Daniels. Nate stared at the plate. A heaping scoop of cheesy grits topped with andouille sausage and shrimp, the entire concoction swimming in a bath of brown gravy. He'd never seen anything like it before and put a forkful in his mouth.

"Is it okay, sir?" Max asked.

"It's damn good, Max."

"You go to school here?"

"No, I graduated a couple of years ago from Cal State Fullerton."

"What brings you to Oxford, family?"

Nate stopped chewing and thought about how to answer the bartender's question.

"Yes, all my family is here in Oxford."

# 36

After his mother's death, Nate continued to live in the family home—the only house he'd ever known. The tragic deaths of his mother and father had left him financially secure. His father's life insurance proceeds had paid off the mortgage to the house, and then some. However, it was a lonesome existence for Nate and he'd do anything for just one more day with his mother and father.

Like all new deputy sheriffs, Nate's first assignment was the county jail. There wasn't much real cop work involved with the job. He and his fellow custody deputies just made sure that the robbers, burglars, drug dealers, rapists, and murderers who were awaiting trial didn't kill each another.

On the anniversary of his mother's death, Nate went back to Oxford to pay his respects to his father, mother, grandfather, and grandmother. This time around, the weather cooperated, but he'd forgotten to pack the belt he wore with blue jeans.

When he walked into Nielson's department store, he was surprised to see the attractive sales clerk who had helped him the year before with the overcoat and gloves. Her name was Haley Somerville. She recognized him as soon as he entered the store; Nate was half-Hispanic and there weren't a whole lot of olive skinned males walking the sidewalks of Oxford's downtown square.

Nate asked her out to dinner and Haley accepted.  At Boure's, over a meal of shrimp and grits, they exchanged life stories.  Nate told Haley everything and they both came close to crying.  A junior at Ole Miss, Haley majored in broadcast journalism.  Haley and her family were from Biloxi.  Her father owned a shrimp boat, but they lost everything because of the oil spill.

Nate spent three days in Oxford and each night they went out to dinner.  The attraction was immediate and mutual.  He became smitten with Haley's Southern drawl.  People in California didn't speak like that and he could spend hours just listening to her talk.  On his last day in Oxford, he took Haley to the cemetery.

Modern technology proved to be a blessing for Nate and Haley's long distance relationship.  Unlimited cell phone minutes and their internet webcams gave them daily communication.  Twice, Nate flew Haley out for long weekends.  On her second visit to Southern California, Haley applied for a summer internship position at the KNBC television station in Los Angeles.

After a year and a half of working in the jail, Nate got his first patrol assignment with the Town of Apple Valley.  Geographically, San Bernardino is the largest county in the lower forty-eight states and the sheriff's department provided police services for nine incorporated cities and towns. Apple Valley was a town of sixty thousand people and located in an area known as the "High Desert".  The town had desert like terrain, but at an elevation of four thousand feet above sea level.  If you live in Southern California and you've driven to Las Vegas, you've driven by the Town of Apple Valley.

For six months, Nate rode patrol with his Field Training Officer.  A senior deputy sheriff who showed Nate how to implement, in real world conditions, everything he had learned at the sheriff's academy.

On the second anniversary of his mother's death, Nate returned to Oxford to pay his respects to his family—and to spend some time with Haley.

Shrimp and grits at Boure' had sort of become their thing. After the server cleared their dinner plates, Nate reached into his pocket for a small box and concealed it in his left hand. Reaching across the table, he looked Haley in the eyes and took hold of her hand. He then handed her the box. Tears ran out of her eyes when she put the diamond ring on her finger. His nerves got the best of him and he couldn't get the words out of his mouth—but he didn't have to say anything. She looked at Nate and said, "Yes."

* * *

By the end of his second full year in the major leagues, Joseph Costa had become the sport's most dominating young pitcher. The Los Angeles Dodgers recognized his value to the team and signed him to a long-term contract—six years and ninety million dollars. In his third full year with the Dodgers, Costa was selected to be the starting pitcher in that year's All-Star game at Washington, D.C.'s National's Park.

On the morning of the All Star game, Costa veered the child's stroller off the Metro subway at the Judiciary Square Station. His son, Mario, looked up at him and smiled. The three-year-old little boy had black curly hair that fell to his neck and covered his ears.

Coming out of the subway station, into the bright July morning sunlight, Costa squinted until his eyes got re-adjusted. He saw the sign and steered the stroller down the sidewalk in that direction. His wife, Angela, had wanted to come along that morning, but he asked her not to. He told her that this was something he needed to do by himself, along with little Mario.

Pushing Mario down the sidewalk, he breathed in the smell of the freshly cut grass. Whenever Costa and the Dodgers played a series in Washington, D. C., he would try to set some time aside to visit a different national monument. He loved the immense grass areas that adjoined all the national historic treasures. They walked under shade trees that lined both sides of the pathway and up ahead he made out the two curving three hundred foot long blue-gray marble walls. The two walls formed the National Law Enforcement Officer's Memorial.

Dedicated in 1991, the memorial honored federal, state, and local peace officers who had been killed in the line of duty. Every spring, during National Police Week, new names were added to the wall. The names of over nineteen thousand peace officers graced the two walls of the memorial.

When Joseph and Mario were almost to the wall, Mario pointed his hand away from the stroller and said, "Cats." The little boy was pointing to a bronze statue of an adult lion watching over its cubs. The adult lion symbolized the peace officer, and the cubs were the citizens they swore to defend with their lives.

The previous night, on his laptop computer, Joseph had run a search on the memorial's website, pin pointing the exact location of the name. He and Mario inched their way along the sidewalk next to the wall. There were so many names. Other visitors before them had left single red roses at the base of the wall. Joseph knew he was getting closer, and then he saw the name:

*Michelle Paz Baxter.*

He stopped pushing the stroller and just stared at the name. Her name was chest high to Costa and he ran the fingers of his right hand over the engraved letters.

"Mrs. Baxter, I hope you don't mind, but I had to come down here this morning and get some things off my chest. It's been eating at me since my folks told me about your death.

"I now understand what happened that night with my brother. I'm still having a tough time with it, but I recognize why you did it.

"I need to apologize to you about the way I treated your son. It was wrong of me to take my aggressions out on Nate. It wasn't his fault.

"I guess Nate and I will, forever, share more than just the perfect game. We've both lost someone in our lives, and that hurt will never go away."

Father and son started back for the subway station when Costa noticed the gift shop in the National Law Enforcement Museum. He wheeled his son's stroller into the gift shop. They both needed a break from the heat.

Costa looked around the shop and his attention was captured by a display shelf full of bronze coins. A sign above the coins explained that they were St. Michael's coins and that St. Michael served as the patron saint of law enforcement. Costa picked one up. On the front was an engraving of St. Michael with the words: *Protecting those who protect others*. On the back was an engraving of an eagle with the words: *Service with honor and distinction*.

When he paid for the coin, Costa saw the glass cooler of single red roses behind the clerk; he bought one. Leaving the gift shop, Costa had the Saint Michael's coin in his shirt pocket and the cellophane wrapped rose in his right hand. He pushed Mario in the opposite direction of the subway station—back towards the memorial wall.

In front of her name, Costa stopped and took Mario out of the stroller. The toddler wore a white Los Angeles Dodgers t-shirt, blue shorts, and sandals. Costa held the rose out to Mario and the little boy grabbed it from his father. Joseph knelt down next to his son and pointed to the other red roses that rested against the base of the wall.

"Mario, go put the flower over there, with the rest of them."

Taking tiny awkward steps, little Mario walked to the base of the wall and dropped the rose. He turned around, with a big innocent smile on his face, and ran into the outstretched arms of his father.

# 37

Nate Baxter walked out of the house and pulled the front door shut behind him. It proved to be a balancing act. His hands were full with his black duty bag and his freshly ironed uniform shirt on a hanger. Like most sheriffs' deputies, he went to work half dressed in his uniform; white tee shirt, green uniform pants, and black boots. He would put the shirt and his gun belt on at the station's locker room.

Walking down the front porch steps, he glanced at his mother's rose bushes, admiring his handiwork. He'd spent the morning pruning them. She would be proud of the way he was taking care of the flowers. Prior to her death, he'd never shown much interest in gardening.

Nate loaded his gear into the old Ford Expedition parked in the driveway. With his one-hour daily commute back and forth from Rancho Cucamonga to Apple Valley, the reliable SUV was getting ready to turn two hundred thousand miles on the odometer. Nate vowed to keep the SUV until he drove the wheels off it. His dad would have wanted it that way.

Nate backed the SUV out of the driveway and pulled up to the mailbox. He opened the mailbox and looked at that day's delivery of mail; mostly junk and Haley's *Better Homes and Gardens* magazine. Mixed in with the junk mail, an envelope stirred Nate's interest. Postmarked Washington, D.C, the envelope had a return address of the Marriott Hotel.

Nate felt something hard and moving free inside the strange delivery. He turned the envelope on its side and ripped it open. When the coin spilled out of the envelope, into his palm, he immediately recognized the object. Every cop recognized the coin—a St. Michael's coin. He held it in his hand and wondered who had sent it to him. His question was soon answered. He read the note, written on stationery bearing the logo of the Washington, D.C. Marriott Hotel.

> Nate,
> I just wanted to apologize for being a butthead. Thank you for
>     saving the game.
> I was very saddened to hear about your mother's death.
> Stay safe,
> Joseph Costa

Nate turned the coin over in his hand several times, grinned, and put it in his pants pocket.

By two o'clock in the afternoon, the swing shift daily briefing had finished and Nate readied his marked patrol unit for that night's shift. He tested the lights and sirens of his unit and made sure that his shotgun was secured in its holder. Before he started the car, he went into his duty bag, took out the empty Starbucks cup, and placed it in the cup holder, just below the dashboard's center console. The cup had red lipstick smudges around its rim. He then reached into his pants pocket, took out the St. Michael's coin, and tossed it into the Starbucks cup.

The call from dispatch came in at six o'clock, just after Nate had finished his dinner—an In-N-Out Double-Double with fries.

"Eighteen Paul Two, we've got a report of an armed robbery at the AM-PM convenience store at the corner of Bear Valley and Kiowa. Shots were fired and the clerk is down with a single gunshot wound to the back of the head.

"The reporting party advises that the armed suspect is a Hispanic juvenile wearing blue jeans and a black Oakland Raiders jersey. The suspect was seen getting into the passenger side of a red low-rider Honda Civic with blacked out windows. The vehicle was last seen heading east on Bear Valley."

Nate gunned the car's accelerator and sped towards the escaping vehicle's location. The St. Michael's coin vibrated from the extreme rpm of the car's engine and rattled, back and forth, against the sides of the Starbucks cup.

17039780R00155

Made in the USA
Charleston, SC
23 January 2013